Treacherous Notion

A Prevalent Notion Novel

Linnea March

Cover design by Getcovers.com

Editing by Heather E. Andrews

Proofreading by Cassidy Kate and A. Berger

ISBN: 979-8-9857188-3-6 (trade paperback edition)

Contents

To Rusty, for saving his dirtiest jokes for me

FOREWORD

This book contains fatphobia, toxic diet culture, and sexual harassment.
And one serious cock-block

Also by Linnea March

Prevalent Notion Series

Faultless Notion

Treacherous Notion

Ruinous Notion

Reckless Liar

The One You Chose

Chapter One

CHIFFON
ILSA

THE LAST THING ILSA Kruger should be doing at an anniversary reception was picture her best friend naked. Particularly revisiting the first time she met him, he was having sex with someone else.

They'd recently hired her as the lead stylist for his rock band, Prevalent Notion. Their personal assistant, Eloise, had directed her to find Nathan in his dressing room. She was expecting to find the bassist alone when she pushed open the third door on the left.

Instead, she found actress and newly minted queen of romantic comedies, Shelby Waters, topless and gyrating on the lap of one naked Nathan Ayers.

Ilsa stood there, dumbfounded, and processed the scene in front of her. The actress hadn't heard Ilsa open the door, but Nathan had. His eyes locked on hers as Shelby moved on top of him. A smile stretched across his face as he watched Ilsa watching him. Flames of heat pulsed through Ilsa's body as she watched Nathan's strong hands, firm on Shelby's hips. Ilsa backed out, trying to be quiet as she left.

Ilsa had worked for several scummy artists in her line of work. Holding firm professional boundaries with her clients was a rule taken seriously in this industry.

When he found her later, instead of cracking a nasty joke about the situation, Nathan came up, standing far enough away not to crowd Ilsa, and introduced himself.

"Eloise said you're the new stylist? Nathan Ayers." Sticking his hand out, he greeted her as if she hadn't walked in on him naked and getting it dirty cowgirl style fifteen minutes before. He never mentioned how she walked in on him, and she wasn't about to bring it up. Instead, he asked her about her ideas for styling the tour so she could switch the topic to her job. They never spoke of that moment in the dressing room.

She hadn't thought about that moment in weeks. Okay, maybe days, and perhaps it was more than a brief thought and more of an *I'm having some quality alone time* type session.

She wasn't into Nathan like that. He was handsome and funny. Above all else, he was a kind man in a city of vipers.

He was her friend. Nothing more than that. Muscular arms and beautiful blue-green eyes aside, he was her friend. Her plans involved opening her shop and expanding her line. They did not involve being distracted by how sexy her friend looked in his suit or wondering what those strong fingers could do to her body.

So, here she was, a year later, standing in the backyard of her friend Eloise and Nathan's bandmate, Keller's home for their party. Beside her was pop star Brenton Michael Phillips, who she'd been listening to for the past seven minutes prattle on about the different EDM influences on his music.

Bringing the champagne glass to her lips, she wet her tongue on the liquid before bringing it down. She wanted to give the appearance of drinking but couldn't trust herself when she got drunk. She might make a poor choice, like sleeping with said pop star. Again. Once was enough of a disappointment. And she suspected he was angling for round two by the way he was droning on.

Rubbing a finger over the rim of her glass, she tried to think of the best way to escape the erstwhile celebrity's clutches. She met him at a club a few months ago and thought, what the hell? How often does a girl get to have sex with the celebrity on that week's cover of Teen Tiger magazine?

Growing up in her little ranch-style house in the Phoenix area, she'd had no run-ins with celebrities. She figured if she went to Hollywood, she might as well have a one-night stand with a celebrity.

Now he was sniffing around as if she was a shoo-in for another round. That was not happening. She liked the idea of a relationship in theory, but she wasn't about to go domestic with a guy who thought the clitoris was in the back. He pushed up the sleeves on the hideous black-and-white striped jacket that reminded Ilsa of a shoe salesman uniform from her local mall. While Ilsa believed in taking risks with fashion, part of good fashion was about tailoring, and this jacket was an ugly pattern, three sizes too big, and smelled like the back room of her grandmother's house, where she kept all her porcelain dolls.

Across the lawn, she caught Nathan looking at her, and she raised her flute in the air. "I'm so sorry, Brandon. Nathan's calling me over."

The pop star floundered for words before calling out, "It's Brenton Michael," to Ilsa's back.

In the three years she'd been in Los Angeles, she found nothing made a bigger impression than calling a celebrity by the wrong name. She hoped that'd get her disinterest across.

Joining Nathan where he was standing next to Eloise's close family friends, she looped her arm through his. She always enjoyed standing next to Nathan. As a woman who stood five-eleven without heels, she'd long resigned herself to the lack of tall men in the dating pool. This wasn't an issue with Nathan, as he was taller than her no matter what heels she wore. Plus, she couldn't include him in the dating pool.

Their friends Keller and Eloise were making a speech on a makeshift dais. Ilsa admired the dress Eloise was wearing with pride. Ilsa had insisted on making the dress herself, using only the finest materials for this woman who took a chance on her and helped her get hired as the stylist for Prevalent Notion.

Eloise asked Ilsa to send over some sketches for the tour when she became their assistant. Ilsa hadn't known who Eloise was or the power that opportunity would grant her.

Ultimately, Ilsa wanted to be free from working for someone else.

The band had loved her ideas and hired her to create all the outfits they'd wear on stage through their North American Tour. From there, Ilsa began securing the connections and funding to open a boutique instead of selling her clothes out of the kitchen of her studio apartment.

Brenton wandered over, his eyes narrowing at Ilsa's arm through the crook of Nathan's elbow. His gaze shifted to Eloise's friend, Ana who was standing beside her husband Xander.

"Hey, I know you from something, don't I?" Brenton asked Ana. This man had no game...

"No, I doubt that." Ana stepped closer to Xander, confusion on her face.

"I do. I'd never forget a beautiful woman, and you are a very beautiful woman." He reached out and took Ana's hand, kissing her knuckles. Ana stared up at him, her hand frozen in the air, genuine revulsion crossing her brow.

"You have definitely never met me," Ana said, pulling her hand back and wiping it against her patterned sun dress.

Nathan stepped between them, throwing an arm around Brenton Michael's shoulders and turning him away.

"Hey, BMP, have you met Aria yet? I bet Theo is dying to introduce you to his date," Nathan said, leading Brenton away.

"So that was Brenton Michael Phillips." Xander patted the baby carrier strapped to his front. "I thought he'd be taller."

Ana snorted into her glass of champagne.

"It would surprise you how many short men dominate the industry," Ilsa said. She told them about the first time she met an action star and how he wore lifts in his shoes.

A waiter walked by with a tray of champagne. Seeing Ana's empty glass, Ilsa waved him over to grab a flute off the tray for her. The waiter, a shorter balding man, stopped beside Ilsa, blinking at her several times. He looked vaguely familiar. He was likely in a car commercial or played hardware store clerk number four on a sitcom. Los Angeles was full of working actors who had to hustle after hours until their big break. Giving him a half-hearted smile, she turned back to Ana and Xander.

Turning her attention back to the group, she saw Nathan had returned from diverting Brenton and asked Xander about the rain gardens he installed in their hometown. Xander lit up at the question, going into detail about its impact on polluted water.

Eloise and Keller finished their speech on the back porch, walking back into their home while making out like teenagers. Smiling, Ilsa moved closer to Nathan, gripping his arm tight. She caught Nathan's eye, and he winked down at her. She knew Nathan was thinking the same thing about Keller and Eloise. While on tour, she'd lost a bet with Nathan on how long it'd take for the couple to have sex. Nathan said four weeks. Ilsa said one. In the end, it was over two months. She loved her friend, but Eloise's lack of getting the dick when it was willing disappointed her. Regardless of how long it took them to finally do the 'dirty,' they were making up for lost time.

The baby on Xander's front fussed, making little squawky noises and a pink fist waving in the air. Ilsa liked the idea of babies. She liked their chubby little faces and their smooth skin. But hearing the noises coming out of the small creature reaffirmed her decision not to have them. They were nice, in theory. But similar to how she knew she'd never develop an interest in skydiving, she was not interested in being a mother.

Beside her, Ana nodded her head to the side, letting Xander know they should probably leave. The couple bid farewells, leaving Nathan and Ilsa alone in the middle of the party.

"I have a new one for you," she said. Nathan grinned at her.

A year before, a woman approached Nathan at a party and, in front of the entire room, said, "besides being a musician, I bet you're a great painter." Before he could ask her to explain, she leaned close to him and whispered, "because I'd let you paint all over my face tonight."

As Nathan declined the pick-up, Ilsa had laughed uproariously at the comment. It wasn't until a few weeks later, when she was propositioned in front of him, that they made it a game of who could get the worst pick-up lines.

So far, Ilsa was winning, as cocksure men were plentiful in LA. Nathan was doing fairly well. As a rock star, he had his share of women offering to have sex with him, but they often would show up naked instead of using pick-up lines.

"Okay, let's hear it."

Ilsa set her wineglass on a small round table and took on a lower voice. "Wanna play war? I'll lay on the ground, and you can blow the fuck out of me."

Throwing his head back to laugh, Nathan attracted the attention of other partygoers. "Oh, that's a great one. Classic. I bet you couldn't wait to go home with that guy."

"He was a charmer, for sure."

Ilsa's smile faded as she caught sight of the relentless pop star making his way toward them. "Oh, damn, here comes Brenton Michael again. Help hide me." Not waiting for him to agree, Ilsa grabbed Nathan's hand and pulled him to the outskirts of the party. Ducking around the corner, Ilsa tucked herself behind Nathan's bulky frame.

She'd managed to wrestle her and Nathan into a small alcove of potted ferns. They were slightly hidden from the party. How Nathan fit was beyond her, but she arranged the greenery above their heads until they were relatively covered.

"Why are you hiding from him?" Nathan looked as if he was trying to fight a smile.

"He thinks I want to go home with him. Which I don't."

"Then tell him no, Illy." Nathan was the only one she let call her that. Ilsa frowned at him, narrowing her eyes. "Right, you did."

"And he isn't taking the hint. You go home with a pop star one time after a few too many tequila shooters, and he thinks you're his personal groupie. It's revolting."

"Him or the presumption?" Nathan grinned.

Ilsa thought back to the pop star's million-dollar home in the hills. The living room and kitchen were covered with towers of beer cans and bongs filled with putrid water. "Both. I'm pretty sure he scratched up my leg with his toenails that night. Like, dude, use some clippers. It's not that hard."

Nathan let out a low chuckle she felt more than heard. The vibrations sent little shocks down her body. She put her foot out to step away, realizing how close she and Nathan had been standing together. She tapped his chest with a single acrylic nail sharpened to a coffin shape. "Don't laugh at me. It was gross. I had scabs from his toenails. I could've gotten sepsis."

He shook his head, rubbing the spot on his chest where Ilsa poked him. "You're not going to get sepsis from Brenton Michael Phillips."

"Not now, because I'm not sleeping with him again."

"Shouldn't have slept with him at all." Tilting his head to the side he looked through the foliage.

"Are you shaming me right now? Mister sleeping with a burlesque dancer in Las Vegas who picked her nose?"

"First, you wound me." Nathan put a hand over his heart and collapsed into the fern dramatically. The green leaves shook from the contact. "Second, I didn't know she was a nose-picker until after we had sex. And third, see if I tell you about my sex life again."

"You love telling me. Stop acting like you don't." Ilsa peered around Nathan's muscled arm to check if the coast was clear. "Ugh, he was the worst. He has to be a Leo, right? He has all those Leo vibes."

Nathan shook his head. "Are you pulling out his zodiac sign? That's not a real thing."

Ilsa eyed him up and down disdainfully. "That's such a Virgo thing to say."

Confident there was no sign of the persistent pop star, Ilsa moved to leave their little fern oasis. Then, down the walkway, she caught sight of Brenton Michael's black-and-white striped jacket.

"Damnit, come here." Before Nathan could resist, Ilsa pulled his face down until their noses touched. Their breath mingled together in the space between them. Her fingers threaded through his soft brown hair. She had never been this close to Nathan before. His glance flickered from her eyes to her lips. She felt him shift closer, the sweetness of his exhale against her lips. For a brief moment, she forgot why she pulled him so close. The rasp of shoes on decorative concrete brought her back. "Stay like this for a second. Let him think we're kissing or something," she said, her words so soft, it was more breath than volume.

Nathan held his face still. His nose brushed against hers. If she shifted at all, their lips would connect. His hand moved from his side to rest on her hip bone, pulling her body closer to his. She could feel every muscle along his body pressing into hers. She moved a step back, and he followed. Her back was to the wall of the house, his firm body pressed against hers. He fixed his attention on her face as they waited to move.

They didn't speak. They were motionless in their embrace. She saw a building heat behind the green-blue of his eyes as they met hers. The thumb that rested on her hip moved, sending a slow heated line that dove straight to her core. She let out a small gasp at the contact, and his pupils dilated. Against her stomach, she could sense something poking her and realized what it was.

He had a boner.

Nathan, her best friend, her confidante. Because he pressed against her. A boner. She wanted to feel disgusted or embarrassed. She felt none of those things. His body's reaction to hers turned her on. Hadn't she been thinking about him naked only fifteen minutes ago? Her tongue darted out, licking her lips. She watched as his eyes flickered to her mouth.

His head tilted to the side. He was going to kiss her. He had a boner, and he was going to kiss her. His head moved against hers, the roughness of his stubble on her cheek until his lips found her ear.

"I think he went the other way," he whispered.

As he pulled away, he kept her gaze. She realized at some point she had set her hands on his upper arms, grasping them. The powerful muscles under her hands tensed.

"Right." She dropped her hands from his muscles, folding her arms across her own chest. "Right."

Nathan stepped back. The absence of his hand on her hip cooled her skin. She felt icy everywhere. She rubbed a hand down her bare arms, wishing she'd brought a sweater to go over her dress. When she left her studio earlier that day, she'd been so pleased with her outfit—an Ilsa Kruger original fitted jade-green dress of charmeuse. Now, bereft of Nathan's heat, being a walking advertisement for her brand was the last thing on her mind.

Nathan shrugged his jacket off his shoulders, holding it out to Ilsa. "You're cold?"

Shaking her head, Ilsa forced a smile. "No, you're a heater. I'm getting back down to a standard fever-free temp."

"Are you saying I'm hot?" he teased.

Giving him a genuine smile, she relaxed. She was back to joking about pick-up lines with her friend. Momentary erections and impulses to kiss him aside, he was the best friend she had.

He was an attractive man. He had a symmetrical face, beautiful green-blue eyes, and fucking dimples, and he smelled good, like leather and clean soap, and he had a sexy laugh, and he—

Nope. He was a good friend. He was kind and funny, and he was her friend. Friend.

"I should get going. I have a nine a.m. meeting with Davis Gallegos tomorrow," she said.

"Is that a person's name or a company?"

Ilsa scrunched up her face. "Both. Thomas Gallegos and Irene Davis."

Nathan held his hand out to stop her as he peered around the corner. "Coast is officially clear. BMP has moved on to chatting up some other girl."

He offered to walk her to the front door, where the valet would retrieve her car, but she declined. After feeling his body pressed against hers, she needed some alone time. Standing on the front porch, she waited as the valet brought her car keys.

"Busy night?" she asked.

The valet shook his head. "Like you wouldn't believe. It's been a bit of a crush since Mr. and Mrs. Grant left for bed." The valet's cheeks colored as he realized he probably said too much. Ilsa waved off his comment. Eloise and Keller were not discreet when they snuck away. In LA, there was always a second party to go to, and most of the Hollywood elite would head there now.

She thanked the valet and tipped him before climbing into her car. The stress of her meeting the next morning must have addled her brain. She needed to focus on her presentation.

She would not think about the way Nathan's muscular arms felt against her hands. Gripping the steering wheel, she ignored the way her fingers still tingled from where she held onto him. Him, her friend. Her best friend, dammit.

Chapter Two

PLEATS
NATHAN

THIS PARTY BLEW. IT was fun for a while. George, the band's personal assistant, had outdone himself in hiring the best party planners in LA. No doubt George's assistants were somewhere on the outskirts of the party, making sure they executed every detail perfectly. The food was amazing. George made sure there was no kiwi in any of the food or drinks, so Nathan wouldn't have a reaction. Nathan always carried his epi-pen, but it was nice to have peace of mind. The DJ was great, some Scandinavian guy who was about to hit it big.

No, the party was fine. Except the second Ilsa left, it wasn't fun anymore. Even after years of living in this world of the elite, he couldn't get used to these parties. If he wanted a beer, they served it in a glass, never in a bottle, or worse, in a can. The whiskey was expensive vintage from Scotland, not his favorite fifteen-dollar bourbon from Kentucky. Adjusting the sleeves of his suit jacket, he longed to get home where he would change back into his T-shirt and joggers. Keller and Eloise wouldn't have cared if he didn't dress up, but in his family, it was a sign of respect to show up in your Sunday best for important events. He loved his bandmate, and he loved Eloise. The band had been together for five years, and in that time, they'd had two albums go platinum and their last one, Hellion, go double platinum. They sold out arenas across the world. They were the definition of success.

Across the lawn, he waved at Theo Blake, their lead singer. Theo was pulling a redemption tour with the media after a disastrous breakup with supermodel Safiya Khan a few months before. Their manager, Tamara, had set up some "dates" with b-list celebrities to help clean up his image. One of those dates was standing by Theo's side, a beautiful Aria Kingston, who recently finished the second season of a teen show. Nathan couldn't remember the plot, but he knew his youngest sister had a poster of the leading man on her bedroom wall. Nathan was also sure the same magazine featured him, Keller, and Theo shirtless. He couldn't imagine the horror of being a teenage girl, opening a magazine, and seeing your older brother shirtless.

Watching Ilsa all night, Nathan saw the way Brenton Michael Phillips had been following her around. Ilsa told Nathan about hooking up with him. It was an offhanded remark about nasty pop stars and lack of showering. It annoyed him. But it wasn't jealousy. Ilsa wasn't his to be jealous over. He didn't get mad when Theo started sleeping with Aria. Ilsa was his friend. Same as Theo and Keller, and Eloise. He couldn't allow any difference in his mind.

Until she pulled him close behind a wall of potted ferns. Hiding in that small area, he could feel all that was Ilsa pressed against his body. Never in the time they'd spent together had she held him so close. He could see the gray flecks in her blue eyes and felt her breath hitch as he held her hip. Through the thin material of her dress, she was warm. He didn't want to notice, but he could feel the texture of lace through her clothing. That got him thinking about her underwear and what color they could be. His thumb twitched, rubbing against the silk of her dress and curve of her hip. Without touching his lips to hers, he knew how she would taste, crisp as the champagne she'd been pretending to drink all night. When she licked her lips, he almost gave in. The need to kiss her thundered through him. His head somehow kept itself together enough to make him pause, but his wayward dick had other plans.

Using all the might he could muster, he somehow stepped away. Once he wasn't touching her, he could refocus on what was important. His friendship with Ilsa. Getting another drink, not kissing Ilsa, talking to other people at the party, not picturing Ilsa's lacy underwear.

After Ilsa left him in the backyard, he waited a few beats before following, making sure she got into her car. His father taught him from an early age, you take care of the people you care about. He knew it was old-fashioned, but it meant something to him. Ilsa could take care of herself. She'd moved to LA at twenty-two and made herself a force to reckon with in the design world. Living alone, she didn't need Nathan to make sure she got to her car. Still, he watched as she spoke to the valet for a minute before getting into her SUV.

Content she was safe behind the wheel of her car, he went back to the dwindling party. Most of the guests had left. There was a rumor that a recently divorced actress was throwing a party at her house to celebrate the end of her marriage to a Broadway director. Most of the guests were happy for a reason to leave Manhattan Beach.

Brenton Michael Phillips sauntered over to Nathan. The black and white coat he was wearing reminded him of those old-time movies of chain gangs working on railroads.

Nathan wasn't the most stylish person, but he also knew it was better to look classic than to take risks he couldn't pull off. The only person who could get him to wear more daring pieces was Ilsa. She had a sense of what would work for his body. Having her tell him he looked good helped a little, too.

"Yo!" Brenton Michael Phillips put out his hand to do some fist bump handshake. Nathan stared down at his outstretched hand. Nathan prided himself on being level-headed, rarely showing emotion aside from a general sense of congeniality. He shook Brenton's hand, squeezing a little harder than necessary. Jutting his chin out, Brenton asked, "Ilsa leave?"

Nathan nodded. "Yeah, a bit ago."

"Cool, cool. You know we hooked up."

Nathan had never liked Brenton Michael Phillips. He had a cool sound and an amazing strategy for promoting his music, but the actual man, not so much. Brenton didn't know Nathan well enough to be telling him about his exploits with Ilsa.

"Is that so?" Nathan asked, glancing away. He understood now why Ilsa wanted to hide behind a fern.

"Yeah, a while back. Saw each other at a club, and she was all over my dick. Girl had some mad sick moves. She was a good one, too. She left right after, none of that groupie shit we get sometimes, you know what I'm saying?" Elbowing him as if Nathan was going to commiserate with him.

Nathan felt his jaw tighten. This dumbass was making a serious faux pas, acting as if Ilsa was like any other girl. His thought must have shown on his face because Brenton stepped back. "Whoa, you two aren't hooking up, right? Cause I wouldn't do that. Bro-to-bro, that's not cool."

"No, nothing like that. We're friends." Nathan wasn't about to explain himself to Brenton Michael Phillips, of all people.

Brenton's shoulders relaxed. "Nice. Look, I'll see you around, right? We should jam together sometime. I bet a collab would be sick."

Nathan let him walk away without agreeing to his request. If he wasn't such a scummy guy, Nathan would have pursued a collaboration with him. But after commenting on Ilsa? No way.

Nathan caught sight of Aria Kingston, sans Theo, standing by the sidewalk. When Brenton Michael Phillips approached, she started walking to the front of the house as if they were leaving together but didn't want anyone to see. So much for "bro-to-bro" conduct.

Theo was sitting alone at a table overlooking the water. Nathan walked over and sat beside him, marveling at the view. Before he moved to California, Nathan had never seen the ocean. The vastness of it shocked him.

Nathan was always a big guy. In school, he was the tallest in his class, barely trying out for sports. He was broad-shouldered and gained muscle easily. He was used to towering over others, making his frame smaller to accommodate sitting in cars and auditorium seats. Standing at the edge of the shore, his feet in the rolling waves, he pictured himself as a speck on the Earth. It was the first time in his life he felt the triumph of being small in an enormous world. He loved the sensation of the ocean nearby, the roar of the water as it crashed into the sand, and the way the horizon looked close enough to touch and yet was always out of reach.

"I think your girlfriend took off," Nathan pointed out.

Theo tipped his beer back, draining it. "She's not my girlfriend."

Nathan waved the balding waiter over to ask for another beer. "That explains why you didn't care when she snuck out the back with Brenton Michael Phillips."

Theo looked over his shoulder at where he left the actress to find no one there. "I guess."

"Ilsa said he doesn't clip his toenails."

Theo blinked a few times at Nathan before chuckling. "Huh, well, I guess Ari will have to figure that out for herself. She wasn't even supposed to come with me. Tamara had us set up to do Nobu and go walk on the beach. Aria asked me if she could come tonight. I figured, why not? She can be fun sometimes, a little weird, but nice enough. Yeah, she's hot, but not, like, crazy hot. She's normal hot, like Ilsa."

The waiter returned with two bottles of beer, setting them on the table. Nathan nodded his appreciation and slipped him a twenty-dollar bill. "Ilsa isn't normal hot."

Theo raised a brow. "What is she, then?"

Nathan grabbed the beer and took a big swallow. "I don't know. She's Ilsa."

Theo studied him for a moment, a small smile playing on his golden boy face. "Right."

Nathan steered the conversation back to Theo's terrible love life. "So, you and Aria? I'm guessing she's not your type."

"Nah, I need to focus on the music. The publicity around me and Safiya messed me up. I can't be serious about another celebrity. Aria knows that. It works for both of us to be seen together. She's trying to get an audition for that Nellie Bly biopic."

Nathan whistled. All of Hollywood was talking about that script. It already had an award-winning director attached to it. The actress who landed that part would be in the running for an Oscar. "Good for her."

Theo looked around. "Where did everyone go?"

"Beatrix Ryan's divorce party."

"That's probably where Aria ended up. I told her I was heading home after this." Theo glanced back at the house. "You going to the party?"

Nathan shook his head. "No. I'll head home, too. I don't want to be hungover for recording tomorrow."

Theo laughed. "Man, how times have changed. Back when we first got together, we'd all stay out until four a.m. and then record all day afterward. You're getting old, man."

Theo gave Nathan a grin. Nathan was the youngest in the group by a few years. "Okay, grandpa." Nathan slapped Theo on the back. "Don't get into too much trouble."

Getting back to his house, he let himself in the front door. The long hallway leading into an open room overlooking the ocean. It wasn't as big as Keller's place or as flashy as Theo's. It had beach access off his back porch, a big soaking tub, and three bedrooms. When he moved in, he had to act like the whole place didn't make him crazy with excitement. Growing up, he thought having a fridge with an ice maker was the height of fancy. Now here he was in an oceanfront house. He took his clothes off, liking to be in his underwear. He had always hated wearing pants. What was the point of being presentable when he was alone at his home? Settling onto the couch, he checked the clock. If it were midnight in California, it'd be three in the morning at his parents' house. He couldn't call them, no matter how much he wanted to hear their voices.

It'd been a while since he was home. He meant to visit after their last tour, *Hellions: North America*, but when they returned to LA, they had to fire their manager, renegotiate a contract with their label, Repercussions Studio, and agree to fast-track their next album.

He barely had time to enjoy the money he was making. They were working so hard. When he got his first big check, he paid off his parent's home and bought his father a bottle of Pappy Van Winkle. His father never opened it, saying his Kentucky Tavern had been fine for years and that wouldn't change, no matter how much money his son made. Now, his family was refusing the money he tried to send home and he was stuck alone in a fancy waterfront house.

He had a house facing the ocean, a car that could go from zero to sixty in under three seconds, and an off-road vehicle. He vacationed in St. Lucia, Iceland, and Singapore.

And it was all for nothing.

Every night he came home to an empty house. He made the mistake one time of bringing a girl home from the club. She refused to leave, locking herself in his bathroom for an hour. When she finally left, it was with thousands of dollars of his personal items stuffed in places he didn't want to picture.

Eloise looked it up online. The woman sold his stuff for a tidy profit. Why someone would want his half-empty cologne, he had no idea. It wasn't worth the publicity to press charges, but he vowed he wouldn't make the same mistake again. Now when he hooked up, he'd go to their place, or they'd get a hotel.

Not that he'd been hooking up much lately. Options were plentiful on tour. There were women at every stop who'd pay extra for VIP treatment, getting backstage passes. Every city afforded him an opportunity to meet a different girl.

But early in the tour, he soured at the idea of taking girls to his dressing room. It'd been months since he hooked up with anyone. They all looked the same—all glossy lips and low-cut tops. He admired the way they went for what they wanted, but he'd leave the next day and they'd stay behind in their town.

Halfway through the tour, Ilsa started coming to his dressing room to talk after the rest of the guys were dressed. She'd save styling him until last each night. They'd talk about her life, the clothing line she was creating, and how she wanted to open her own shop. He'd tell her about moving from small-town Kentucky for school in LA and the culture shock of it all. They talked about the music they liked and the books they didn't. The correct toppings on pizza and which college had the best basketball team—his UK Wildcats obviously being the correct answer.

On the day he met Ilsa, he was so worried. When she walked in on him and Shelby having sex, he thought she must be another girl who went backstage to hook up with a band member. It'd happened before, and Shelby had gladly welcomed the extra girl into their bed.

In walks this long-legged, blonde bombshell with full lips begging to be kissed, and Nathan was more than willing to let her in. A moment into Ilsa walking in, he realized she wasn't a fan but someone else. After Shelby left, Nathan pulled Eloise aside and asked her about Ilsa. Realizing how badly he screwed up, he put on a brave face and introduced himself. She was a professional, and she deserved his respect.

Nathan wouldn't pretend that moment hadn't played in his mind a few times over the past year and a half. Ilsa was gorgeous and amazing to look at, but she was also smart, had more dirty jokes than most men he knew, and was confident in her sexuality. Most of all, Ilsa was a good friend. She listened to him when he missed his family. She supported Eloise as she tried to break into the business. Ilsa treated her employees well. He swore he'd never again make her uncomfortable around him. No matter how she made him feel when he finally turned the lights off.

Scrubbing his hand over his face, he tried to banish the memory how Ilsa felt against his body. He could have his pick of almost any woman in LA. Why was he was thinking of the one who might never choose him?

Chapter Three

Ruching

IF THERE WAS A word Ilsa would use to describe herself, it was determined. When she was fifteen, she was determined to win the local pageant to secure scholarship dollars for college. As a young student at the Fashion Institute, she was determined to be at the top of her class. When she moved to LA with little more than a few references and a dream, she was determined to get a job working with some of the top names in town.

And today, standing in front of the nondescript skyscraper in downtown LA, she was determined to nail her meeting with Davis Gallegos. If this meeting went well, she'd have the funding to expand her line from ten items to over fifty pieces.

Like the pageants and school, she relied on her sheer determination to help her succeed. She put in the time creating a financially sound business plan. Her online sales had already been strong for years and the press around her designs were always on a positive trajectory. Her limited line was featured in a few smaller publications about her styling of Prevalent Notion for the Hellion tour.

Walking into the lobby, she was directed to the 32nd floor where the venture capitalists were waiting to meet with her. The elevator was a mirrored thing. She fought the urge to smooth her dress in the reflection. The outfit she picked was painstakingly created. All her own designs, she paired a periwinkle leather top with chiffon sleeves softened by a midi tulle skirt. The only thing not of her own design were the sky-high nude heels with red bottoms. They cost a fortune but were, fortunately, a gift from her mentor, Allegra Cuoco, who already owned several pairs. Ilsa finished the outfit with simple earrings and a thin bangle bracelet. She'd curled her long blonde hair and pulled it into a low side ponytail, showing off the undercut on her left side. She waffled over if she should take out her nose piercing, finally opting to leave it in. Her half-sleeve tattoos were mostly covered by the dolman sleeve of her top. She looked fashionable and professional. Before she could second guess herself, she took a picture of herself in the reflection for Eloise.

Ilsa's shoes made a clacking noise as she made her way down the long marble hallway to their office. Greeted by a bored-looking young man behind the desk, she was asked to sit and wait. Taking a seat in a white chair that was more art than furniture, Ilsa resisted the urge to check her phone again. Pulling out her portfolio, she studied the numbers she'd collected. Fashion, art, and design were her talents. Things like budget, cash flow projections, and collateral were out of her wheelhouse. She worked hard at understanding the answers to those questions.

Fifteen minutes past their meeting time, and Ilsa was still waiting. She wasn't sure if this was a power move or if it was poor time management on their part. Giving up on the portfolio in her lap she pulled out her phone from her oversized bag. There was a text waiting for her from Nathan.

Nathan: *Do you know karate? Because your body is kicking.*

Ilsa smiled to herself. His joke was exactly the reprieve from her nerves she needed before going into the meeting. She was relieved to see they could resume their jokes with one another. She tried not to think about how Nathan's body felt against hers in that little space. Or how she'd drifted off to sleep with the image of his lips so close to her own. She texted back.

Ilsa: *Thanks. Pervert.*

Before she could slide the phone back into her purse, he responded.

Nathan: *Knock 'em dead.*

The phone rang at the desk, and the bored man picked up, answering questions with a blasé "Okay, alright." He hung up and called over the tall counter, "Mr. Gallegos and Ms. Davis will see you now."

Ilsa shoved her phone into her purse as she fumbled with her portfolio. When she walked by the man's desk to the office, the receptionist snapped his fingers at her. "Hey, be tee dubs, cute skirt."

Ilsa flashed him the steadiest smile she could muster and made her way to the meeting that'd determine the fate of her business.

Two hours later, Ilsa was approaching the coffee shop where she was meeting Eloise. Once she got to the ground floor of the skyscraper, she took her heels off, replacing them with the flats she'd stashed in her bag. The leather top was cute that morning, but under the unforgiving California sun she was sweating. Her air conditioning had crapped out a month before. The quote to fix it was so high she knew she'd have a choice between AC or paying her employees. It was an obvious choice.

She'd hoped this meeting would've solved her lack of cash flow, but she wasn't so sure when she left. The man, Thomas Gallegos, had looked engaged, asking questions about not only the line and business plan but about Ilsa herself. Irene Davis sat stone-faced, watching Ilsa through dark brown eyes. The few times she asked a question, they were tricky ones that Ilsa stumbled over. In the end, they both shook her hand and let her know they'd be in touch.

Eloise was already settled at a small table in the back. Raising her arm over her head, she waved, her gigantic diamond ring catching the light. Eloise wasn't famous enough to be recognized, unlike her husband and his bandmates. Ilsa sensed that was about to change soon, with Eloise's debut record coming out.

"Sorry, I'm late. The meeting ran long." Ilsa dropped into the chair opposite Eloise. God bless her. She'd already gotten Ilsa's cold brew with oat milk. "Oh, you got my drink already. It was my turn, Lou."

Eloise knocked the comment away with her hand. "It's a small price to pay since you wouldn't let me pay for my dress from last night."

Ilsa had worked for weeks on perfecting the dress for Eloise and Keller's wedding reception. While a large part of creating the dress was to give Eloise the wedding of her dreams, since she'd married Keller in a Las Vegas Chapel after drinking too much, Ilsa figured she deserved a redo. Also, Ilsa couldn't pretend that the exclusive coverage by the nation's largest celebrity magazine didn't play a part. Under each picture of Eloise and Keller looking adorably in love would be the words *Bride in an Ilsa Kruger original.* A person couldn't pay for that kind of press.

"You know it'll work out for me in the end. You did me a favor. I know you had designers beating down your door to style you."

Eloise wrinkled up her nose. "As if I would use any of them over you." Shaking her head, Eloise's pastel, rainbow-colored hair moved as she talked. Ilsa liked the way Eloise was always changing her hair color. The boldest Ilsa dared was an undercut. She wasn't touching her blonde hair with color.

"How did I do last night? Keller was tired, so he wanted to go to bed early."

Ilsa laughed. "That is a bald-faced lie. I know exactly what you two were up to when you left your own wedding party early. I hope the orgasms were worth it."

Eloise straightened up haughtily. "They were. Now, what did I miss while having the best sex of my life? I saw you talking to Brenton Michael Phillips. Is there something going on there?"

Ilsa groaned. "No, definitely not. That was a one-and-done situation. I'll never go there again." Ilsa had never been ashamed of her sexual exploits. She had urges, the same as anyone. She was always careful and never put herself in an unsafe situation. Every time she hooked up with a guy, she'd send Eloise a copy of his driver's license with a text saying *If I die, it was this guy.*

Ilsa had been so busy with work she rarely had time to get dinner or drinks with a friend, let alone hook up with a random guy. It'd been a long few months of battery-operated tools and the internet.

"He's cute if you like that scrubby look. Not my type, but where I'm from, guys who dressed like they could be homeless took up about half of my graduating class." Eloise said, referring to her Pacific Northwest roots.

Ilsa shook her head. "Trust me, I am not going there again."

"Was there anyone else who caught your eye at the party? Did you talk to Keller's friend from New York? Abraham? He was cute, right?"

Ilsa struggled to remember the man. She'd talked to him briefly—a jazz musician a few years older than her. He was cute, but there was no spark. "Yeah, he was cute, but he lives in New York. Besides, he's a musician."

"So is Keller," Eloise responded.

"And so are you. That's fine for you. I'm sure a lot of girls would love to be with a musician, but that's not what I want. Keller is great, and I know you love him, but he's not normal. Sorry, but most musicians are like Theo, or even worse like Brenton Michael Phillips. Some guy who thinks his dreams are bigger and more important than mine? No, thank you."

Ilsa had been at the party the previous year where Theo and his supermodel girlfriend, Safiya, had loudly broken up. She liked Theo reasonably well. He was always kind and respectful to Ilsa. But the stuff he said to Safiya while they were fighting? If that's what a woman had to tolerate being with a rock star, she'd pass.

"Theo was going through a rough time." Eloise paused before adding, "but yeah, it was not a good look for those kinds of men. I can see that. What about Nathan?"

Ilsa was startled at the question. "What about him? Did he say something? Did you see something? What have you heard?"

Across the table, the hand holding Eloise's latte was frozen halfway to her mouth as she stared at Ilsa, bewildered. Bringing her coffee slowly back down to the table, Eloise leaned forward. "I haven't seen or heard anything. I was asking if he had met anyone? Is there something I should know?"

"No." The word came out more forceful than Ilsa intended. Softening her tone, Ilsa repeated herself. "No. Nothing. I didn't see him talking to anyone."

Eloise pursed her lips as she studied Ilsa. She let out a noncommittal noise before taking a drink of her coffee. "Tell me about the meeting. Did they love your designs?"

Somehow, Ilsa managed not to let out an audible sigh of relief at the change in subject. She was mixed up enough about her moment with Nathan. Talking with a happily in love Eloise was only going to confuse her more. Knowing Eloise, she'd push for a double date. As if Ilsa had time for anything more than to-go food in between working.

Ilsa gave Eloise a rundown of the meeting, lamenting that she had no real idea how well it went. Eloise assured her that the company would be foolish not to invest in Ilsa's company. After thirty minutes, Ilsa's timer went off on her phone, alerting her to get back to the shop.

"Lou, I'm so sorry. I want to chat longer, but I have to get back to the shop."

"Those clothes aren't going to make themselves." Eloise rose to give Ilsa a hug. "Remember, I look terrible in red, so make sure you have something I can wear in the collection."

"Something? You're going to be my spokesmodel. I'm using you as a brand ambassador." Pressing a quick kiss to Eloise's cheek, Ilsa left her in the coffee shop.

Back at the studio, she met her lead seamstress, Trinh, about the newest piece in the line. Something wasn't working on the three previous versions, and it was going to bother her until she figured out a solution. After working together under their mentor, Allegra Cuoco, whose real name was Angela Cook, Ilsa brought Trinh with her when she branched off into her own line. She never regretted it for one minute. Trihn balanced her out with calm and brevity. Their working styles complemented each other.

As Ilsa walked in, Trinh waved at her with a deep-purple manicured hand before hunching back over the sewing machine she was working on. While Trinh worked over the fabric, Ilsa walked to the bolts of cloth hanging on the wall. Talking with Eloise about the dress inspired Ilsa to try a new direction with the problem piece she'd been laboring over. Trinh's favorite music played lightly on the speaker, and they worked alongside each other as Ilsa filled Trinh in on the meeting that morning. Trinh believed in the label so much that she turned down more lucrative offers from other designers to come with Ilsa. Ilsa hoped she could soon pay Trinh what she deserved. So far, the profit sharing was working okay for Trinh, but if Ilsa couldn't expand, she might risk losing the most talented member of her team.

A beep sounded from Trinh's phone. Looking at the screen, Trinh cursed under her breath. "Shoot, I have to get going. I'm meeting a guy at Proper Bar for a drink."

"Oh, a date. Sounds fun." Ilsa couldn't remember the last date she'd been on. "Good for you, getting a little excitement in your life."

Trinh put the phone down, frowning at Ilsa. "You could too, you know. If you wanted a quickie, I bet you could find a guy in fifteen minutes on an app."

Ilsa picked up the bolt of fabric from the table, stretching it out to test how the color contrasted with the periwinkle fabric. "I don't have fifteen minutes. Plus, 85% of those men don't know the difference between a clit and an asshole. What's the point of spending all night leading up to a hook-up to go home and finish the job myself?"

Trinh's face brightened. "I have the perfect stuff for you! Franny is branching into intimate items."

Ilsa groaned. Trinh's cousin, Franny, was often dabbling in new business ideas. She tried being a pastry chef, a jewelry maker, and a handmade crochet rug maker. Apparently, she was now creating personal care items. Ilsa loved Trinh dearly and trusted her business acumen and talent for design, but when looking at the faults of her family, Trinh was blind. Ilsa admired her loyalty.

Ilsa only had her mother in Phoenix, and if she could limit their communication to once a month, it was too much.

"Trinh, I love you, but Franny has some terrible ideas. Remember those lavender jalapeno macaroons she tried selling at the farmer's market? I'm not so sure I want anything she's selling on my body."

"It's totally organic."

"So is arsenic."

Trinh ignored Ilsa as she dug through her purse. Pulling out a small bottle labeled *exxxcitement oil,* Trinh shoved it in Ilsa's hands. "I think she's finally got a winning product this time. Try it. I love it."

After Trinh left in a cloud of bergamot and lemon, Ilsa tentatively opened the bottle and took a small sniff of the oil. She was taken aback by the pungent scent of mint and something else. She couldn't put her finger on it. It wasn't an unpleasant smell.

Putting a small dab on her finger, she rubbed the oil into the back of her hand where it tingled slightly but not unpleasantly. Deciding it was harmless enough, she threw the bottle in her bag. Ilsa turned back to the sewing table where she needed to get three dresses out by the end of the day.

With Trinh gone on her date, she was alone in the lofty room. Ilsa called out to her smart device to change the music. The opening bass chords of a song played as the familiar sound of Prevalent Notion filled the room.

Her hand stilling on the fabric before her, Ilsa remembered the way Nathan looked the first time he played this song for her. She had no musical experience. When she did pageants as a teen, her talent was speed drawing. She couldn't tell what made for a good song or not, but the way Nathan held her eyes as he played, the tentative thrum of his fingers along the frets when he finished, his velvet voice warm from singing when he asked her if she liked it. It was a heady feeling to have a man of such talent look at her and want her approval. Like the first time she heard the song, her finger wandered to her lips, tracing them as if his voice was a kiss she never wanted to be parted from.

In the band, Theo was the golden one—golden hair, golden voice, and golden persona. But deep inside, Ilsa always felt Nathan was the best of them all. He was the strength that held the band together. For a moment, she wanted to know what that strength would feel like around her.

Chapter Four

Jersey
Nathan

THE CRASH OF THE cymbals reverberated around the room as Nathan played the last note of their new song. Since letting go of their previous manager, Arnie, the year before, the band had been experimenting with their own material. Arnie always brought them songs he said the label wanted to hear them play, limiting the number of original songs they had on each record. They discovered Eloise had been ghostwriting many of the songs they played and decided to fire Arnie at the shortest band meeting they ever had.

Since hiring their new manager, Tamara Sullivan, they've been branching out into more creative songwriting. Keller was working on a new jazz compilation album with some of the genre's biggest stars and brought that influence into their songwriting. Theo was writing lyrics with a depth and sensitivity they rarely saw from him. Nathan wanted to bring more bluegrass to their music.

He was heavily influenced by the music of his childhood and the sounds of county fairs and festivals in the rolling green areas of his youth. Together, they were melding these sounds into something unlike their previous albums. It might be a complete flop to take such a departure from their target audience, but they decided as a group, they'd go all in. If they failed at this genuine attempt, they'd do it together. The arena rock sound was fun for a while, but they knew they could only play the same sound for so long before the audience got bored.

After grabbing a water bottle from the mini fridge, Nathan picked up his phone to check messages. When he and the guys began playing, they'd get wrapped up in the music so much they'd forget to eat. There were emails from Tamara reminding him of an upcoming interview and photo shoot, confirming the date of their album cover shoot. Tamara said the album cover shoot would be sexy. Nathan fought back the groan in his throat.

Keller was the kind of guy who had to exercise to let out pent-up energy. He liked to run, for God's sake. It was inhumane. Nathan had hardly ever seen Theo work out, yet he still maintained a fit physique. Nathan never let himself get too flabby, but he was softer. As much as he enjoyed lifting weights and building up muscle, there was a layer of cushion created from his love of gravy and beer-battered foods that he struggled to get rid of. He'd never be the sex symbol of the group, and he knew it. But that didn't mean that he didn't enjoy looking his best. Working out daily, he tried to keep himself as much to celebrity standards as he could, but it was exhausting.

He wondered if Ilsa would help dress him. Moving to his messages, he went to type out a request that she come over that night. There was already a text from her, waiting for him.

Ilsa: *If I said I work for UPS, can I handle your package?*

Nathan let out a loud laugh, getting the attention of Keller and Theo.

"Sorry, Ilsa sent me a joke." Nathan typed out a message asking Ilsa to come over that evening to help him pick out clothes. She responded that she'd pick up some dinner, suggesting Thai. After telling her she should come over around five, he set his phone down.

"What's up with you two?" Keller asked as he made a note in his songbook. "You guys hooking up yet?"

"Yet? What makes you think we're going to hook up?" he asked, a strange flush creeping up his neck.

Theo and Keller glanced at each other, a silent conversation happening between them. He recognized the look. It was the same one he and Ilsa would give each other when Keller and Eloise would bicker the year before. That was before the two of them had a few too many drinks and got married by an Elvis impersonator in Las Vegas, hours before they kicked off the North American Tour.

Nathan shook his head. "We're friends. I wouldn't want Ilsa to feel weird around me."

"You totally want to bone her," Keller said.

"Don't say 'bone' about Ilsa. That's gross." Nathan's voice was sharper than he intended it to be.

Keller threw his head back and laughed. "I'm gross? Do you remember how much shit you gave me about Eloise when we got married? Every day you'd asked me if we'd done it yet."

"That's different—"

"Yeah, because she's my wife." Keller picked up his drumstick, twirling it around on his fingers as he talked. "All I'm saying is, weirder things have happened. I mean, look at me. I married a woman after kissing her once. And I'm the luckiest bastard on the planet."

Keller was disgustingly happy, too. Happier than Nathan had ever seen him. Somehow, the man-whore of the group had turned into the most straight-laced overnight.

"I'm telling you, nothing is going on with Ilsa and me. We're just two super sexy-looking friends."

Theo snorted into his drink. "Bro, you are a terrible liar."

Nathan picked up a balled-up piece of paper off the floor, throwing it at Theo's head. "Let's get back to it. I think we might need a key change at the beginning of *Vermillion*."

Forty minutes into his workout, and Nathan was covered in sweat. He never enjoyed exercise. As a child, his body was too big, his limbs tripping him at every turn. As an adult, he'd grown into his long arms and legs, filling them out with muscles. Weight lifting was his favorite part—the act of building muscle mass, of becoming strong. But cardio, never. He ran on his state-of-the-art treadmill, hating every minute. Keller talked of the "runner's high" he got, but Nathan only felt abject annoyance at the activity. Still, he needed to stay in shape. Performing on stage was an endurance sport. He had to perform night after night with energy, or the fans wouldn't enjoy the experience.

Running always had to happen first in his daily workout, or else he'd be tempted to skip it. Saving the best part for last was the only way he could get it done.

The 90s rap music blasting through his phone stopped for a moment as a text came through. Stabbing the stop button with his finger, Nathan picked up his phone to unlock it.

Shelby: *Hey, sexy. What are you doing tonight?*

Nathan groaned. His ex-girlfriend Shelby had recently been dumped by her director boyfriend. Since the very public breakup, she'd been reaching out to Nathan. Shelby had been the one to break things off in the first place. She told him that if she was going to transition from TV to movies, she needed someone with more star power beside her.

After being dumped, Nathan spent a few days wallowing, before realizing he was more upset with the dating pattern that'd emerged in his life since he became famous. In the few years since the band hit it big, he'd gone out with a few different women. All of them left him, saying that they couldn't see anything serious. The first few times, he could brush it off, but after the fifth girlfriend said the same thing, he got worried. He didn't love these women, but all of them saying the same thing felt damning.

He wasn't in a rush to settle down or anything. He just wanted to know that it was possible to find something genuine. So far, he was failing. All he'd found were one-night stands and celebrities who wanted him for his bedroom prowess. Even when Shelby was dating her producer boyfriend, she tried to invite him over for a late-night 'chat.' There were lines he'd never cross, and being the other man was one of them. He made the mistake of seeing Shelby once after the breakup, but it was obvious she only wanted sex. There were hundreds of men who'd have cut off their right arm for a night with Shelby Waters. But Nathan couldn't do it.

Ignoring the string of texts, which included a nude photo, Nathan picked up the dumbbell, starting another set of reps. As a man raised in a more traditional house, he liked the idea of monogamy and commitment. He wanted someone to confide in and to share his day with. His parents may not have been passionate with each other, but they were good friends. In a few months, they'd be celebrating their thirty-fifth wedding anniversary. Nathan talked them into letting him pay for a trip. He suggested one of the Caribbean Islands, but his parents insisted that a few nights in a nice lodge in the mountains of Tennessee was more than enough. Even that had been a tug of war between them.

He wondered what Ilsa would think of his parents. They refused to come out to California. His dad blamed his work at the power company. Nathan knew his father had more than enough personal leave saved up. He'd never taken a sick day in his life, worked holidays when asked, and was an all-around model employee. But his father also hated change. The one time he got his parents to LA, his father was miserable the whole time. His mother was easier, wanting to see the sights and dip her toes in the Pacific Ocean. He was sure his parents would love Ilsa. He'd rarely seen anyone work as hard as her. Her steadfast determination was striking compared to so many. His father would appreciate that.

Nathan shook his head. Why would he be wondering what his parents would think of Ilsa? He didn't worry about what his parents would think of Theo or Keller. Hell, he didn't even think about whether his parents would like Shelby—he suspected they wouldn't have liked her at all—but the idea of his mother meeting Ilsa made him smile.

He knew he liked Ilsa. As much as he tried to believe in the speech he gave his bandmates earlier, he'd admit to himself that he was full of shit. He thought about her all the time. When he had news, Ilsa was the one he wanted to tell. When he had a bad day, talking to Ilsa made him feel better. Even when she was incredibly busy, she always made time for him. He trusted her with things he told no one. She was gorgeous, funny, and smart. She understood him. Ilsa was the total package for him.

For a moment, he allowed himself to fantasize about what he'd do if given the chance to be with her. He thought about the way her soft hair would feel under his fingers as he brushed it from her face. Her lips were against his, as he took her mouth. The way her body would become pliant under his. Her skin was soft as he roamed his hands across her hot flesh.

He gulped. His erection was straining against his underwear. Setting the weights on the bench, he stared down at his bulging appendage. He could take care of himself. With the images in his head, he knew it'd only take a few minutes. But fantasizing about Ilsa like that felt wrong— cheap, even. She wasn't some random girl to him. She was his best friend. He'd take a cold shower instead.

Slinging a towel over his shoulder, he made his way to the bathroom. A knock on the door stopped him in his tracks. Glancing at the clock, he realized it was five. Exactly when he'd told Ilsa to come over. He'd somehow lost track of time. Cursing, he raced back to his bedroom, where he pulled on a pair of sweatpants and hoped his dick would behave enough to not be noticeable. He had to get himself together. It could only be a fantasy. He could never risk the best friend he had for a lover who, like the others, would never stay.

GODET
ILSA

$\mathbf{I}$LSA TAPPED ON NATHAN'S front door with the toe of her high-heeled boot. On the other side, she could hear the shuffling of footsteps and a low curse before the door swung open. Nathan stood on the other side with what looked like denim print athletic shorts slung low on his waist. He wore no shirt, and sweat glistened on his bare chest. As Nathan ran a towel over his sweaty face, Ilsa allowed herself a single glance down his body before snapping her eyes back up to a more platonic spot.

"Working out?" she asked. Holding up the plastic bags in her hands, she handed one to Nathan.

"Yeah, we have a photo shoot for the new album cover in a few weeks. According to Tamara, it's going to be *sexy*. I'm making sure I don't look like a sea sponge next to Theo and Keller." He took both bags from her hand and turned to walk down the hall, knowing she'd follow him.

"You work out in denim shorts?"

He looked down at his lower half and scowled. "These are not just any shorts. These are replicas of the best uniform the Cats ever had in '96."

"I didn't understand half of that statement." Ilsa shook her head. "Doesn't matter. Fashion is subjective."

As if he decided that arguing the fashion merits of the University of Kentucky's basketball team wasn't worth it, he changed the subject.

"You're early."

"It's five. You said to come over around five."

"I meant five in a vague sense, like five-thirty-ish."

"Then you should have said five-thirty." Ilsa dug the chopsticks out of her bag and set them on the table next to the takeout containers. "I got you two-stars because I know you don't like it too spicy."

"I like to actually taste my food, not burn my taste buds off." Nathan ducked down the hallway, leaving Ilsa alone in the kitchen.

"Wimp," Ilsa called out to his back.

Ilsa turned to the cabinet, pulling the plates down from their shelf to the right of the fridge. Nathan returned to the kitchen, wearing a faded T-shirt. His hair looked less messy, and she wondered if he ran a comb through it.

"Do you have any white wine? I'm in the mood for a white." Ilsa got up from the table and was already halfway across his kitchen.

"In the door, there should be a bottle I opened last night."

Ilsa opened the stainless-steel fridge door, peering inside the monstrosity. Once the doors were open, Nathan's fridge was half the size of the kitchen in her studio. "I don't see it."

"It's right here." Nathan pulled a bottle out of the door, holding it up for Ilsa.

"Nate, that's not wine."

Crinkling his nose, he scoffed. "Yes, it is. It says wine on the bottle."

Ilsa took the bottle from him. "Moscato? This is grape juice. Do you have any idea how much sugar is in a glass of this? It's like drinking a lollipop."

Nathan took the bottle back, holding it to his chest. "I happen to like this wine."

"It's a travesty to sommeliers everywhere."

"Good thing I went into the music industry then and not winemaking."

"I'm surprised is all, a big tough guy like you? I was expecting three fingers of bourbon or IPA, not—this."

"I'm disappointed in you, Ilsabeth. Have you no sense of adventure? This happens to be an excellent vintage I had Alexis get from the gas station," he said, referencing his assistant Alexis.

"You're a manly man. It's just not a manly wine."

Nathan raised a brow, shaking his head. "I was unaware wine had a dick."

Ilsa fought back a laugh.

"I'm 29 years old. I'm rich beyond my wildest dreams. I've traveled the world and met amazing people. In all my life experiences, I think I've earned the right to drink whatever fruity wine I choose. You or anyone else cannot denigrate my choices."

"Denigrate, huh? That's an SAT word. Been holding on to the speech for a while?" Ilsa asked with a smirk.

Nathan smiled. "Maybe a little."

Ilsa got two wine glasses out of the cabinet to the left of the sink. She held them out, and Nathan filled them almost to the brim. Taking a tentative sip, the wine hit her taste buds. It was as sweet as she expected it to be, but no more than if she would've ordered a cosmopolitan. Beside her, Nathan took a large swallow before grinning at her.

"See, it's good."

"Okay, I'll admit it's good."

Nathan grinned over the top of his glass before setting it down. "You hold tight. I gotta wash this sweat off me. I'll be back in five."

"Hurry, the food will get cold," Ilsa yelled to his retreating back. He waved a hand at her, flicking her comment away. She heard the click of his bathroom door down the hall. His house was well insulated so she couldn't hear the water running, but her mind went there, anyway. She imagined his body, slick with water, his head tipped back under the spray, the rivulets falling down his bare chest.

Ilsa had to admit she liked the image a little too much. She liked that he refused to be shamed for his drink choices. She liked that he let her take control over what they ate. And as much as she didn't want to admit it, she liked the way he looked when he opened the door. Bare-chested, sweaty, and oh so strong.

Ilsa had every intention of taking home the leftovers from the dinner, but between Nathan's appetite and having forgotten to eat lunch earlier, there was only a single carrot and bean sprout at the bottom of the takeout box. While her hometown had amazing options for a variety of Mexican, southwestern, and prickly pear everything foods, what they lacked was quality Thai food. The first time she had Phad Thai in LA, she was blown away by how different it was from the tomato-based noodle dish she'd had in her hometown. Rising from her spot on the floor, Ilsa went to grab the boxes to throw them away. Nathan grabbed her wrist. A tingle shot up her arm and into her chest. It was as if her whole body lit up from his touch.

"Let me take care of the garbage," he insisted.

Ilsa settled back down on the floor, bringing her legs up to her chest. Nathan had changed into a thin gray shirt that clung to his muscular back. The sleeves were tight around his upper arms. Most of her ex-boyfriends had been thinner men, tall and waifish. She was sure if she tried to wrap her hand around Nathan's biceps, her fingers wouldn't touch. They were the arms a man used to pick a woman up and hold her against a shower wall. A shiver of pleasure at the thought raced down the back of Ilsa's neck.

Don't go there, Ilsa.

"More wine?" Nathan called out from the kitchen.

Ilsa hesitated. She already had two glasses and was feeling the heat from the drinks. More wine could lead to poor choices, like mauling her best friend.

"I have an early day tomorrow. I should probably get going."

Nathan returned, wiping his hand on a dish rag with red roses all over it. She remembered him saying once that his mother sent him a bunch of kitchen items when he moved into his house. The floral print was as far from the typical chic LA style as anything could be. Ilsa liked that he used the dish towels his mother sent him. She liked that he drank sweet wine and that he had muscular arms.

She liked him.

"You said you'd help me pick out what to wear to the interview tomorrow. I can't let you leave until I'm fully decked out."

Ilsa had said that. It was the whole point of her coming over. Pulling herself up to standing, she nodded at him. "You're right. I did. Let's do this."

Ilsa hung the three options for outfits on the back of the door. It was likely the stylist for the photo shoot would have clothes they wanted the band to wear, but for the actual interview at least Ilsa could get him in an outfit that suited him.

"You nervous?" Ilsa asked.

Nathan lounged back on his elbows, watching Ilsa work. "No, it's all pretty standard by now. Theo and Keller are the ones the press is primarily interested in. Everyone is wondering about Keller's marriage or Theo's new actress girlfriend. They don't ask me as many questions."

Ilsa paused, turning to him. She never understood the way Theo got the attention. As the lead singer, he was put out front, sure, but Nathan was talented, handsome, and funny. How the press never seemed to pick up on that was beyond her. "Does that bother you?"

Nathan shook his head. "Nah, I'd rather have them ignore me than dig into my personal details. You hear these horror stories of the press going after family members for gossip. I'd hate for my family to get targeted if I got too famous. I like where I'm at. I have the money, and cool clothes, and fun parties, but I don't get hounded by the paparazzi the way Keller and Theo do."

"You know you're as talented as them, don't you?" Ilsa asked. Nathan's cheeks colored at the compliment. She wondered how often he was told that. Vowing to tell him more often, Ilsa smoothed her hand over the hanging clothes. "There we go. You should be all set."

Ilsa chose a print that she knew would stretch his comfort zone. It was a fabulous pattern with a color she knew would look incredible, contrasting the green of his eyes. Ilsa flopped down beside him on the bed, something she did often when over at his house. She sunk into the downy of his white comforter. She tried to remember if he had a housekeeper who did his laundry or if he could keep his bedding this white on his own.

Nathan looked over at the outfits. "Why is it so hard to dress myself, but you come over, and it's easy?"

Ilsa turned her head to look at him. He was close enough that she could see the small scar below his lip. Her finger itched to trace the edge of that white line to where it met his lip.

"We all have our talents," Ilsa responded. She shoved her hands under her back, fighting against the urge to touch him. Staring up at his high ceiling, she counted the exposed beams above her head.

"You more than others." Nathan turned on his side so he was facing Ilsa.

"Okay, Mister Grammy-nominated rock star. I'm the talented one, sure." She could feel his gaze on her, but she couldn't turn to face him.

Nathan was silent for a moment. She could hear the way he leaned closer to her and felt the blanket move beside her. His voice was more serious than before. "Ilsa. I think you are the most amazing person I've ever known."

His words burrowed inside her, filling the little space she allowed for kind words. She learned from an early age how hollow those words can be. Actions were the currency, and she was forced to earn every cent. From her pageant days to working harder than every other person at school, she never let the words of affirmation sink in, never allowed herself to revel in them because, in the end, they'd never get her what she needed. She had to do that.

But how tempted she was by Nathan's words and the honesty in his voice. "Can I ask you a question, and you promise not to get weird on me?"

"Sure."

Closing her eyes, she willed the words to come. Or the will to get off the bed before she crossed that line. She wasn't sure which she wanted more.

"The night of the party. When we were hiding from Brenton Michael Phillips…" she trailed off. Beside her, Nathan watched her, waiting quietly as she found the words. "Did you want—"

"Yes."

Ilsa opened her eyes, turning her head to look at him. He was staring intently at her. There was no hint of joking in his normally jovial face.

"You didn't let me finish."

"You were going to ask if I wanted to kiss you. The answer is yes."

She blinked at him a few times, the stark truth of his statement shocking her. It'd been years of games and allusions. Of ghosting men and men ghosting her, of playing these dating games. Her mouth popped open as she realized it was the truest statement she'd heard in years. The weight of this was crushing her chest.

"Oh."

Reaching forward to brush a lock of hair off her face, Nathan tucked it behind her ear. "Did I scare you?"

Ilsa shook her head, her word more air than voice. "No." Her heart beat hard in her ears. She wasn't scared by him wanting her. A thrill coursed inside her body. She was excited.

Nathan's hand was in her hair, his finger tracing the shell of her ear until it reached her jaw. Stilling there, he watched her face. His touch was light, more heat than pressure. "What did you want?"

Ilsa opened her mouth, her lips making a soft pop sound as they separated. Nathan's gaze dipped from her eyes to her mouth.

"You're my best friend," Ilsa whispered.

Nathan pulled his hand away, a shadow descending over his face. "Same."

As he studied her, Ilsa took in the hesitation on his face. "Should we?"

"I would never do anything to make you uncomfortable, Illy."

Ilsa loved when he called her that. Ilsa was already such a short name. No one ever made a nickname for her. But Nathan did. He was different. She'd always known he was different. He was special.

"I know. You're one of the last true gentlemen out there."

He leaned in closer, his breath fanning over her face. "If you knew some of my thoughts, you wouldn't say that."

"Tell me."

Nathan's eyes fluttered shut, "I can't. I don't want to scare you."

Ilsa wiggled closer, her knee bumping against his on the bed. "You thought about kissing me at the party."

"Yes."

"Would you have held my head in your hands, or would you have held my waist?" She knew her questions were dangerous, that she was passing a point that neither of them could return from.

"Both. One hand in your hair and the other around your waist as I pulled you against me." His gaze dipped down her body before coming back to rest on her face.

Ilsa let out a shaky breath, heat climbing over her body. That moment at the party had replayed repeatedly in her mind, and now here he was beside her, saying he wanted more.

"Did you think about what my mouth would taste like?"

"No." His eyes flashed to hers, resolute. A flash of uncertainty coursed through her. He moved closer, placing a hand on her hip. "I knew exactly what you'd taste like. I watched you all night. You'd have tasted like champagne and strawberries."

She edged closer, her mouth inches from his. Her eyes fluttered shut. She couldn't stop the words, couldn't stop her body from reaching for more. "What do you think I'd taste like tonight?"

One hand came up to rest on her face, his thumb on her cheekbone and his fingers diving into her hair. He brought her mouth to his, a slight brush of his lips against hers. The touch of his lips was more a whisper than a kiss, barely enough to count. Her body felt like a live wire, every spot where they connected sizzling with heat. Tentative, Ilsa brought her hand up to his head, pulling him closer. With this encouragement, his kiss deepened, his tongue tracing the seam of her lips.

Their bodies flush as they lay beside each other, Nathan's hand moved from her hair to her waist. His large hand rested on the smallest part of her stomach. His thumb was on one side, and his fingers swept over her spine.

A loud beep sounded, breaking their kiss. They pulled away, their eyes locked on one another. Their breathing came in heavy pulses. Ilsa couldn't remember the last time a simple kiss had made her so breathless. They stayed still, staring at one another in silence. Ilsa tried to discern what was behind his heavy gaze. She could feel the physical effect of their kiss pushing against her leg. But whether he would regret it, she couldn't tell.

The phone on the table behind Ilsa beeped again. Slowly, Ilsa turned away from Nathan, grabbing the phone off the nightstand. A picture flashed on the screen of a pair of bare breasts. Ilsa fought to keep her face composed. She couldn't react. He was a rock star. He had legions of fans who loved him. Nathan Ayers was an international sex symbol. Of course, he would have women sending him nudes.

With much more composure than she thought she could have, Ilsa handed the phone to Nathan. Taking it without looking, he shoved it into his back pocket. Ilsa couldn't bear to ask him about the text. She had no rights to Nathan. He was her friend. Nothing more.

Her friend with muscular arms. Her friend with a kiss that could turn her to goo. Just a friend.

"I should get going." Ilsa sat up, throwing her legs over the side of the bed. "You're all set for tomorrow."

She glanced around the room, trying to remember where she left her phone and purse. *What did Nathan think of the kiss?* Did she have a jacket? *Why would someone send him that picture?* Where did she put her shoes? *Why did she kiss her best friend?* What the hell was she thinking?

"Ilsa." Nathan sat up, rubbing a hand over his face. "Wait."

Shoving her feet into her heels, she focused on the way the leather felt against her toes, not Nathan's heat behind her.

"I know you'll be great in the interview. You'll have to let me know how it goes," she said, avoiding the elephant in the room. She couldn't turn around to look at him.

She didn't meet his eyes as she left the room. Her heels made a loud clacking noise as she made her way down his hardwood hallway. The floors were polished to a sheen, so different from the worn linoleum flooring she had in her apartment. Another reminder she was out of her depth with this. Nathan was someone important. Not like her.

In the bedroom, she heard Nathan as he clambered off the bed and followed her to the door. As Ilsa gathered her things, she prayed Nathan wouldn't want to talk about it. She needed time to think, and she couldn't do that when he was around. He must have sensed she wasn't ready for a conversation because, instead of asking about the kiss, he said, "I'll walk you out to your car?"

She glanced over his shoulder at her car in the driveway. The chivalry warmed her. He had a gate across his driveway. The chance of something happening to her between the doorway and her car was slim.

"No, I'm good. You go to bed. You have a big day tomorrow," she argued.

Despite her assertion, he was already pulling the front door open, holding it for her to walk through. She knew better than to disagree with him on this. It was a silly thing to fight over. Walking her to the car fulfilled some honor code he had instilled in himself. Approaching the car, Nathan bent over the front, grabbing a flower that was resting on her windshield wiper. Ilsa furrowed her brow.

"Where did that come from?" Taking the purple flower from his hand, she studied the small bloom before glancing around them. It didn't look like it came from any of the trees or bushes surrounding his home, but the Santa Ana winds had produced odder things than a flower on her windshield.

"Maybe I have a secret admirer." Ilsa laughed as she twirled the stem between her fingers. There was a quick flash of something dark behind Nathan's eyes at her words. Hesitating for a moment, they stared at each other, the smile slipping off her face. Before she could question if it was the wrong choice, she leaned forward to press a quick kiss to his cheek. Breathing in the male scent of him, all musk and warmth, she whispered in his ear. "Thank you for inviting me over."

Before he could say anything else, she climbed into her car. Nathan stepped back as she pulled out of his driveway. With a single glance in her rear-view mirror, she saw Nathan pull his phone out of his pocket, waving it in the air to let her know she needed to text him when she got home. He always asked her to do that, reassuring him she got home safe.

As the gate closed behind her, she saw his face go to the screen of his phone and looked away. A second later, she turned the corner, driving away from him and his mansion by the ocean.

DEMASK
NATHAN

I

N A LOW-BACK CHAIR, celebrity reporter Fernanda Alvarez sat across from the band, her long, tanned legs crossed. She'd finished asking Keller about his relationship with Eloise. Keller answered with his trademark charm and dangerous edge that garnered him the bad boy edge the label liked to play up before he was married. The bulk of the interview was spent having Theo talk about the musical process and his relationship with Aria Kingston. Theo was the most skilled at talking with the reporters, hinting at a relationship that was only on paper and still making it sound as if he was single enough for the fans to have a chance at him.

Being famous was never what Nathan intended with his life. He didn't move to LA hoping to become a musician. He moved to attend college. In his sophomore year, a friend from class mentioned she was going to an open mic night at Proper Bar, and he should come along.

It was there he met Theo. At the time, he was a single performer on an acoustic guitar. From the start, Nathan knew he had a talent few would possess. Not only did Theo have the perfect voice for rock music, but he had a stage presence. When he stood on stage, it was as if he was playing for thousands of people, yet he made every audience member feel like he was singing just for them.

Nathan was man enough to admit he was a little jealous of Theo's skills. Nathan had played bass and guitar in junior high. While he was talented in his hometown, he knew he was only one of thousands in LA.

After Theo's set, Nathan bought him a beer, and they talked about music for hours. When Nathan mentioned he played in a band in high school, Theo invited him over to jam. A few months later, they found Keller, and Prevalent Notion was born.

Nathan knew what he brought to the band—he was a hard worker. He practiced day and night to get the notes right. He brought a playful energy to the stage that complimented Theo's soulful attitude and Keller's edge. They balanced each other out, and together they'd proven successful. But there were days when he wondered if he was cut out for this lifestyle.

In the beginning, Nathan tried to keep up with his studies as an engineering student and play in the band. But one had to give between nightly shows and the heavy course load. He quit school a few terms before graduation. While the band took off, he sometimes wondered how different his life would've been if he'd been content playing bass in someone's garage on the weekends.

He wondered what Ilsa would think of him if he was some electrical engineer with a bass in his den and no water views from his apartment. He wouldn't have met her, most likely. A woman like that, successful, creative, beautiful, driven? Those kinds of women were rarely around when he was in college. The few women in his program were great people, but they weren't like Ilsa. No one was like Ilsa. She was unlike anyone he'd ever met before.

He knew he screwed up the second he pulled out his phone the night before. The picture of Shelby's bare breasts and a text asking him if he was still up, displayed on his lock screen. He wasn't ashamed of having been with Shelby, but he didn't talk about her. Who would want to hear his complaints that an award-winning TV star wanted to use him as a booty call? It was a ridiculous thing to take issue with. Ilsa had no idea how he really felt about Shelby.

As Ilsa always did, she texted him that she got home twenty minutes after she left his house. Nathan thought about calling her and explaining what she saw, but to do so felt like confirming something. Ilsa wasn't his girlfriend. She was his friend. He wouldn't justify himself to Theo or even Eloise.

He knew how he felt about Ilsa was different than his standard friendship feelings. But aside from her scorching kiss the night before, he had no idea what she could want from him. She owed him nothing, and how he felt had no bearing on what she wanted. To justify Shelby's message would admit something more than he was ready to give.

Ilsa had long told him she was independent. She was frank about sex in a way he hadn't experienced around other girls. He never thought less of her for going after what she wanted, whether it be in her career or with men. He only wished he was the one she wanted.

"Now Nathan, all the ladies want to know, is there a special someone in your life?"

Fernanda's question shook him from his thoughts. "I'm sorry, ma'am. What was the question?"

Her face pinched at the use of the term ma'am. Nathan knew she was about his age, but he was raised to be respectful. In LA, it seemed to bother women to be referred to as 'ma'am,' but he didn't feel right calling a thirty-year-old woman 'miss' when she was three years older than him.

"There have been insider reports that you and Shelby Waters have been getting chummy lately," Fernanda repeated the question. Nathan laughed before taking a sip of water.

"Right now, the only lady that matters in my life is my music. Getting this new album out has been a great experience for all of us, and we're excited for our fans to hear it."

Nathan suspected Shelby had tipped the press off to that tidbit, but he wasn't biting. He refused to say anything negative about Shelby in the press—he was a gentleman. Still, he wouldn't act like something was going on either. Fernanda gave him a devilish look that said she saw right through his maneuvers.

"I'm sure your fans will be pleased to hear that at least one member of the group is available."

Nathan wanted to snort. He'd never felt less available in his life. His thoughts went to Ilsa. If he thought kissing her would scratch some itch he had, he'd been sorely mistaken. If anything, the need intensified. He could hardly concentrate for wanting her. It was barely even a kiss, and it was the hottest thing he'd ever experienced. He had a threesome with two swimsuit models a few years back, and it paled compared to those minutes on his bed with Ilsa.

Fernanda wrapped up the interview, thanking them for their time and letting them know the article would come out in a few weeks. As she was about to walk out the door, she turned back, stepping close to Nathan, a small business card in her hand.

"You should call me sometime. I can be very discreet," her voice dropped low. A few months before he might've been tempted. Fernanda Alvarez was gorgeous, and he'd never heard any rumors about her she didn't want out. He had the feeling he could trust her for a quick fling. But the temptation wasn't there.

Shaking his head, he gave her the best smile he could muster. "I'm sure you are. I appreciate the offer."

She seemed unfazed by his brush-off. "If you change your mind, you have my number." She winked before pulling on her coat and leaving him in the interview room.

The door had barely closed behind the reporter when Theo asked incredulously, "Did Fernanda Alvarez proposition you?"

"Maybe." Nathan's voice sounded tired. He hadn't slept well the night before, with images of Ilsa beside him in bed playing in his mind. He wondered what would've happened between them if Shelby hadn't texted him at that moment. Why didn't he put his phone on silent? Or block her number? Something, anything, to have a few more minutes alone with Ilsa.

"I tried to ask her out years ago, and she kept turning me down." Theo shook his head as if he couldn't understand what Nathan had that he didn't. "What kind of magic dick do you have?"

Nathan shrugged. The idea of Fernanda Alvarez, all tanned legs and long dark hair, held no temptation for him. When he lay down, he wanted blonde hair splashed against his pillow. He wanted hazel eyes and a tattooed back. He wanted Ilsa.

"I don't know. Maybe she wants a nice guy."

Theo snorted into his coffee cup. "Yeah, right? A girl like that doesn't want a nice guy. She wants to be—"

"Stop talking, now." Eloise interrupted from the doorway. Theo had the decency to look chagrined. Walking over to Keller, she handed him a coffee cup from the carrier she held in one hand. Keller leaned down to kiss Eloise. Their kiss lasted longer than was publicly appropriate. As they broke it off, Nathan felt a pang of sadness in his chest. There was so much love in the air between the newlyweds.

Nathan wanted someone to bring coffee to. He wondered how Ilsa would react if he showed up at her studio with a latte. Ever since she left the night before, he wished he'd said more to her. He wished he'd stopped her from leaving and asked her what the kiss meant to her. Instead, he'd let her drive away.

Eloise pulled away. "You guys, don't forget—I need you to be on your best behavior at the release party tonight." Her words were more directed at Theo than Nathan. Eloise had shot to fame the previous year when a video of her singing one of her songs was posted on YouTube. She got an album deal within weeks, followed by much fanfare.

Nathan hadn't forgotten about Eloise's album release party. Though, he may have misplaced it in his mind. "Right. Tonight."

"Ilsa said she was going to take an Uber, but I was hoping someone could arrange a car for her." Eloise shot Nathan a pointed look and raised her eyebrow. "She should arrive in style."

Nathan already had his phone out, texting Ilsa that he'd pick her up in his car, and they'd go together. Maybe they'd talk before the event.

Eloise took out the two remaining coffees, handing them to Theo and Nathan. "Tell me about the interview?"

Chapter Seven

BIAS
NATHAN

K NOCKING TWICE, HE STEPPED back and glanced down the hallway. Ilsa's next-door neighbor was an older woman who'd always narrow her eyes at Nathan. He wished Ilsa lived in a better place, but he wouldn't tell her that. The one time he mentioned it, Ilsa joked she could barely afford her rent as it was.

Ilsa opened the door, gaping at him. "Crap, you're here." Clutching her fuzzy black robe around her body, she stepped aside to let him through the door. Her hair was loose, curling down her back in long blonde spirals. She wore a full face of makeup, including deep purple lipstick. He could smell the perfume on her skin as he walked past her. She turned away, heading into her small walk-in closet.

Nathan walked into the small room that served as her bedroom, dining room, office, and living room. "Exactly what every man wants to hear when he arrives at a beautiful woman's home."

She popped her head out of the walk-in closet to frown at him. "That's not what I meant. If you're here, then I'm running later than I thought."

"I'm a little early." Tapping a rhythm on his thigh, he glanced around Ilsa's small space. Her bed was in the middle of the room beside a corner desk. A half wall separated the small kitchen. In there was a tiny table with a vase of flowers and two chairs set to the side. If he sat on the bed, he'd be able to see the entire place. Her entire apartment could fit into his living room.

Ilsa told him once that she didn't mind the small space as long as she had her walk-in closet. He could hear her rustling around, likely picking out her clothes. This wasn't the first time he'd been to her place while she changed, but something about tonight felt different. He'd kissed her. He'd felt her body under his hands, and now she was changing a few feet away from him.

"Your neighbor still doesn't like me," Nathan called to her.

Ilsa stuck her head out of the closet again, her black robe hanging off her shoulder. Ilsa wrinkled her nose. "She's a grump. Don't mind her."

Nathan walked to the table, scanning the stack of mail against the wall. He noticed the red "payment is past due" printed on the top mailer. Glancing over his shoulder, he saw Ilsa was still in her closet. He picked up the stack of mail, flipping through the unopened envelopes. There were past-due notices from the apartment building, the power company, credit cards, and a wireless provider.

He knew Ilsa didn't have the money he did, but she never told him she was struggling to pay her bills. He gathered up the stack and walked to the closet, stopping outside the door.

"Are you decent?"

Ilsa laughed. "Never. But I am still wearing my robe if that's what you're asking."

He turned the corner to stand in the closet's doorway where Ilsa was holding up a dress in each hand, comparing them. "Illy, what are these?" He waved the bills in the air.

Glancing at the envelopes in his hand, her jaw flexed. "Bills."

"Past due bills? Do you need help?"

Turning her back to him, she hung one dress back on the rod and grabbed a new one. "I'm fine, Nathan."

"Why didn't you tell me—"

Ilsa interrupted him. "Look, I know you think it's your job to take care of people, but I don't need you to take care of me. The girls needed to be paid. They need their paychecks a lot more than Visa does."

"Ilsa, if you need help, I can help you. You know I have the extra money."

"I don't want to take your money, Nate. You're my friend—"

"Exactly, I'm your friend. Friends help each other."

"—and I'm not asking a friend for money. I'll be fine once the new line launches."

Nathan shook his head. "It won't matter to me. Let me pay these for you."

Ilsa slammed the dresses down on her dresser, her mouth a purple line of frustration. Stomping over to him, she ripped the envelopes out of his hand. "I don't want to hear how rich you are right now, and I don't want you paying my bills. I'm not some groupie looking for a sugar daddy, Nathan."

Taking a step back, Nathan put his hands up in surrender. "I never said you were. All I see is a friend in need of help, and I want to help them. I'd do the same for any of my friends."

Ilsa picked out a gold dress, holding it out in front of her. Her voice was softer as if she was talking to herself more than him. "I need to do this on my own. All my life, my mom had men who took care of her. I told myself I'd never let that happen to me. The men get bored, and then they leave, and you have to survive on ramen and powdered milk. I'd rather be broke and on my own than rely on a man to pay my way."

Ilsa rarely talked about her mother. She lived in the Phoenix area, and Nathan had heard that she asked Ilsa for money from time to time. He also knew Ilsa hadn't been home in a while. His own upbringing felt pampered compared to the occasional stories Ilsa would let slip in moments like these. "Do you think I'd do that to you?"

Ilsa's face softened. "No. No, of course not. I'm just..." she trailed off, her hands hovering over her cheeks as if she wanted to scrub her face but couldn't. She took a deep, shaky breath before leveling her eyes at Nathan. "I still haven't heard from Davis Gallegos. They said they'd get back to me by the end of the week. I'm nervous, is all."

"What can I do?" Nathan asked.

Lowering the gold dress, Ilsa shook her head. "Let me get dressed. Take me to this album release party and help me forget about my impending doom for a few hours."

Nathan nodded, retreating until he was back into the main room. As much as he yearned to grab those bills and secretly pay them, he had to respect Ilsa's wishes. She wanted to pay her own way in the world and break free of the constraints and lessons her mother created around her. He respected that. To undermine Ilsa now would be to undermine the very thing he respected the most about her.

Ilsa emerged a minute later, clutching the gold dress to her front. "What do you think about this one? Does it scream, '*Eloise deserves a Grammy?*'"

"You look incredible as always. And while the Grammy statue is a gramophone and not human-shaped, I'm sure Eloise will appreciate the thought."

"You look fantastic. Didn't I tell you that the velvet would look good? And you doubted me?" Her smirk was a welcome reprieve from the heavy subject of her bills. She clapped him on his chest and wiggled her eyebrows dramatically. "I think you should be a zombie for Halloween and practice by eating me."

He laughed at her joke as he smoothed the front of his jacket. Ilsa had picked out the deep velvet suit a few weeks before. He had balked at the odd choice in material, but she insisted he could pull off the look. Once again, he was shown how believing in Ilsa made him better. The last time she talked him into wearing something that pressed against fashion rules, he was put on a list of best-dressed celebrities. His sister called him and told him, telling him he looked weird, but LA couture and his hometown fashion were two very different things. His 17-year-old self would've balked at the patterned suit, but after the time he'd spent in the business, he was more willing to take risks.

Reaching her hands behind her back pushed Ilsa's boobs against the low-cut top of her dress. Nathan tried not to look anywhere but at her face. Ilsa struggled to zip her dress for a moment before dropping her hands to her side. "Can you help me?"

Nathan stepped forward as Ilsa turned around to show him her bare back where the dress gaped wide.

"I guess this is a good trial run for this dress. I had no idea it would be so hard to button by myself. You'd think, as the designer, I'd have planned this better."

Nathan cleared his throat as he gazed down at the creamy expanse of her bare back. She moved her blonde curls over her shoulder, and all he could see was the line of her spine trail downward to the top of the silk and lace of her underwear. Down her spine was a tattoo of a single green stem with watercolor flowers shooting from the middle. She wore no bra—it was all smooth skin. There was a small freckle to the right of her spine halfway down her back, and he wondered what it would taste like if he pressed his lips to that exact spot.

"Yeah, I can help." His hands hovered over her back. His palms were warm from wanting to touch her. He must've taken too long to move because Ilsa turned her head to look at him. Their eyes met and the words she was prepared to say died on her lips. Stepping closer, Nathan touched the knot at the top of her spine. His fingers trailed slowly down the length of her back. Her skin was soft under his finger as he brushed down, tracing the edge of one tattoo bloom. Her breath hitched, and she turned her head to look away. He could feel her relax under his touch. She let out a gasp as his fingers stopped at the base of her spine. Drawing a small circle on her bare skin, he took his time memorizing how her body felt under his touch. He wasn't sure why she was allowing this, but if he had this chance, he was going to take it. His finger dipped lower, pressing into the small dimples above her ass. He wanted to go further, to feel all of her under his hands, but he didn't dare. Not yet.

Pulling his hand away from her skin, he grasped the small hook closure and pulled it tight against her lower back until he could fasten it. There were several thin straps he hooked to the other side, creating a line along her back. Once he'd secured each strap, he laid his palm flat on her back. His voice husky, he leaned close to her ear.

"Done."

Ilsa turned to face him. Their bodies were close enough that if he wanted to, he could wrap his arm around her waist. His eyes dipped to her lips. The feel of her kiss the night before pulsed inside him. He wanted to taste those lips again. Her mouth parted, her tongue darting out to wet the very spot he'd been staring at.

"Do you want to kiss me again, Nate?" she asked, her words breathy.

"Yes," he whispered back.

She leaned closer, her lips grazing against his, before landing on his cheek. Her cheek was warm against his skin. "What's happening between us?"

Wrapping his arms around her, he pulled her body flush with his. He could feel the swell of her breasts against his chest and the curve of her stomach. His mouth near her ear, he breathed in the sweet scent of her skin.

"I don't know," he said.

"I don't want to stop." He closed his eyes, feeling her words soak in. It wasn't a promise. It wasn't a declaration. But it was something. It was enough for that night.

Pulling back, he cupped her cheek in his hand, her smooth skin fitting perfectly in the palm of his hand. "I don't think I could stop even if I wanted to."

She closed her eyes at his words, nodding. When she opened them, she swallowed hard. "We should get going. We don't want to be late."

Nathan rubbed a circle on her cheek, relishing the way her skin felt under his hand. "After the party, we need to talk about this," he said, and she gave him a barely perceptible nod.

Nathan stepped back, gathering up Ilsa's coat and throwing it over his arm. As they stepped out into the hallway, he double-checked the door was locked before they left. Placing his hand on the small of her back, he savored the heat of her body as they made their way to the waiting car.

Chapter Eight

LEATHER
ILSA

PULLING UP TO THE album release event, Ilsa gazed out the window with trepidation. She was becoming more used to attending parties in the public eye. As the stylist for the band, she was often in the back at events, helping them get ready. Her proximity to fame meant she was included on the invitation list for several up-and-coming artists in the area.

But this event was something else entirely. At the other events, she was a third-tier guest. The press never looked at her as she walked in the door. Alongside the assistants, the new screenwriters, and the hangers-on, she would walk in the background of the celebrity photos.

This night was different. The guest list still included the music industry's elite, but Eloise had made sure Ilsa was included as a VIP. She was expected to walk the red carpet of the event, answer questions, and be seen.

Luckily, public speaking came easily to her. She didn't spend her teenage years talking into microphones for scholarship dollars only to freeze up when talking to a random D-list celebrity reporter. Ilsa knew how to make the camera work for her. She knew how to present herself to make an impact. In pageants, they tell you to make them laugh, make them cry. She was a master of this. In her experience, she knew what people wanted to hear and how to get on the good side of the media.

No, the press wasn't the issue. It was the man beside her in the town car. The car should have felt roomy, but everywhere in the backseat of that car was the essence of Nathan. His scent of leather and musk, the heat of his body only inches from her. The sensation of being touched by this man only an hour before and how badly she wanted him to push her further.

When did the lines they'd drawn become smudged? Where was this boundary between friendship and lovers they were edging treacherously closer to?

Standing beside Nathan, she yearned to be closer. She wasn't a fool. There'd been an attraction from day one, at least on her side. If he felt the same way that first day, he hid it well. Nathan was unfailingly kind to everyone, and the friendship that'd blossomed between them meant the world to her.

She was accustomed to the way men looked at her—the wanting, the lust in their eyes. It'd been this way since she was thirteen.

Her mother was thrilled when Ilsa hit puberty, her body shooting up to be taller than her peers. Tall meant modeling, it meant pageants, and it meant money that her mother didn't have to work for. From a young age, she was stuffed into tight clothes and paraded around the valley for modeling jobs. It didn't matter that she was fourteen. Her mother approved of all the photo shoots they asked her to do. Ilsa's height made her look older than she was. Her partners in photo shoots were often men closer in age to her mother than her. By the age of sixteen, she was used to the adult attention of men. The photographers, the male models, the pageant coaches, and the talent agents.

The boys her age were a different story. Ilsa was six inches taller than almost all the boys and flat-chested. The petite girls with sweet smiles were the ones getting boyfriends, not Ilsa. Her relationships weren't based on affection but on what they could get from her.

Ilsa never regretted the choices she made in sex, but she did sometimes wish she could've had something sweet as a young teen. What would it have been like to fall in love the way her classmates did? To go to school dances where the boy she liked picked out a cheap corsage from the grocery store? While her friends at school were getting felt up on their parents' couches to the sound of reruns, she was at the dance studio practicing her evening gown walk or at the gym, making her already thin body more gaunt.

She learned early on that her beauty would only get her so far. If she wanted something more than what was offered by second-rate upstarts, she'd need to get out of Phoenix. The typical teenage girl would've been shocked arriving in LA and seeing the culture of what it took to get ahead. But by the time Ilsa moved to the city at twenty-three, she was a professional. She knew how to make her mark. She knew how to dodge unwanted advances while making a man think he had a chance with her.

She knew how to play the game.

And it was exhausting.

When she met Nathan, she assumed he'd be like every other guy in the area—every other guy she'd known. But he wasn't. He was kind, funny, and sweet. She waited for him to make the pass that always came. They spent months together, and aside from the first night when she caught him having sex with Shelby, he never once looked at her like he wanted her. Until the night of Eloise and Keller's party.

That was the hardest part of all this. In the year she'd known Nathan, she'd let her guard down. She relaxed in a way she never had with another man. How could she risk her friendship with him over a little lust?

Okay, a lot of lust.

The wanting him had always been there. Even when she told herself they were only friends, she still found him attractive and still allowed herself to think about him naked a time or two. Though she'd had several close-up fitting sessions with Theo and Keller in their boxers, she never once considered what they looked like naked. But with Nathan, it'd always been a different story.

She couldn't act on it, could she?

The town car stopped at the curb, and Ilsa took a steadying breath as Nathan walked around the car to meet her. A tuxedoed valet opened the door, and Nathan was there, his hand outstretched and the flash of hundreds of bulbs behind him. Setting one gold stiletto onto the concrete street, she allowed him to pull her up and into the lights of the waiting press. For a second, she thought he'd dropped her hand. Instead, he pulled her arm through the crook of his elbow, guiding her to the first reporter waiting on the side of the red carpet. Nathan was naïve about show business, but he knew what message it sent to walk the red carpet alongside someone, even at a small event like this.

"Nate, maybe we should walk separately. You don't want the press to think—"

He held tight to her arm. "I don't give a damn what the press thinks. I want you beside me."

The first photog waved them over, snapping pictures as he shouted questions. "Nathan, tell us who you're wearing tonight."

"The suit is from Dynotos."

"And who is your date?"

Ilsa smiled at him, trying her best to hide the apprehension bubbling inside her. She wasn't afraid to walk the carpet and be asked about her connection to Eloise, but to stand beside Nathan, to be called his date? That was entirely different.

"Ilsa Kruger. We're longtime friends. Ilsa was our designer on the Hellions tour and has a new fashion line coming out soon."

The reporter's camera trained on Ilsa. "And Ilsa, who are you wearing?"

"This is my design. An Ilsa Kruger Original. I also designed Eloise's dress for her anniversary party."

Nathan interrupted, "As well as the dress Eloise is wearing tonight. Make sure you mark that down. Ilsa Kruger." Nathan spelled Ilsa's name out to the reporter.

A warmth bloomed in her chest as they made their way to the doorway, stopping every few feet for more photos and questions. Ilsa might've talked with a few reporters, but Nathan was steering the conversation to Ilsa at every stop. He commanded their attention using his star power, then allowed her to talk.

As much as she wanted to make her own way of promoting herself, she couldn't help but be grateful for the way he brought attention to her. If they weren't talking about how excited they were about Eloise's album, they were discussing Ilsa's new line.

This extended inside, where Nathan introduced her to several musicians whom she'd previously only seen from a distance. The whole time, Nathan didn't touch her. Not like he did in the confines of her apartment. But she could feel the heat of his body as he stood beside her. A warm shock traveled through her every time he slid against her.

Eloise was in high demand at the party as music insiders chatted with her. A year ago, she was fetching coffee for the same people who now praised her. How quickly fame was sneaking up on her.

The guests were a mix of industry elite and fans who won behind-the-scenes tickets. Before the event, Eloise confided she'd let her manager know that she didn't have any friends from her hometown to attend the event. Ilsa and Eloise were similar in that way. Both had left their homes at eighteen for better opportunities and didn't look back. LA was full of these kinds of people. It was a running joke that no one was ever from LA. Eloise and Ilsa included. Eloise only had her surrogate sister, Ana, and Ilsa had no one. For them, it was better this way.

They made their own group of friends and their own family within the confines of Prevalent Notion. Ilsa didn't regret the friends she left behind in Phoenix. The phone went both ways, and aside from one classmate asking to crash on her couch a few times each year, she hardly heard from her high school friends.

Nathan stuck by her for a long while until she told him to mingle on his own. She told him she was fine. And she was. Making small talk with people came easy to her. The vapid conversations prevalent in LA weren't that different from what she'd found in the modeling and pageant world. Everyone is more than a little self-involved. Ask them a question about themselves and then stand back and listen as they prattle on. People didn't want to listen to her. They wanted to feel like they were important enough for her to listen to them. Ilsa maintained that thin line of looking slightly engaged but also like she was waiting for a more important person to talk to. Nothing held their attention more than the sense of being her second choice in conversation.

Ilsa excused herself from a conversation where a hotel tycoon's son was spewing nonsense about cryptocurrency. At the same moment, Nathan returned to her side, handing her a flute of champagne.

He held his own glass in his large hand, the comically delicate stem balanced between his thick fingers. Only two hours ago, those fingers had been tracing a searing line down her spine. If their presence wasn't required at this party—if the party was for anyone but Eloise—she'd have said, "Fuck it" and turned around to kiss him at that moment.

"Having a good time talking to real estate magnates?"

Ilsa smiled. "Oh him? Not really. But you know how it is. You let a man talk about himself for ten minutes, and they think you're in love with them."

"You're trouble," Nathan teased.

"The best kind, I hope."

"Absolutely."

Resting her hand on Nathan's shoulder, she smiled up at him. Champagne always made her a little giggly, a little sleepy. The third glass she held in her hand was no exception.

"I like that you're so much bigger than me. When I wear heels, I always feel like some giantess. But with you—" Lazily, she closed her eyes, her fingers rubbing the velvet of his jacket, a small smile pulling at the corners of her lips. "If there was an emergency, I bet you could pick me up and sling me over your shoulder. I like that idea."

Nathan stepped forward, closing the gap between them. "Who says there has to be an emergency?"

Crouching down, he wrapped his arms around her upper thighs, lifting her until she was aloft above him.

Ilsa let out a hoot of laughter, catching the eyes of partygoers turning to see them. Across the room, she saw Eloise watching them with a knowing glint in her eye. Ilsa looked down at Nathan. His bright green eyes watched her with humor. "Bet you didn't think I'd do it."

His hands were tight around her legs. She could feel the heat from his forearms as her ass rested there. "I should never doubt you."

His touch was fiery against her skin. His head was level with her chest and his green eyes flickered from her face down to her breasts in front of him. She could feel the muscles in his forearms and then the strength of his chest against her stomach. His gaze became more serious. "Lesson learned."

Loosening his grip, he let Ilsa fall slowly down his arms until her face was level with his. They were a breath away from each other, her air and his mingled in puffs of warmth and champagne. Her long nails scratched at the nape of his neck as her hands drifted from his shoulders. Her stilettoed feet hit the ground, but his arms were still wrapped around her. She wasn't sure if it was the expensive champagne or the feel of his arms around her body, but Ilsa's head was swimming. The party faded away, and all she could feel was the warmth of his hand on the small of her back and the rasp of his pant leg against her bare legs. Faintly, she could hear someone speaking into the microphone. Nathan's thumb rubbed a circle on her spine, mimicking her memory of his touch hours before in her studio apartment.

"Nathan Ayers. Calling Nathan Ayers!" Someone called from the stage. With the sound of Nathan's name being called, their spell was broken, and they glanced from each other to the stage where Eloise was waiting with Theo and Keller. Ilsa blinked several times, clearing her head. They'd forgotten that Nathan had agreed to play a few songs with the band for the party.

They broke apart, Ilsa wavering slightly on her tall heels. Her heart was beating against her chest as she lost contact with him. She glanced at the stage, focusing on the waiting band members. She couldn't look back at Nathan. "Looks like you're on."

"Yeah." She could feel him watching her. "Any special requests?"

"No, it's not my party." After taking a steadying breath, she glanced back at him. "But you know, I love everything you play."

He winked at her, shooting her a devilish smile. She felt her knees get weak.

'I love everything you play?' What a juvenile response, Kruger. What are you? Twelve?

From her spot in the audience, she watched as Nathan climbed the stairs to the stage, picked up his bass, and walked to the microphone. He came alive on stage. Whether it be for a crowd of only a hundred or ten thousand. The fans who won tickets rushed to the stage, hoping for an up-close performance from their favorite musicians. Eloise took her spot in the front. While Eloise had her own band, she wanted to open the night with a few songs with Prevalent Notion. Theo stood behind her, taking the background vocals as Eloise started belting out the words to one of their first hits—*Unnoticed.*

The fans in the front sang along to the words. A year before, Eloise had won back songwriting credits for the songs she'd helped co-write for Prevalent Notion. Part of the deal was she could play them in concert if she chose to. It was fun to hear Eloise's version of the songs. Once played as arena rock anthems, they were stripped down for her alto voice and acoustic guitar. After the intro, the song morphed back into the song played on the radio.

All the while, Ilsa watched as Nathan played the bittersweet love song. The fans around singing the words.

Standing there silent,

three steps behind

You sing your songs

and I'll be fine

As the band launched into the bridge, Theo and Eloise stood together, sharing the microphone. Even though she was several rows back from the stage, Ilsa watched as Nathan played. His eyes looked up and though she knew from her pageant and modeling days that it was unlikely that he could see her, she still felt like his eyes were locked onto hers. As Eloise and Theo sang, Nathan watched her, his long fingers moving across his bass guitar. Even though Nathan wasn't singing the words, it felt like they were for her alone. His fingers plucked those strings as if each strum was against her skin.

You were here, right here, waiting to be

I was a fool, everyone else's fool, you see

She let out a shaky breath. This situation was getting too messed up. Her brain was jumbled up with the need to protect herself and the desire to have him closer. If Nathan was any other man, she'd dive into these impulses. She'd take him to bed and not think about it the next day. Sex was simpler that way. Always with birth control, always with a condom. Always with the protections she needed to save herself.

She knew it would be different with Nathan. Because *he* was different.

Watching him as he played on the stage, she wished he could be a normal rock star for one night. That he could be a little more callous. It would be so much easier that way. Why couldn't she have been attracted to Theo? At least with Theo, she knew he'd never entice her again. It didn't matter how attractive that man was. Despite him being golden outwardly, inside, he was anything but warm and soft.

A man approached Ilsa, his sleeve brushing against her elbow. She felt his eyes on her before she turned to look at him. Tall and thin, he had jet-black hair styled in a high pompadour that made his already thin face look gaunt. His eyes were so light blue they didn't seem real.

"I love this band." He leaned in, and Ilsa could smell the gin on his breath.

Ilsa gave him a halfhearted smile. She wasn't in the mood to be hit on by some random at Eloise's party.

He motioned to the stage. "Have you seen them perform before?"

Ilsa blinked at him a few times. There was no reason this guy would know that she was on every stop of Prevalent Notion's last tour or that she attended dozens of Eloise's recording sessions.

"A few times."

"I know the bass player."

"Do you?"

Of course, he did. Nathan made friends everywhere. Ilsa could see that this smarmy guy was all overpriced suit and no substance. Nathan might have rocketed to fame in the past few years, but some of his sensibilities were all small-town. While most of the time, she loved his sense of credence, she worried about him getting taken advantage of. Several smaller stories were sold to the tabloids from people he thought were friends. The band's previous manager, Arnie Phelps, was a grade-A douchebag, but he knew how to squash a story.

"That's nice," Ilsa said as she looked down at him, glad she wore her tallest heels. Being taller didn't always deter men, but she wasn't too petty to use her height as a power move.

The man stared at Ilsa, a confused look on his face as Ilsa didn't ask him to elaborate. He was a persistent man though, leaning closer instead of backing away. "How many times have you seen them?"

"Which ones?" Ilsa asked, raising an arched brow.

"What?" he yelled over the crash of Keller's cymbals. He leaned closer, and Ilsa could see where he missed a spot shaving his jaw.

"I asked, Which ones? There are two separate artists up there. Are you asking if I've seen Prevalent Notion or Eloise Grant?"

The man blinked a few times. He glanced at the stage as if he didn't notice Eloise up there, as if it wasn't Eloise's album release party.

"Oh, well, either, I guess." This man was not getting the hint.

"Like I said a few times." Ilsa brought her champagne up to her mouth and downed the rest.

"I'm Mike, by the way."

Of course, he was.

"Ilsa." She took his proffered hand, letting his sweaty palm glide over hers. Fighting back revolt from his weak handshake, she pulled away and discreetly wiped her hand against the rough beading of her dress.

"Nice to meet you, Lisa."

"Ilsa." She corrected him, then she wondered why she bothered. She didn't want to talk to this man any longer than necessary.

"Ilsa, sorry. Let me get you another drink. Prosecco?" He turned away before she could tell him not to bother. As frustrating as it was to have to decline a free drink, especially on her budget, she could tell this guy was an *'I bought you a drink, what are you going to do for me?'* type of guy. She had no problem telling those kinds of men off, but she wasn't in the mood tonight.

Glancing back at the stage, Ilsa saw Nathan watching her, or at least looking in her general direction. Her pageant and runway days showed her it wasn't always possible to look out at the audience and see people. The song they were playing was at the end of the setlist. Ilsa knew this because she'd been there for a few of the meetings, and she knew it was important for Eloise to sing *Faultless* with Keller at the end. It was the song that first brought her attention. Eloise's drummer, Todd, came out, and Keller stepped forward, taking the spot where Theo was standing earlier.

With no glass in her hand, Ilsa had nothing to keep herself grounded. Watching as Keller and Eloise stepped closer, the way their bodies were drawn together, the light in her friend's eyes as she looked at her husband. Ilsa had never wanted something like that before. The whole of LA was full of people who had their hearts broken by the city. Since Ilsa was already fractured to pieces when she arrived, she considered that a head start.

Eloise and Keller sang the bridge. It was all about loving each other with torrents and moats or something. Ilsa wasn't a songwriter but she didn't doubt they loved each other. She'd seen them fall for each other. While Ilsa had doubts about Keller being right for her friend, he came through in the end. The sticky-handed man came back to give her another glass of sparkling wine.

"I really didn't need another glass, Mark."

"Mike." He leaned in, pushing the glass toward her. "I'm always happy to get a beautiful woman a drink. I'm a gentleman like that."

In Ilsa's experience, any man who has to tell others what kind of man he was ended up being the opposite. "I said I'm fine."

"No, I insist. I already bought it. No need for it to go to waste."

Ilsa opened her mouth to refute him, but then a heavy hand rested on her shoulder.

She looked up to see Nathan standing beside her, glaring at Mike. She hadn't noticed the song was ending, and the boys from Prevalent Notion were now off stage. Nathan walked back wearing his velvet jacket over the tee shirt he wore on stage. His hair was damp from a quick splash of water backstage.

"Illy," Nathan said, more to the man than to Ilsa. "Who's your friend?"

"Holy shit, it's you! You're Nathan Ayers. Oh man, I'm such a big fan." Mike pushed his glass of prosecco at Ilsa. The man grabbed Nathan's free hand and began shaking it. "I've loved you guys since the early days. I saw you at that spot in Solana Beach."

"I thought you said you knew the bass player?" Ilsa asked, lifting an eyebrow.

"What?" The guy looked from Ilsa to Nathan.

"You told me you knew the bass player. Nate, do you know this man?"

"Nope, can't say I do."

Ilsa put her free hand to her chest and leaned back dramatically. "Was that a lie, Matt?"

"Mike. And I mean, we met once. Like I said, at that concert in Solana Beach. We talked for a few minutes."

"I don't remember you, man. Sorry," Nathan said with a tone as close to rude as Ilsa had ever heard from him.

"I can't believe you were lying to me, Morris. For what? Did you think I was going to go home with you over a little lie like that?"

Nathan stood beside her, a small smile ticking up on the corner of his mouth.

"Oh, well—" Mike scratched his nose, his eyes darting around the room. "I think I see someone I know."

Grabbing his drink out of Ilsa's hands, he hurried away.

"Bye, Marcus!" she called to his back.

Beside her, Nathan pursed his lips to keep from smiling. "I can't take you anywhere, can I?" Nathan teased as he plucked the glass out of Ilsa's hand.

"Oh, I wouldn't—" her words died out as he downed the glass. He handed her the glass back. "...drink that."

Wiping his mouth with the back of his hand, he looked at her. "Why?"

"Woman rule number one—don't accept drinks from people you don't know. He could've roofied that thing."

Nathan stared at the now empty glass. "Seriously?"

"Yeah," Ilsa said. "How do you not know that?"

Nathan narrowed his eyes at the man's back, now across the room and chatting up a young woman in a small pink dress. "I should ask security to throw him out."

"For what? Nate, if security threw out every man who might've spiked a girl's drink, they'd never allow men in bars."

"Well, I didn't like how he looked at you."

"You were on stage for most of my brief conversation with that man. You couldn't see a thing," Ilsa scoffed.

"I saw you. I can always find you in the crowd." Nathan stepped closer.

"Because I'm so tall?" Ilsa teased.

"I'm always looking for you. Because when I'm on stage, yours is the only face I see."

Ilsa's sharp inhale burned in her throat, the words she wanted to say dying on her tongue.

Nathan glanced around the party before his eyes caught on something. Ilsa followed his gaze to see Theo and Aria Kingston standing together, talking to some record executives. Eloise was in her own world, being fawned over with Keller beside her.

"I think we've fulfilled our appearance obligation. Let's get out of here." Nathan offered his arm. The soft bristle of his velvet jacket rubbed against the inside of her elbow, as they walked to the door.

Outside, Ilsa wrapped Nathan's coat around her shoulders tighter.

As they'd stood on the gray concrete sidewalk waiting for their car, Nathan shrugged off his coat, placing it over Ilsa's bare shoulders. She'd thought about protesting, but between the silk lining and heady scent of Nathan that clung to the jacket, she'd shut her mouth. When the car pulled up to the curb, Nathan opened the door for her, allowing her to get in before walking to the other side. As he slid in, Ilsa opened her mouth to say something, but the space between them was too small—she had to look away, or she might be tempted to say too much.

Leaning against the back of her leather seat, Ilsa wrapped Nathan's coat around her shoulders tighter. Nathan broke the silence. "Did you have fun?"

Blinking a few times, Ilsa focused on the sparkle of her shoe, watching the way the light cast rainbows against the floor of the car.

"What did that mean? You always see me?" Isla asked, getting to the crux of what was happening.

Beside her, Nathan scratched the side of his nose with his thumbnail, letting out a sigh.

"Did it freak you out?"

Ilsa considered the question. Did it? If she was being honest with herself, it freaked her out a bit. But not for the reasons Nathan thought. It freaked her out because until he'd said the words, she hadn't realized how much she wanted to hear them. She hadn't realized how much she wanted somebody to see her in a crowd. And that scared her more than anything. To be wanted that way.

To be seen that way.

She couldn't let Nathan know that. It sounded pathetic.

"No, it's fine." Straightening her spine against the seats, she focused on the cool slide of leather against the backs of her bare thighs. She stared ahead. "It's not like it's the first time a man said that to me."

Beside her, Nathan stilled. "I'm not any man, Ilsa. You know that, right?"

She couldn't look at him. Not yet. The streetlights of the city cast shapes against his face as they drove. She swallowed hard and looked at him. Her voice was softer now, "Yes, I know that, Nathan."

Pulling up to her apartment, Nathan gazed up at the glass building as if he could see her door.

"Let me walk you up to your apartment." Nathan unbuckled his seatbelt.

Putting out a hand, Ilsa stopped him. "No. It's better if you don't. Let's leave this here until later."

Studying her for a moment, Nathan seemed to weigh his chivalrous nature against the heat climbing between them. Understanding what she wasn't saying, he leaned forward and took her cheek in his hand. He pulled her face toward him, and for a moment, she thought he was going to kiss her. Instead, he tilted her head down to press a kiss on her forehead. His warm lips pressed against her widow's peak of hair; she took a deep breath. His kiss sent waves of warmth down her body; not the familiar rush of lust, but something else, something headier she couldn't place because she'd never felt it before.

Inside her studio, she dropped her bag on the small table at the entrance and plopped down on her bed to remove her stiletto shoes. Despite all her years of walking in heels, she never figured out how to make them more comfortable. Heels off, she laid back on the bed. She knew she should take off her beaded dress and wash off her makeup. Her mother instilled in her from an early age that if she didn't remove her makeup every night, she'd age three days. She should've done those things. Instead, she picked up her phone and texted Nathan.

> Ilsa: *Roses are red. Violets are fine. You be the six. I'll be the nine.*

His answer was immediate.

Nathan: *Please don't tell me that asshole at the party said that to you.*

Ilsa smiled to herself. She thought about teasing him, but it felt wrong. There was jealousy in his gaze when he walked up to Ilsa and the random M-named guy. Clicking over to a selfie she'd taken with the group earlier, she looked at herself squished between Nathan and Keller. Eloise was so much shorter than the group, even in heels, that she stood in the front like a child in a family photo. Or at least the family photos she'd seen in other people's homes. Her mother, Mitzie, was never one for those types of photos on the walls. She was more the *spring the child on them later when they're hooked* type of gal.

Nothing in their rotating homes suggested that Ilsa ever lived there. This changed when she met the chiropractor, who had walls of family pictures of children whose ages sat between Ilsa and Mitzie. Suddenly, there were family photos up on the walls of Ilsa. Not that it mattered anymore. She had a family. Eloise was her family. Trinh was her family. Nathan. Even pain-in-the-ass Keller and emo-boy Theo. They were all closer to family than Mitzie was.

Zooming in on the photo, she looked at each of their faces. For so long, it felt easier to work hard and focus on her job, her designs, her clothes, and her life. Ilsa's hand clasping Eloise's, whose side was being held tight by Keller. Beside Ilsa, Nathan has his arm wrapped around her shoulder. Ilsa is looking at Eloise, and Nathan is looking at her.

Ilsa: *No, I read that one online. No creepy come-ons tonight.*

Nathan: *Except for the guy.*

Ilsa: *He was harmless. Maybe. How do you feel?*

Nathan: *Fine. Nothing more than a nasty mix of bourbon and champagne.*

Smiling to herself, she bid Nathan goodnight and hefted herself out of bed. The cold linoleum floor soothed her aching arches. Standing in front of the bathroom mirror, she reached behind her to unclasp her dress. Nathan had to button her into the dress, and now she couldn't get the hook closure undone. After trying a few times, she dropped her hands.

"Well, fuck."

Chapter Nine

Drape
NATHAN

Once he dropped Ilsa off at her apartment, he watched as the door closed behind her. He knew if he stayed where he was, he would catch one last glimpse of her as she walked past the long window of her floor. He watched from his spot in the parking lot as she walked by the window on the fifth floor before slipping out of his eye-line. That was going to be safe enough for him if he couldn't walk her to her door. He instructed the driver to take him home, his mind going over the night.

They say it's hard to see the audience when you're on stage. That can be true sometimes. Despite the light on him, he could pick out where Ilsa was in the crowd the whole time he played. The way she stood back, watching the set, her hand clutching the half-empty glass of champagne. Her eyes never left him. He wished he didn't agree to play, but he had to honor what Eloise wanted. The support of Prevalent Notion helped get her songs to the masses. If it was anyone else, he would've been tempted to bail, but not for Eloise.

While on stage, he let himself go into playing by rote, which only occurred on songs he'd spent years perfecting. He could play these songs in his sleep. The change was the charged air between him and Ilsa. He didn't want to let her go when they called him to get on stage. The whole way up those stairs, his fingers tingled from the feel of her bare back against his hand. His arms were heavy from the weight of her ass resting on them as he held her above him. Her body felt perfect against his.

He saw the guy approach Ilsa, standing a little too close to her. In her heels, the man came to her chin, but his hair was styled up high enough, so the top of his hair was the same height as Ilsa. Nathan could appreciate that other men wanted to spend time on their hair. Theo certainly had enough products to stock his own hair care aisle, but Nathan liked to keep his own brown hair cut short. It didn't get in the way when he played, and he didn't have to worry about looking presentable when he was in a rush out the door. It wasn't rock star hair, but if Flea could have short hair, why couldn't he?

He wondered if Ilsa liked his hair shorter or if she wanted him to look more like that guy. Scrubbing a hand over his face, he tried to banish the thought. He'd look ridiculous trying to style his hair like that guy. His whole aesthetic, carefully crafted by stylists, was that of down-home charm. Nathan was the attainable one, the one a guy thought he could be like and girls thought they'd have a chance with. He was glad his look was the more no-nonsense one. And Ilsa was the one who helped create that look. If she didn't like it on him, she would've helped him dress differently.

Leaning against the back of the leather seat, he watched as the car rushed through the city and toward his house. He cracked his knuckles, the feel of her bare skin still lingering in his muscle memory. He wasn't sure what came over him to pick her up and hold her that way. They were in the middle of a crowded party full of industry people, not a house party. But when she cracked the joke about him carrying her away, that was exactly what he wanted to do.

He'd been too forward with her, telling her he always looked for her in the crowd. It was too late to take it back now. He was earnest to a fault; he knew this about himself. It'd gotten him in trouble a few times in LA. Everything here was coded messages and mind games he never learned the rules to. Ilsa knew the rules, though.

Pulling into his driveway, he leaned out the window to key in his security code for the gate. He never pictured he'd live in a place with a security system, but the house came with it. Once the car pulled up to his door, he got out, sliding the driver a large tip.

Staring up at his large home, he was struck by how different the house was from where he dropped off Ilsa. There was no cracked facade or vandalized windows. Rows of well-manicured plants led up to his front door, where Ilsa's place had brown rock landscaping with shrubby brush accents.

Walking into his foyer, he toed off his shoes—black leather things that likely cost more than his parents earned in a month. Moving down the hall, he got to his bedroom. Flopping down on the bed, he pulled out his phone. Eloise had texted the group a picture of them tonight. Nathan's arm wrapped around Ilsa's shoulder as she looked over at Eloise. Ilsa fit so well under his arm. They fit together. As he was zooming in closer to them, a text came through from Ilsa. Another dirty pick-up line.

When they started telling each other these jokes, it all felt so innocent. Now it was anything but. He wondered if she'd taken that guy's phone number. If this guy had said that to her. Ilsa didn't seem interested in his attention, but how could Nathan tell? She was making fun of Brenton Michael Phillips, and she admitted to sleeping with him. While on stage, he watched as the man leaned closer to Ilsa, his mouth almost on her ear. The whole time Nathan willed the set to be over, willed Ilsa to tell the guy off.

This wasn't the first time he'd felt the twinge of jealousy while watching Ilsa, but this was the first time he felt like he'd had a right to the jealousy. Ilsa was her own person. Her life belonged to her alone. It was one of the things he admired most about her. The past few days had him wondering if he had a right to be a part of that life as more than a friend.

Before he could second guess himself, he asked her if that guy had given her the pick-up line. After a few long minutes of no response, he was relieved when Ilsa set his mind at ease and joked about him being hungover the next day. After wishing her goodnight, he set his phone down beside him. While he was a little too hot in his suit jacket, he couldn't move to take it off yet. He could still smell Ilsa on him—the clean floral scent that lingered in her hair. Closing his eyes, he imagined holding Ilsa in his arms again. If only he had the chance.

The phone beside his head trilled an annoying sound. Scrambling his hand over the covers, he found the phone wedged between two pillows.

"What is it?" Eyes still closed in half-sleep, he set the phone against his ear, letting it rest there without holding it in place. He'd been having a wonderful dream—something about Ilsa, a beach, and no swimsuits.

"Time for our run, buddy. I'm on your porch," Theo said.

Bringing his hand up to hold the phone, he rolled to his back, cracking one eye open to see the pink light of dawn on his ceiling. "What time is it?"

"Six AM, like we agreed, little buddy." Theo's voice was annoyingly chipper. A year before, Theo had been heading down a destructive path that almost cost the band everything. It came to a head when he tried to kiss Eloise after a nasty breakup with his supermodel girlfriend, Safiya Khan. Since then, Theo's been on a health kick, working out all the time, eating clean, and doing what their new manager told him to do. Most of the time, Nathan was happy about this change in Theo's discipline. But not today.

"I'm hanging up now," Nathan mumbled as he disconnected the call. Closing both eyes, he buried his face into his blanket.

He was almost back to sleep with the image of Ilsa wrapped around his body when the blanket was ripped off his body. Nathan struggled to a sitting position to find Theo standing at the foot of his bed.

"Up and at 'em, Hoss." Theo raised a brow at Nathan's clothes. In his fatigued state the night before, he never took off his dress pants and a button-down shirt. "Might want to change first."

Nathan grabbed the blanket from Theo's hand. "How did you get in here?"

"I have a key. I know your code. Come on. I can't run with Keller because that guy's a beast at sprints and he lets me know it."

"So, you want to run with me because I'm slower than you?" Nathan swung his legs over the side of his bed, scrubbing his rough stubbled face.

"A guy needs an ego boost somehow."

Nathan glared at Theo. There wasn't a single girl in his graduating class who was prettier than Theo. "Give me ten minutes, fucker. And you buy me breakfast."

Two hours later, they walked into Dot's Diner on jelly legs and took a seat by the window. A little hole-in-the-wall diner above a pub—the greasy spoon boasted homemade bread and raspberry jam. And best of all—anonymity. Dot herself waitressed every day and didn't care who they were as long as they paid their bill. The place reminded him of the diner in his hometown, only this one overlooked the water instead of a tobacco field.

Taking off his moisture-wicking ball cap, Theo ran a hand through his blond hair. Nathan's head was too big for those fancy hats.

Nathan's phone on the table lit up with another text from Shelby. He hadn't responded to the last few texts she'd sent, but he'd need to soon. Most were simple check-ins, with a few naked pictures sprinkled in. If Ilsa saw another one, she might get the wrong idea. Not that he knew what the right idea was.

Stretching his long legs out under the table, Nathan leaned back in the wooden chair, tipping it on its back legs.

"You break my chair, you're buying me a new one, young man." Dot turned over the ceramic mugs, pouring coffee into each. There were no fancy artisanal cappuccinos here. It was drip coffee or chamomile tea if you asked nicely.

Nathan righted the chair. Scooting it in and straightening his posture. "Yes, ma'am.

Sorry about that." He let his drawl slip a little more than usual.

With pursed lips, the woman's eyes narrowed at him. "What's it going to be, boys."

Theo ordered first, then Nathan.

"You got that special still going? The one you had around Valentine's Day?"

Dot stuck the pencil in her gray and black bun. "You mean the big platter?"

He grinned at her. "That's the one."

"That's a two-person breakfast."

"It's perfect. That's what I'd like, ma'am."

Dot harrumphed, but once she got to the window barked out the order to the cook.

Theo shook his head. "Man, I don't know how you can eat like that."

"One bite at a time, brother."

Dot left Theo and Nathan alone, and there were only a few glances from the other customers. In the many times they'd come to the diner, no one ever bothered them. Across the table, Theo ripped the lid off a small half-and-half, dumping it in his coffee.

"So, you going tell me what's going on with you and Ilsa, or do I need to speculate like everyone else?" he asked, his eyes focused on stirring his coffee.

Grabbing the sugar canister, Nathan tipped it over his coffee. His nutritionist would be appalled, but he rationalized it by the long run on the beach they'd just done.

"Nothing's going on."

"Come on, man." Theo cocked his head to the side. "I saw you two canoodling last night."

"Canoodling? Who says canoodling? What are you, eighty?" Nathan asked, deflecting.

"You going to tell me I'm wrong? I know you, man. That was not friendly behavior."

Nathan tipped his chair back, staring at the ceiling. "What do you want me to say? Do I like her? Yeah. Do I know what's going on or if something's going to happen? No. She's got her business, and I have the album coming out. What I want for us would complicate things."

"So, you want her." A knowing smirk crossed Theo's face.

Across the restaurant, Dot yelled out. "What did I say about my chair, young man?"

Nathan set the legs back down, grimacing at Theo, who was laughing behind his mug of coffee.

"Sorry, ma'am," Nathan called out, waving good-naturedly.

"Don't ruin this place for me. I like it here," Theo chided.

A young woman with curly black hair and tanned skin walked up to the table, a notepad clutched against her chest. "Are you, um," she swallowed, her hand shaking. "Are you Theo Blake and Nathan Ayers?"

Theo turned to the young woman with a warm smile stretched across his face. "Yes, we are. How can we help you?"

"I'm such a big fan. I have all your albums. Your song, *Dig Deeper*, helped me get through a nasty breakup last year. He was a musician, and listening to your song made me feel less alone, you know?"

Theo's smile got wider and he nodded at the girl. "I appreciate you saying so. You know we have a record coming out in a few months. We'll have to send you a copy. How old are you, anyway?"

The girl preened, flipping her dark hair back from her face at Theo's attention. "Um, seventeen. I'll be eighteen in April, though."

Nathan set his chair down, about to interrupt the dangerous direction of the conversation. He knew Theo wouldn't date an underage girl, but even flirting with one could be grounds for tabloid fodder. Theo was on thin ice as it was. It turns out he didn't need to worry, though. Theo leaned in and asked the girl. "Seventeen. Okay, seventeen. Can I give you some advice?"

The girl nodded wordlessly.

"Work hard in school, focus on your education, and don't let any boy make you feel that way again. Men aren't worth your tears, no matter how cute they look or how well they play the guitar. You feel me?"

The girl took a step back, nodding. "Ye—yes, Mr. Blake, I understand."

"And by the way, if you like the lyrics in *Dig Deeper*, you need to check out Eloise Grant's album. She wrote the lyrics for that song."

The girl nodded at him, her face serious. "I will. Could I ask you to sign this for me?"

Nathan took the notepad, "Sure thing. Who should we make it out to?"

"Lola."

"Dolores, you leave those boys be." Dot nudged the young woman with her hip before setting the food down in front of them. "My granddaughter may have gotten my name, but she doesn't have a lick of sense yet."

The young woman looked away sheepishly.

Nathan handed the notepad to Theo, who signed it before giving it back to the young girl. Nathan smiled up at Dot and her granddaughter. "It's really alright, ma'am."

Dot narrowed her eyes. "Where you from?"

"Kentucky."

"Humph." She looked him up and down. "My second husband was from Tennesee."

Nathan wasn't sure if this was a positive reference and was more than a little intimidated by the woman, so he didn't ask.

"You're a long way from home, young man," she said, her eyes squinting with suspicion.

Nathan nodded at her in agreement. Without another word, she turned away, Lola walking behind her. Nathan shot her thumbs up to let her know it was okay.

"Look at you giving a teenage girl, advice." Nathan teased as he shook pepper over his eggs.

Theo shrugged. "She reminds me of someone I knew once. Stop trying to distract me, though. What are you going to do about Ilsa?"

Handing the pepper shaker to Theo, Nathan shrugged. "I don't know."

Chapter Ten

PINKING SHEARS
ILSA

I LSA WAS RESTLESS. SLEEP eluded her all night and through the morning.

The feel of his hand on her cheek the night before and the playful glint in his eyes as he held her raced through her mind. She was thankful for Trinh's calm demeanor when she came into the studio, still wearing her dress from the night before. With no admonishment, she helped Ilsa out of the gown. Some of the beadwork had loosened in the night, and it would need to be fixed if it was going to be used as a display. Ilsa changed into a simple pair of shorts and a white button-down and tried to get some work done on the payroll. She wanted to hire an outside firm to handle this task in the future, but she was still paying off so much debt.

With numbers blurring together, Ilsa kept seeing Nathan before her. She felt the weight of his hand on her shoulder, the scratch of his cheek against her hand as she cupped his face.

Staring at the screen in front of her, she checked her emails again for news from Gallegos and Davis. Still no word from the venture capitalist firm. She had a few more people she could reach out to for possible funding or investment—a model she met a few times when she was a teen, a socialite she met in New York when the band was touring who had complimented her designs, and a tech wizard from Silicon Valley she met at a party the year before. They were options, but they felt even less likely to bear fruit than the Gallegos and Davis firm.

Switching screens to her bank statement, she groaned. Funds had not magically appeared in her account overnight. Before she could talk herself down, she sent emails to the three potential investors, asking if she could take them out to lunch the next time they were in town.

In her bag, the distinct trill of her phone sounded. Only one person had been assigned that tone. Grumbling to herself, Ilsa scavenged through the lipstick tubes and fabric squares crowding her purse, to retrieve the phone.

"Hello, Mitzie." She hadn't called her mother a maternal name since she was a young child. At first, it was rebellion. But then her mother ended up preferring it. Probably so they could be mistaken as sisters.

"Darling, you will never believe what I saw online today," her mother's breezy voice was low. She'd worked for years with a vocal coach to take away the harshness of her northeastern roots.

"I couldn't guess." Ilsa balanced the phone between her shoulder and her ear, her neck bent at an angle. With her free hands, she pulled out and smoothed the bolt of cloth she was going to work with.

"A picture of you. On the internet! Did you know?" At the end of the line was the distinct click of ice cubes in a glass. Ilsa could picture her mother, the tall glass filled to the brim with ice and diet soda, as her mother lay by the pool in her backyard. They didn't live anywhere with a pool as a child. Still, Mitzie had wasted no time securing herself another money maker once Ilsa's modeling fountain ran dry. Mitzie married Doug, a chiropractor twenty years her senior, three months after Ilsa moved out. Doug was a nice enough guy, but Mitzie was his third wife. Ilsa wasn't holding out hope this marriage would last.

"I'm sure there are a few pictures of me on the internet. I was a model for ten years."

She gave a heavy sigh indicating she felt Ilsa was being impertinent. "Not from your teen years. From last night. It's a nice enough picture of you, I suppose, though you look a little heavy. Have you tried that Keto diet? I heard it works wonders."

Ilsa ignored the jibe about her weight. It'd taken a few years of deprogramming to get to a place where she was confident in her body, but her mother would never understand that. To Mitzie, she could never be thin enough, graceful enough, or simply *enough*. Getting out of the valley and away from her mother's control was one of the best things she'd ever done for herself.

"What site was the picture from?"

"Oh, well, let me see." Mitzie's nails were clicking on the screen before her voice returned. "It was on *allceleb.com*. It looks like you are at an album release party for some chubby girl named Eloise, something-or-another. Wearing a gold dress. Though I will say, I don't think gold is your color, darling. You know it washes you out."

"Eloise Dunning-Grant. She's a good friend of mine. I made that gold dress myself. I like the way I looked in it." Despite knowing it was never a good idea to look yourself up online, Ilsa walked to her desk to pull up the photos.

"If you say so. Black is more slimming."

"Mitzie, if you continue to talk about my weight, I will hang up." Ilsa had to do this frequently. Her mother would pout for a few weeks, posting vague inspirational quotes about how you can't always trust family to love you unconditionally. Still, then she'd call a few weeks later asking for something.

Mitzie sniffed in an affronted tone but didn't press on.

"I'm looking at them now." The pictures from the album release party loaded on the search engine. There were a few unflattering shots of her, of course. It was a given when you're being shot candidly, but she was pleased with the way she looked in the photos.

There was a slideshow of different photos from the event, including her and Nathan on the red carpet as they walked in. Her arm was draped through the crook of his elbow and he's looking down at her while she faced the cameras straight on. It was a posed picture—where she strategically stood for her best angles. Nathan looked as handsome as ever, his bright smile stretching his face into a thing of beauty.

"You didn't tell me you were dating someone, Ilsabeth."

Ilsa hated when her mother called her by her full name. She was gearing up for some talk, Ilsa knew it. "I'm not."

"Oh, come now. I see how the young man is looking at you. And a successful musician too. You should try to hold on to this one."

Ilsa was inclined to agree with her mother, but she wouldn't admit that. She didn't want Nathan for the same reasons her mother married Doug—money, status, and connections. No, Ilsa wanted Nathan for who he was—for his sweet smile and kind words, the rough touch of his hand on her back and the heat of his gaze. But she'd never tell her mother that. Knowing her mother, if she confirmed anything related to Nathan, Mitzie would have a word to the tabloids by noon.

"I'm not talking about Nathan with you."

"I'm your mother. If you can't have girl talk with me, then who can you talk to?"

Ilsa opened her mouth to answer, then closed it. It wouldn't help anything to argue with her. Mitzie lived in her own world; keeping distance and peace was a bigger priority than proving she was right.

"I have to go. A client walked in," Ilsa lied.

"Love you, darling. Maybe we can meet up for a weekend trip like last time. Palm Springs again?"

Ilsa rolled her eyes. There was no way she'd make the mistake of being caught in Palm Springs again with her mother, half-carrying her back from the bar after she hit on men younger than Ilsa.

"I'll check my schedule. Bye Mitzie. Give Doug my love." Ilsa hung up before her mother could add anything.

Setting the phone down, Ilsa started clicking through the slideshow from the night of the album release. There were the customary pictures of various celebrities on the red carpet and standing around tall tables that could barely fit a plate of hor d'oeuvres. Eloise and Keller rightfully dominated the photos. There was a group photo of the boys from Prevalent Notion with Eloise. Ilsa jotted down a quick note about getting a copy of the photo as a gift for Eloise.

Scrolling through the random candids, one picture made her stop short. In the background of a picture of Theo and Aria Kingston, she could see the moment Nathan had picked her up. Held above his head, her hands resting on his shoulders, her face was bright with laughter as he gazed up at her. She sucked in a breath seeing the picture. From the outside, knowing how it felt at that moment as he held her close, it was obvious how much she cared for Nathan. Rubbing a hand on her chest, Ilsa felt like she was splitting open. She wanted this man.

"Ilsa."

Ilsa blinked a few times at Trinh, who'd appeared in the office's doorway, a stack of papers in her hands and a concerned look on her face. "What?"

"I asked if you're okay?" Trinh set the papers down on a table and turned to face Ilsa. "You look a little...." She waved her hand dramatically in front of her face.

"Tired?" Ilsa supplied.

"Sure, let's call it that and not what I was going to say," Trinh agreed.

Ilsa squeezed her eyes shut and tilted her head back. With her hands in her hair, she scratched her scalp with her long nails. Her mother used to do that to help her go to sleep at night. It was one of the few maternal things Mitzie did away from the public eye. The feel of long nails against her scalp calmed her and made her feel confused all at once. She didn't want to think about her mother and what her mother would think of Nathan.

Ilsa knew her determination was from her mother. Mitzie taught her to go after what she wanted in life. Only what Mitzie wanted in life was a good husband to take care of her and a daughter she could brag about. She was never interested in having her own life or accomplishments. Mitzie's approval of a relationship with Nathan rankled her.

"Listen, I don't know what has you in such a funk, but it is seriously affecting the energy of this space."

Ilsa narrowed her eyes at Trinh. "I'm fine."

"Lying liar filled with lies." Trinh wagged a finger at Ilsa. "You have something on your mind, and it's toxic. The negative air is so thick I could swim through it."

Ilsa knew better than to argue with her seamstress when she began on a *law of attraction* rant. "Fine, I guess I'll go get a smoothie or something. You want anything?" Ilsa asked as she hurried to the door.

Trinh shook her head. "No, I got a kombucha. I'm good."

Getting in her car, Ilsa leaned back against the seat and stared at her storefront. Can she cope with these emotions now, after all the hard work she'd put into that little shop and her dreams?

Pulling out to the street, she wavered at a stop sign. To the left was the smoothie shop. To the right was the onramp for the highway that'd take her closer to Nathan.

Chapter Eleven

THREAD
NATHAN

WHEN HE PULLED INTO this driveway, he was surprised to see Ilsa's beat-up SUV parked in front of his house. She had a key and knew his security code but was never one to drop by unexpectedly. Locking his car, he walked into his foyer, calling for Ilsa. He caught sight of her sitting on his deck overlooking the sea with a bottle of water beside her.

To someone else, it'd annoy them when their friend let themselves in. Admittedly, he was irritated with Theo a few hours before for doing what Ilsa was doing. But having Ilsa in his home and seeing her feel comfortable enough to be at ease in his space made him happy.

Grabbing his own bottle of water from the fridge, he joined her on the deck, plopping himself into a lounge chair beside her. Her blonde hair was up in a high ponytail, with her distinct undercut on the left side of her hair. When she turned to look at him, he could feel the warmth in her hazel eyes behind her oversized sunglasses. Her legs stretched in front of her in some pleated red shorts that made her tanned legs look longer than normal. A white button-down shirt was tied below her navel, showing a small swatch of soft skin.

"Hey, you." Her voice was soft, and she gave him a smile that made his stomach clench. It was the same smile she'd given him in the middle of the party last night. It made him feel like he was the only man in the world.

Studying her, he tried to think of something to say, but all the words he had said to Theo earlier, all his feelings clogged his brain, and he couldn't get any rational words out. Instead, he eeked a small "hey" in return.

"Where were you earlier? I called, but you didn't pick up," Ilsa asked as she took a sip of water.

"On a run with Theo. He woke me up at six."

"Ouch." Ilsa smiled at Nathan. She knew he wasn't a morning person.

"Yeah, I was hurting a little. How about you? How'd you sleep last night?" he asked.

"Terrible."

Nathan wondered if it was because she was thinking of him, but she quickly dispelled that thought. "I couldn't get out of my dress. I had to sleep in it."

Annoyance laced through him at the image of Ilsa sleeping in that beaded dress. "Why didn't you tell me? I would've come over to help you."

Ilsa let out a snort. "I'm not going to ask you to drive all the way back to my place because I can't unbutton my dress. I'm not a child."

No, but I want to take care of you. He could never say that to her.

"Sleeping in it is the better option?"

"Yeah." Ilsa put her palms up with a look of *obviously, duh*. "I wore it to work, and Trinh helped me out of it. We'll have to fix some of the beading, anyway. Apparently, it's not meant to be slept in."

"Imagine that. Maybe you need to put a disclaimer on the dress: *only to be worn when someone can get you out of it.*"

"You're not going to use this as one of your *this is why a woman needs a man* things, are you? Because I'd like to think that you hold your gender in more regard than opening pickle jars and unclasping dresses."

"Sometimes I do." If she had asked him, he'd have been over there in record-breaking time. The image of him helping her out of the dress, her soft skin under his fingers, the weight of the gown falling to the floor as he turns her to face him. The heat of her skin burning under his fingers. Fighting the urge to reach out and touch her, he clenched his fists, squeezing hard enough for the impulse to ebb. Luckily Ilsa didn't seem to notice his hands. A small breeze picked up, lashing a strand of hair against her face. She brushed it away as she glanced at him.

Turning to face her, he set his water bottle between his legs. He felt a little like a frog in the position he was in. The lounge chair was too low to the ground for his long legs.

He studied Ilsa. She looked calm as if she was relaxing. But Ilsa didn't relax. And Nathan knew she certainly didn't come over to his house this morning for relaxation.

"You want to tell me why you stopped by?" he asked. Could he dare wish for her to want him?

Ilsa pushed her oversized sunglasses up to rest on her head and blinked at him a few times. "Do you want me to leave?"

"No, definitely not. I'm happy you're here, but you don't normally swing by for fun. Did something happen?" He wondered if that guy from the night before had called her.

No, it couldn't be that. She wouldn't talk to Nathan about that. It had to be the investors and the funding for the line.

"Did you hear from the investors yet?"

She shook her head. "No. I emailed to check in, but there's no response yet. I hope they're not giving me the brush-off. That meeting was hard enough to schedule."

"I bet I could make some calls for you if you wanted."

"No, absolutely not." Ilsa's voice had a hard edge to it. "I won't allow you to do that. I'm doing this on my own."

Nathan knew better than to argue with her. It was her business. She never told him how to play music. What did he know about fashion design and running a business?

"What's going on?"

"Trinh sent me packing earlier. She said my nervous energy was bringing negative energy into the shop, and we could fail because of it."

"Do you honestly believe that?" he asked.

Ilsa shook her head. "No, but I needed to get out and clear my head, anyway. I don't know. I got in my car, and I was going to get myself a smoothie, but I drove here instead."

It wasn't a declaration, but it was something. A morsel for him to cling to and build upon. Nathan reached over to take her hand lying on the side of the lounge chair. Her nails were long and multicolor. He wasn't sure how she worked with such long nails, but she made it work. Lacing his fingers through hers, he pulled her forward into an upright position.

"So, you were unhappy, and you came here."

Ilsa nodded. "I don't know why."

"I do." Nathan dragged his lounge chair closer until his knees hit hers, and he leaned forward. "I think you do, too."

Ilsa glanced at him with an unreadable gaze.

"Tell me," she whispered.

Reaching forward, he took her other hand, holding it up before him. His finger skirted down her palm to her wrist, where he traced the blue-green veins with his fingertip. Her breath shuddered at his touch, and he knew she was reacting to his touch. His eyes still on her wrist, he drew a line down her arm and back up until he was holding both her hands.

"I was thinking about you all night," Nathan admitted.

"Me too." Her face was solemn, but his heart soared. She leaned forward, bringing her legs up to set them between his open thighs. Looking down at their entwined hands, she watched as their fingers clutched each other.

"I like the way your hand feels in mine." She looked up at him. "I like the way *you* make me feel."

Dropping one hand, he reached forward to cup her face. Her cheek fit his hand perfectly. The brush of her undercut was soft on his fingers. His thumb touched the corner of her mouth.

"How do you feel now?" he asked. He waited for her to pull away, to tell him to stop. Instead, she leaned forward and rested her forehead against his.

Chapter Twelve

NEEDLE
ILSA

NATHAN'S HAND ON HER face felt so right.

Something had felt off all day. She couldn't concentrate. Couldn't do what needed to be done. Couldn't calm down.

For days she'd been actively fighting against the urge to be close to Nathan, to have his hand on her face, to feel the warmth in his gaze. This felt right. His hand was large on her wrist, with long fingers grazing her skin. His touch sent warm waves down her body. She wasn't a blusher, never had been, but her face felt warm from his touch. The heat of his gaze intensified, and she was back at the party, being held in his arms and the loud music fading away as he held her above him.

"What were you thinking about?" he asked her.

"Last night, standing beside you," Ilsa put her forehead on his shoulder, looking down at the small space between them. This wasn't a lie. She'd been thinking of that moment. About what it might mean for both of them. What it meant to her. But how could she tell him that? "I like how tall you are. It makes me feel small and dainty."

Nathan wrapped his arms around her, his hand resting on her back, rubbing a small circle on the base of her spine. Heat traveled up her body at his contact.

"I don't want you to feel small. You should never be small. I love that you take up all the space you deserve. I love the length of your legs and the lushness of your hips. The sharpness of your elbows and the way your arms can wrap around me to hold us together. You make me feel powerful."

Ilsa stilled at his words. She never tried to make herself smaller to fit into the world around her. Being tall was something she just was. But she'd never been told it was her strength, that it was her power. With Nathan staring down at her, she felt like a goddess who could conquer the world. Until he said those words, she had no idea how much her heart had longed for them.

He pulled her face to look at him and brushed a strand of hair off her face, his palm cradling her cheek as if it were breakable. "Never let anyone make you feel like you don't deserve this world you've created. You deserve all of this and more."

A lump grew in her throat at his words.

"I like you, Illy." Ducking his head down, his lips brushing against the softness of her cheek.

Her eyes fluttered shut at the feel of his soft lips, warmth traveling down her body.

"I like you too," she whispered.

"No, I really like you." He pulled back and stared down at her, his green eyes pensive. "Tell me I'm not the only one who feels this between us. Tell me I'm not alone in this wanting."

Ilsa shook her head. "You're not alone. I feel it. I want it. I want *you*."

Nathan swiped his thumb across her cheek and leaned his forehead against hers. The connection made her feel so strong.

Ilsa struggled to get past the lump in her throat. "You're my best friend." She hesitated, "Did you know that?"

Nathan stared at her, his face serious. "Yeah, I did. I know."

"Tell me I won't fuck this up, Nathan," Ilsa asked. "Tell me, no matter what, you'll still be my friend."

"We're not going to fuck this up." He cupped her cheek, running his thumb on her cheekbone.

"You have no idea how many ways a relationship can be ruined. I've seen firsthand, and I *need* you as my friend." Her voice hitched at the word *friend*. The idea of losing him brought such intense emotion it terrified her. She gazed up at him. He had no idea. He was still so sweet, so naïve when it came to heartbreak.

"This isn't about sex, for me. You know that, right?" Nathan asked.

Ilsa nodded. If he wanted sex, there were scores of other women he could call up, including Shelby Waters.

"This is about a choice we are making today—you and me. Together." Nathan's voice sounded reverent on the word *together*. Ilsa sucked in a breath. "We make this choice. We do this," he motioned between them with his hand. "What's happening here. I can't be casual with you."

Ilsa nodded her head. She knew. She'd always known the connection between her and Nathan would be many things—special, wanton, unforgettable—but it would never be casual.

"You're my Illy. If we do this, if we cross this line? That's it for me. I'm not seeing other women, and you can't see other men. You understand?"

Ilsa nodded again. His words—*My Illy.* Her heart beat loudly in her ears. He wasn't touching her, and yet her body was flush with something more than the lust she was familiar with.

My Illy.

She'd never wanted to belong to someone. Until he said those words, she had no idea how much she needed Nathan to want her like this. All her life people wanted pieces of her—sections of her smile, her body, her hair. Never had someone wanted her for herself, for all of her? But Nathan did.

"Are you, my Nathan?"

Reaching forward, he cupped her face in his hands, his thumbs rubbing a line on her cheekbones. "That's all I want to be."

Reaching up, she mirrored his hands, cupping his face in her hands. The bristle of his unshaven cheek was rough on her palm. *"My Nathan."*

"Say it again." He asked, his eyes growing darker as his face inched closer.

"Mine." Her words were a whisper against his face.

"Again." His nose brushed hers as he tilted his head.

"Mine."

His lips brushed against hers, the feather-light touch of caution. "Again," he asked against her lips.

Instead of speaking, she moved into him, parting her lips over his. His mouth descended on hers and then she was on her back on the lounge chair, his body over hers. She could feel all of him, the lines of his thighs as they rested between hers. Wrapping her legs around the back of his legs, she pulled him closer, bringing his length against her core. She could feel him harden through the thin fabric of their clothes.

His kisses were demanding as his tongue urged against hers. One hand reached beneath her, gripped her ass, and pulled her into him while his other hand tangled in her hair. She felt a sweet sting as his fingers pulled the hair at her nape. His mouth left hers, kissing a line down her throat to the front of her shirt. With one deft hand, he unbuttoned the top button, licking the newly exposed skin. Heat blazed through her, and she thrust her center upward to grind against him. Nathan hissed at the contact.

"You're going to kill me." Looking up at her, his face in line with her breasts that were threatening to burst out of Trinh's sports bra she'd borrowed earlier. It wasn't the sexy underwear she'd wanted to show him for their first time together, but he didn't seem to even notice. Instead, his fingers traced the edge where the bra and her skin met.

"This is far too tight; we need to get this off you." He unbuttoned the rest of her shirt and pulled it open. She sat up, shrugging her shirt off her shoulders.

He met her in the sitting position, his mouth covering hers in a frenzy. The shirt was thrown on the ground beside the lounge chair. Nathan pushed the shoulder strap of her bra down. He ducked his head to press a kiss to her bare skin where the material had been digging into her skin.

"It won't come off, that—ah," she started to speak, but his mouth distracted her.

He sucked her skin into her mouth, his tongue moving in circles over her tender flesh. Her hands went to his hair, her nails scratched at his scalp.

Far off, she heard a bird cry, and she opened her eyes. They were still outside, on a lounge chair, no less.

"Wait, we can't do this out here." She gasped as his kisses descended across the top of her breasts.

"It's fine. No one can see us," he assured her.

Ilsa wasn't sure if that was true. Drone cameras were a thing in the area, and Nathan's address wasn't a secret. But that wasn't the issue. "Nate, I want you in a bed. As sexy as this, on a lounge chair...."

He pulled away, resting his head on her chest, breathing heavily as he nodded against her breasts. "You're right. It's not good enough."

Quicker than she thought possible, he stood up, scooping her up in his arms. She wrapped her legs around his waist as he walked through his open patio door and into the house. His hands were rough on her ass as she kissed him, her tongue diving into his mouth to caress his. His house felt big before, but never had the bedroom felt so far away as when he was carrying her down that hall.

He must've known the layout by heart because he never stopped kissing her as they made their way to the bedroom. Taking one hand off her back, he steadied himself as he lowered her to the bed.

He was on top of her, their kiss barely breaking. Bracing himself over her, she could feel the muscles in his arms on each side of her body. Running a hand over his forearms, she marveled at the form of his body. She knew he was strong; she'd felt the might of him when he held her aloft in his arms. But she never imagined such strength could be encased within the silk of his skin.

Safe in the quiet of his room, he moved down her body, kissing the tops of her breasts. When he got to the sports bra, he pushed the fabric down but was met with resistance.

"Hold on." She smiled down at his attempts to take the bra off. "It's too small for me. I had to borrow it from Trinh." Sitting up, she reached for the band of the sports bra and wiggled until her breasts were free. Nathan's eyes darted to her exposed nipples, and he reached forward to take one breast in his hand. Ilsa tugged on the sports bra, trying to get it over her head. The bunched-up fabric stuck under her armpit. She tugged a few times more, but the bra barely moved. Nathan dropped his hand and watched her.

"Do you—"

"No, no, I'm fine. It's just a little—snug." The last word was said like an expletive. She gripped the band again and pulled harder. Wedging it into a tense band across her chest, she cursed. "Fuck."

Over her, Nathan chuckled.

"It's not funny." Her arm came down on the bed beside her. "I was trying to be sexy here."

"Obviously." He grinned.

"The bra is too small."

"I can see that." He didn't hide his smirk. "You want help?"

Screwing up her face in anguish, she let out a loud sigh, "Yes, okay."

"What were you saying about women not needing men, again?" He reached under the band and pulled it over her head in a quick movement. The bra had been pushed to its elastic limits and snapped out of his hand, hitting the wall with a low thud.

Ilsa crossed her arms over her bare chest, covering herself. "Don't be a dickhead."

Smiling, Nathan reached forward, his fingers combing through her hair as he pulled her mouth to his. This kiss was teasing, a brush of his lips against hers. As his kiss deepened, she leaned back on the bed until he was over her again, his hard body pressing her into the mattress.

"I got a dick head for you," he whispered against her lips.

Despite herself, Ilsa laughed until his mouth traveled down her body and to her bare breast. His tongue laved the tender pink skin where the bra had been holding her in.

"Never again put these beauties through such torture," he said, his words against the tender flesh. His lips kissed the red spots as if to heal them.

She arched her hips into him, and he let out a hiss that went straight to her core. Reaching down, she laid her hands on his shoulders as his tongue swept across her breast.

"Such delicate skin. So ready for more." Holding one breast in his hand, his lips closed around her nipple, sucking into his mouth.

"Oh, God," she moaned as his tongue circled her areola. He watched as she writhed beneath him. His green eyes were dark with desire.

He pinched her nipple as his mouth left her breast. Her skin flushed pink at his touch. "Look how you bloom beneath me."

Ilsa nodded at him, urging him back onto her skin with her hands. He made a tsking sound. "I'll say where I go, *Petal*."

The term of endearment, at the moment, only made her hotter. Her legs wrapped around his waist. She urged her center closer to him, friction building inside her.

"I need you."

"Need me? Where?" Sucking her other nipple into his mouth, his teeth scraped against her sensitive flesh deliciously. Sensation built up between her legs as his tongue flickered across her pebbled nipple.

"Lower, please." She moaned. "More."

Releasing her breasts with a pop, his words were hot on her skin. "Need more here."

His hand traced below her breast, moving over her stomach. "Or here."

"More," was all she could gasp out as his fingers dipped into her shorts. His deft fingers skimmed her clit before circling her entrance. "Here? Is this where you want me?"

Ilsa nodded, the words failing her as his finger parted her folds. When his long finger plunged inside her, she gasped, grabbing his shoulders and folding in at the pleasure. Nathan's lips kissed her stomach below her navel. His finger disappeared from inside her, and she groaned at the loss of contact.

"I want to see you, all of you." Looping his fingers on the top of her shorts, he pulled them down over her hips and thighs. His motions were slow and methodical as he slid her shorts over her legs and threw them to the floor. Clad in only her thong, she clamped her thighs together to hold in the sensation building from just the heat of his eyes on her body.

Once her shorts were off, he slid down between her legs. Placing one hand on each knee, he pushed them apart and ducked down until he was face to face with the thin scrap of fabric between them. Cupping her mound, his hand covered her heat.

"You're so wet. Are you wet for me?"

"Yes." Ilsa moaned as his fingers moved over the fabric, teasing her.

Bending down, he kissed the top of her pubic bone, moving over her with featherlight kisses until his face was between her legs. His mouth closed over her as he sucked the fabric and her skin into his mouth. As his mouth moved, the cold air hit her wet skin, the contrast sending heat to her chilled skin.

"You like that?"

He took her moan as approval. Through the wet fabric, he found her clit, sucking it into his mouth. She still had her underwear on, and he was edging her faster to orgasm than any man ever had before.

As his mouth worked over her, his hands came up, tweaking her nipples. Between his tongue moving over her sensitive flesh and his rough hands on her breasts, she was climbing higher. She cried out, and his hands moved to her hips as she bucked against his face. She brought her hands up to her hair, pulling her strands as his tongue moved faster.

There were no words, only cries as she spiraled up, energy crackling behind her eyelids as she hit her climax. His rough touch held her in place as he wrought every drop of pleasure from her body.

Her arms flopped down beside her head. Her mind was empty of all coherent thought as she came down from her orgasm. Nathan slid up to lie beside her. Her eyes were still closed, and she felt his hand on her forehead as he brushed hairs off her face. Opening her eyes slowly, she found him watching her with darkened green eyes.

"That was incredible," she whispered.

A small smile brightened his face as he gazed at her. "Yeah?"

Ilsa nodded before turning over to climb on him, straddling him. Her core was still tender from her orgasm, and his hard length pressing against her sent shivers through her body. She was pretty sure if she rocked against him a few times, she could get both of them off from friction alone. But she wouldn't do that. She had a better idea.

"You had your fun with me. Now it's my turn." Ilsa winked at him before climbing off him and moving into the hallway. She returned a minute later with a small bottle of clear liquid.

Nathan seemed more than willing to have Ilsa take the lead. He laid back against the headboard, his arms behind his head as Ilsa kneeled between his legs. Palming his erection that was straining out of his boxers, Ilsa licked her lips. She'd never been one to enjoy giving blowjobs, but she had the urge to take Nathan in her mouth and suck him down.

Pulling down his boxers, she took out his cock. She knew he'd be large. For a man of his size, it was likely, but looking at his girth, she was surprised by how big.

"Whoa." He sucked in a hard breath and gave her a wicked smile.

"You've been packing this thing around and never once boasted?" she asked.

"I'm a humble man."

"If the world knew how gorgeous this cock was, you'd be on the cover of every rock and roll magazine."

"Gorgeous?"

She ran a finger down the length, reveling in the feel of the soft steel. "This has to be the most exquisite cock I've ever seen."

"I don't want to think about you seeing another cock," he said, a wrinkle forming between his brows.

Taking him in hand, she gripped him at his base, running her hand up the length. "Then don't think about it. Think about what I'm doing to you right now."

Pumping her fist over him, he groaned from the contact. With her free hand, she grabbed the small bottle of lube she'd had in her purse. Squeezing the gel into her palm, she returned her hand to his cock, gliding down the long length of him.

"Oh, that's hot." He gasped as she moved.

"You like that?" She moved faster, pumping her hand over his length.

"No, I mean, that's hot." He sat up straight, out of her reach. "It's burning. Oh, fuck!"

He jumped off the bed with a grimace. "What is that stuff?"

"Arousal gel. It's for hand jobs and oral."

He groaned as he gripped his dick, squeezing it. "It hurts. Oh, God. What the fuck?"

Before she could ask what was going on, he rushed out of the room and into the bathroom. She heard the water running for the shower.

Sitting on the bed, Ilsa grabbed Nathan's shirt that he'd discarded and wiped her hand off. So much for sexy time.

In the bathroom, the water continued to run, and she could hear Nathan cussing. Dejected, she grabbed her shirt off the floor, putting it back on.

"Nathan," she called out. "Are you okay?" Ilsa walked into the bathroom. Through the opaque shower door, she could see the outline of Nathan scrubbing himself in the water.

"No. Maybe." There was a long pause before the water turned off. "I don't know."

Retrieving a towel from under the sink, she held it out for him. A quick glance showed her that his dick looked wrong. Redder than it should've been. Swollen and not in a sexy way. She glanced away as he wrapped the towel around his hips. While she was excited to see him naked moments before, it felt wrong to ogle his broken dick now.

"Um, I think you might need to go to the hospital."

"Seriously?" He shook his head. "I'm not going, Illy. It's just a little allergic reaction."

He moved past her and into the kitchen, where he grabbed a bag out of the freezer and pressed it to his front.

"Your dick looks like an eggplant and not in the cute texting way. Do I need to call an ambulance, or will you get in my car?" she yelled, her voice edging on shrill.

She could tell he was trying to hold it together, but the pain was getting to be too much.

"An ambulance for my dick? No, you can drive me." His face screwed up in pain, and he sucked air between his teeth. "Oh, fuck! It really hurts."

"Okay." Ilsa turned to gather her things. Nathan managed to put on a pair of athletic shorts and a T-shirt. Waddling with the bag of frozen vegetables in front of him, he made it to the car, collapsing inside.

In her haste to pull out of the driveway, Ilsa almost struck the black sedan parked in front of Nathan's driveway. Careless driving. If she got in an accident, Nathan's dick would never get fixed.

On the road, Ilsa called Trinh's cousin Franny.

"Fran, what is in that gel you gave Trinh?"

"Oh, did you like it? Who are you using that on? You or someone else? I had no idea you were seeing someone. Tell me all about him, or her, I don't ju—"

Ilsa interrupted, "Tell me what was in the lube. Seriously."

On the other end, Fran huffed. "Well, I can't disclose all the ingredients, you know, proprietary informa—"

"Tell me! I think we're having some sort of reaction. What's in it?"

"A little menthol for that special tingle, a little aloe vera, some coconut oil, and a few fruit extracts"

"Like kiwi?" Ilsa sucked in a breath, her eyes darting to Nathan as he bunched over in her front seat, a bag of frozen broccoli over his junk.

"Yeah! It's great for skin regeneration. Did you know that? In fact, I heard of a study where—"

Ilsa hung up on her. Nathan groaned, his eyes shut tight in pain. "I hate that fruit. Fucking kiwi."

Nathan rested his head against the window, grumbling. "Why is it so hot in here?"

"Hot? This isn't hot. You have no idea what hot means. Try living in Phoenix in the middle of August with no air conditioning."

"Isn't it a dry heat?" He gritted his teeth as he spoke.

"It doesn't matter how hot it is. Day after day of 110 degrees is still a hell of a lot hotter than you could handle."

Nathan groaned again. "But why is it so hot in here?" He bent forward to mess with the knobs on her dashboard. Musty, hot air blowed out at them. "Why isn't your air conditioning working."

Ilsa checked her blind spot before moving over to the left lane. "Because it's broken."

"You don't have AC?"

Ilsa shook her head no before focusing back on the road ahead. "It was AC or pay the girls at the shop. I made the right choice. I can handle it."

Beside her, Nathan straightened up, grunting in pain. "Ilsa, you need AC."

"It's not a big deal, Nate. All you have to do is roll the windows down, see?" To demonstrate, she pushed the button on her car door to let the breeze in. "Fresh air, no need for a two-thousand-dollar bill from the mechanic."

"Who told you two thousand dollars? Most AC work should only be around five hundred."

Ilsa glanced at Nathan, who was trying to sit up straight but failing. "Why don't we worry a little more about your precious appendage and a little less about the state of my air conditioning?"

"Fine," he grumbled as they approached the hospital. "This conversation isn't over, though."

Ilsa got out, walking around the car to pull open his door. She could see from the darkness in his eyes that he didn't like how she opened the car door for him, but he'd need to get over that. "Let's go save that gorgeous cock I love so much."

Chapter Thirteen

TWEED
NATHAN

AllCeleb exclusive report.
Rock Star Hospitalized?!
By Trinity Flay

Eyewitness accounts have reported that Prevalent Notion bassist, Nathan Ayers, was hospitalized at Cedars-Sinai on Wednesday afternoon. The Grammy award-winning musician was escorted to the hospital by an unnamed woman.

It's unclear at this time the reason for his hospitalization, but sources close to the musician report that the medical emergency could have been caused by an underlying medical condition Ayers suffers from.

Hailey Lucas, another patient in the emergency department, shared this, "He was very kind as he waited his turn. I think whatever happened must've been his stomach because he kept doubling over in pain. He's cute, I guess, but I'm a Theo girl through and through. He's so hot. Nathan's kind of boring, you know?" When asked about the unnamed woman who brought the musician, Ms. Lucas shrugged. "I don't know, tall, blonde. She's no one famous, I know that."

A spokesperson from Cedars-Sinai responded to questions with this statement: "Cedars-Sinai takes the privacy of all their patients seriously. We will not comment on Mr. Ayers or any other patient's medical treatments."

All we can say here at AllCeleb is we hope Mr. Ayers isn't living up to the rock star persona. Bandmate Theo Blake has been trying to clean up his image after his public affair with married supermodel Safiya Khan. No stranger to scandal, drummer Keller Grant shocked their fans last year when he married an unknown songwriter, Eloise Dunning. AllCeleb requested a follow-up quote from Ayer and his team. Tamara Plein, manager of the rock group, declined to speak. Ayers typically provides the least amount of tabloid fodder out of Prevalent Notion. Let's hope Ayers has a speedy recovery.

If you have information regarding this story or have any other celebrity news, please email us at our tip line at gotcha@allcelebs.com

W ITH A MEDICAL-GRADE HYDROCORTISONE shot and strict instructions from the doctor not to further inflame the area, Nathan was discharged from the hospital. His dick had never been abused so badly in his life. Ilsa brought him home and offered to stay with him, but he sent her away. Seeing him bent over with a bag of frozen vegetables was one thing, but to have her try to take care of him and his dick injury felt wrong.

Determined to make sure he was okay, Ilsa stopped by a few times, brief visits where she brought him food, before having to rush back to her studio. Ilsa had always been devoted to her work, but he suspected she was as embarrassed as he was about what happened. The last time she was over, she dropped off a burger and fries from his favorite restaurant and let him know she'd be preparing for work meetings for the next few days and wouldn't be able to stop by. It was just as well. While his dick was healing, his ego was still bruised.

It was humiliating having to go to the hospital with Ilsa like that. He knew a lot of people had allergic reactions. He could run a mile in six and half minutes, he could bench press 250 lbs., and he was a world-renowned musician. Allergies weren't something he could fend off, no matter how manly he felt.

Still, did it have to be his dick?

He wallowed at home for three days, watching TV and taking calamine baths as the doctor encouraged. His assistant, Alexis, was kind enough to reschedule an interview he had. As good as Alexis was at her job, she couldn't help him when the news of his visit to the ER hit the internet.

Halfway through a rerun of American Pickers, his phone rang. Glancing at the screen, he groaned. He could avoid most of his friends at his pity party, but he could never ignore a call from his mother.

"Hi, Momma."

"Nathan Allyn Ayers. What is this I'm reading on the internet about you going to the hospital?" Jean Ayers was a small but formidable woman and took her role as his mother seriously.

"It was nothing, Momma. A little allergic reaction. I went as a precaution."

"Where was your epi-pen? You know you're supposed to always have it with you."

"I did. It was a skin reaction. Nothing happened. I got some medicine, and they sent me home."

"Humph." He could hear her rustling around in the background with something. His mother liked to keep busy, never sitting for long. The familiar sound of her making paper flowers came across the phone. She liked to do it on her days off from her job as a school psychologist. It made him a little homesick.

"Where did you hear about this?"

"Well. I *should* have heard about it from my son, but no! I had to find out on the internet with the rest of the world."

Nathan was certain that the hospital wouldn't have disclosed his visit. But the hospital was a public place, and there was a chance he was seen by another patient.

"What website?"

"Oh, well, let me look here." He heard the clack of her nails on the old desktop computer his parents kept in their spare bedroom. He offered to buy them a better one last year, but they refused, saying they hardly used the thing as it was. "Ah, AllCeleb. Darla down the street called me and told me to check it. She said Janessa, you remember Darla's daughter. Well, Janessa was a couple years younger than you in school."

"Yes, I remember Janessa," he said, rolling his eyes.

"Now Janessa told her mom, who asked me about it. Can you imagine hearing about it from the neighbor whose daughter read it on the internet and not from you?"

"Sorry, Momma. I didn't think it was a big deal. I didn't want to worry you."

"Worry me! I'm always fixing to worry. You know that. It's my job to worry 'bout you."

"Sorry, Momma. I'm really fine. It was no big deal." No matter how close he was to his mother, he wasn't about to tell her the circumstances of his injury. He'd known that if he'd called her when he got out of the hospital, she'd be asking these questions. Better to avoid the conversation altogether if possible.

"Well, if you say you're okay, then I believe you. Now, when were you going to tell me about this girlfriend of yours?"

Nathan scrubbed a hand over his face, his two-day-old stubble rough against his palm. He really needed to shave. "I don't have a girlfriend."

"Doesn't look like it to me. From the report, it sounds like some girl brought you to the hospital. Now, who was she?"

If talking about his injury was hard, talking about Ilsa was worse. As the oldest in his family, he knew his parents wanted him to settle down. His sister, Ashleigh, had given them one grandchild, and he knew his parents were itching for another one. If Nathan had a girlfriend, they would think he must be thinking of marriage, and if he was thinking of marriage, then children weren't far behind.

He didn't have the heart to let them know he wasn't the type for kids of his own. As much as he loved his nephew, the idea of being a father never appealed to him. He was more the fun uncle type. But discussing that with his mother right after his allergic reaction wasn't wise, so he let the subject pass.

"She was a friend, Momma. Ilsa. You remember me talking about her? The fashion designer?"

"The one with the shaved head?" his mother asked. Ilsa was in a few of the pictures he texted his parents when they were on tour the year before.

Nathan wasn't going to argue with his mother about Ilsa's hairstyle. While they only lived an hour outside of the college city of Lexington, his parents were skeptical of big-city fashion trends. While Ilsa's undercut hair was tame by Los Angeles standards, he was pretty sure it was the first time his mother had seen a woman like Ilsa.

"Sure, Ma. Yeah."

There was a long stretch of silence on the other end before Jean said, "Well, funny hair or not, she sounds like a nice girl. Taking you to the hospital was good of her. So, she's not your girlfriend?"

"No, she's not."

"You want her to be?" Jean interrupted.

Nathan hesitated, and his mother kept talking.

"She seems a whole heck o'lot better than that actress you were seeing. What was her name? Sadie?"

"Shelby. You know her name was Shelby, Mom."

His parents never met Shelby, but after their breakup, when Shelby moved on with a new man, his parents were quick to say they never trusted her. Nathan wasn't sure it was called for, but he knew better than to argue with his parents.

"Right, Shelby. That Ilsa seems like a better girl. She's pretty, too. And tall. Tall enough for you." Nathan had to bite back a laugh at the comment. His mother was five-one on a good day. It was from his father, Tobias, where he got his height and build.

"I'm glad you think so." He was nervous his mother would start asking him more questions about Ilsa and what their relationship was. He could never lie to his mother. Best to change the subject to her favorite topic—her one and only grandchild. "Now, tell me about how Kaiden is doing in school."

This did the trick, as his mother launched into a long explanation of how his sister, Ashleigh, and her son, Kaiden, were doing.

He wasn't off the phone for fifteen minutes before his security system let him know someone had entered the code for this front gate. He'd told Ilsa he didn't need her to stop by, but she must not have been listening to him still. Jogging to his bedroom, he tore off the old T-shirt he'd been wallowing in and pulled on a new one. There wasn't time to shower, so he wiped on some deodorant. When he still smelled some funk, he sprayed on a little cologne as well. Couldn't hurt.

Getting to the door before she could knock, he swung it open with a smile. Instead of a beautiful, tall blonde on his stoop, he found his bandmates.

"What's up, fucker!" Keller said as he walked in without invitation. As he passed Nathan, he wrinkled his nose. "Are you wearing cologne?"

"He probably thought we were a girl," Theo said, walking in behind him. Nathan held the door at the top as the guys walked down the hallway and plopped down on his couch.

"Come on in, guys," Nathan drawled. "Make yourself at home."

Keller stretched his long legs out in front of him, putting his feet on the coffee table. "I might do that."

Theo grabbed a French fry out of the takeout container Nathan had left out on the table. He held it up to his face before popping it in his mouth.

"How do my cold fries taste?" Nathan asked, settling into a chair across from them.

"Could use some ketchup." Theo grabbed another fry, popping it in his mouth.

"So, when were you going to tell us you had to go to the hospital?"

Nathan groaned. "Come on, not you guys, too. First, I have to hear about it from my mother, now you?"

Theo shrugged. "Tamara told us. I guess they called her for a quote."

Keller leaned forward, clasping his hands in front of him. "But you're good?"

"Yeah. I didn't even want to go to the hospital, but Ilsa said she'd call an ambulance if I didn't."

"Wait, Ilsa was with you? That was the unidentified blonde?" Keller put his hand out to Theo, opening and closing it in a gesture of gimme-gimme. "Fork it over. I told you."

Theo grumbled but dug out his wallet, slapping a hundred-dollar bill in Keller's hand. "Bullshit."

Theo looked back at Nathan with a mischievous glint. "So, you two fucking?"

Nathan groaned. "I'm not having that conversation with either one of you."

"He is," Keller said as he got up from the couch and headed into the kitchen, where he opened the fridge and pulled out three beers.

"I told you I'm not saying anything," Nathan said.

Keller handed a beer to Theo and Nathan. "You might not, but Ilsa told Eloise, who told me, so I've known for a few days now."

"Cheater. You knew?" Theo narrowed his eyes at Keller. "Give me my money back. You can't use insider information to make a bet."

Keller shrugged. "I'm using what I got."

"Give me my money back, fuckwad," Theo growled.

Keller frowned at Theo before digging into his pocket and handing the money back. "Fine. Ya, dick-crumpet."

Theo shoved the money back into his pocket before turning to Nathan. "I can't believe Keller knew before me. After I asked you over *homemade jam* at Dots and you were all, '*Nothing's going on. We're just friends.*'"

"First, don't act like you made the jam. And second, we weren't—doing that the last time we talked. This is a recent development. A non-thing, honestly." He wasn't normally so tight-lipped about his conquests with the guys but talking about Ilsa was different.

"You two don't tell me anything. I have to find out through the newspaper that Keller got married last year, and now you're keeping me out of the loop with your stuff. I'll tell you guys everything," Theo said.

"Yeah, maybe don't do that," Keller offered. "I don't need a play-by-play of your exploits with random groupies."

Theo rolled his eyes. "Like you're some saint. Before you got with Eloise, you were the worst of us."

Keller crossed his feet at his ankles, kicking back with his arms behind his head. "What can I say? Love changes a man."

Nathan snorted, and Theo shook his head. "So, tell us what happened. None of this BS Tamara told the news about an underlying medical condition." Theo asked.

Nathan hesitated. Yeah, it was embarrassing, but he'd observed the both of them doing far worse things. Before Keller married Eloise, he got a black eye from a woman who elbowed him while changing positions. Theo was no better. He was once so drunk while having sex doggy style his knees buckled, and he fell, taking the girl with him. They frequently shared these embarrassing stories with each other.

"I had an allergic reaction to the lube she had."

Keller opened his mouth to say something, then closed it, and lifted a finger up to interrupt before his hand closed back into a fist and settled into his lap.

"That's... huh," Theo said.

"So, you went to the hospital because of a little allergic reaction?" Keller asked, a chuckle in his words

Nathan groaned. He loved both these guys like brothers, but like family, they gave him the most shit. "Oh, I'm sorry. Next time the skin of your dick blows up to twice its size and burns like it's on fire, we can talk."

"I mean, it was just a little allergic reaction," Theo joked.

"On my dick. I can't believe I told you guys. I should've kept it to myself."

Theo laughed. "And you say I talk too much."

Nathan picked up a cold French fry and tossed it at him. Catching it with one hand before it hit him, Theo popped the fry in his mouth with glee.

Chapter Fourteen

CASHMERE
ILSA

S TANDING ON HIS FRONT step, Ilsa wondered what she was doing. There were so many reasons Nathan would want nothing to do with her. She was never any good at this next-day stuff with men. Most men never stayed around long enough for her to have a conversation with them, and she preferred it that way. It was different with Nathan.

This was exactly why her kissing Nathan had been a mistake. He was her friend. Her best friend, for God's sake. What was she thinking? Not only had she jeopardized her friendship with him but possibly his chance to have future children. Children he no doubt wanted. He seemed like the type.

Nathan opened the door, shirtless. Ilsa blinked a few times at him, her eyes going over his bare chest in a wanton way she'd never let him see before. "Wow, look at you. All hot and sweaty. I sure know the right time to come over to ogle you."

He seemed surprised to see her. She hoped it was a good surprise. His mouth ticked up with a small smile. "I guess you do."

Holding the door open, she ducked under his arm, stopping in the doorway to look up at him. A small bead of sweat lingered on his temple. Ilsa raised her hand to brush it away, her fingers lingering on his face. She wanted to apologize for putting him in danger with that stupid lube. She wanted to lean forward and press a kiss to his lips. Instead, she chickened out, stepping back to get space between them. "Are you a taxidermist? I have a beaver I need stuffed."

Nathan let out a relieved sigh at the pick-up line. If they could joke, they could be okay. "I bet you do, Petal."

Ilsa felt her cheeks flush a little and stepped away, making her way into his house. "I know you said you had enough food, but I brought you some dinner. If that's okay?"

She hated the way her voice went up at the end. In her pageant days, her vocal trainer had worked hard to contain the up-speak in her voice. But it came out when she was nervous. The familiar surge of panic clenched at her stomach. Her feet wanted to flee.

"You know all the rest of my body works fine, right? My dick got hurt. My legs still function."

"I know that!" Ilsa said a little sharper than she meant to. This was why she shouldn't have come over. She was looking needy. What did she know about how to help take care of someone. She couldn't keep houseplants alive. "I was driving by and thought you'd like some sushi. If you don't want it, I'll take it back."

Clutching the bag of food closer to her chest, she took a step toward the door. Nathan put his hand out, stopping her.

"No, don't go. I like sushi."

"No. If me coming over is an imposition, then I'll leave."

Nathan grabbed the plastic bag in her hand. "I love sushi."

Ilsa held on tighter, regretting the choices that led to this moment.

"Don't go. I want sushi. I appreciate you coming over." He tried again to take the bag, but Ilsa held on. As he tugged it from her hand, Ilsa drew back, pulling it in the other direction. They struggled with the plastic bag before the telltale sound of a rip sounded, and the paper containers flew in the air between them, spraying soy sauce, sticky rice, and various fillings all over the wall and each other.

"Agh!" Ilsa screamed as soy sauce dripped down her face. She looked at Nathan, who was equally covered in bits of cucumber and soy sauce.

A smile crept across his face, and his shoulders shook with silent laughter.

"It's not funny, Nate."

Flicking a green bit from his cheek with a finger, he shook his head. "Oh, come on, it's a little funny."

"Sushi is expensive. Now it's ruined. Ugh." She wiped a hand over her face, bits of food and sauce falling to the floor. Nathan stepped closer. Using his thumb, he wiped her cheek. The feel of his hand sent sparks through her body. He closed the distance between their bodies, stepping into her space. She took a sharp intake of breath. Feeling him so close after not seeing him for days was overwhelming.

Her body betrayed her when he was around. To give in would be foolish. Besides, they were covered in food. Stepping back from his touch, she bent down and gathered up the food, scooping it into the ripped plastic bag.

"I'll clean this up. Don't worry about it."

"No, I made the mess. I'll clean it," she snapped.

Nathan bent down until he was eye-to-eye with her. "*We* made this mess. Not you."

Ilsa grumbled a bit as she wiped at a spot of wasabi on the ebony hardwood floor. Nathan took the bag from her, setting it to the side. "Let me clean this up while you get cleaned up, and then I'll take you out to dinner to make up for it."

She frowned at him. "Sushi?"

"If that's what you want, yeah, sushi."

"It's what I had my heart set on for the night, yeah."

"I'll take you to Yamashiro."

Ilsa narrowed her eyes. She wouldn't tell him that the sushi she bought was from Lucky Teriyaki, the gas station-turned restaurant down the road from her studio. A single item at Yamashiro was enough to buy seven people sushi at Happy Teriyaki. She waved a hand over her ruined dress. "I can't go to Yamashiro. I'm covered in sauce."

"So, take a shower. We'll both scrub up, and then we'll get ready for dinner."

Ilsa's thoughts on the price of sashimi stuttered to a stop. "Take a shower? Here? At your house?"

Nathan nodded. "Yeah."

Thoughts of seeing him naked flooded her mind. It'd been all she could think about before the kiwi lube incident.

"What am I going to wear? I don't have extra clothes."

Nathan furrowed his brow. "Let's figure that out after we shower."

"So how are things..." she pointed her hand down, "down under?"

"Recovering."

"So, I didn't break your dick?" she asked.

"No, you didn't break my dick. Only slightly injured it."

"So, it's working now?"

Nathan grimaced. "It's not in 100% working order, no." He stepped closer, peeling her shirt off her shoulder. His finger traced a line from her throat to her collarbone. "My fingers are working fine, though."

Heat flooded through her. "Does this mean you'll let me see it again?" she asked.

Nathan paused. "Do you want to?"

A small smile ticked up on the corner of her mouth. "Yes, yes, I do."

He shook his head at her, cursing too low for her to hear, but the effect was the same. "Later," he told her before walking down the hall, leaving her to follow.

Nathan left her in the spare room with its adjoining bathroom and a large towel. She undressed quickly, wrapping herself in the plush towel. The house was insulated enough that she couldn't hear the water running in Nathan's bathroom. But she knew he was in the shower, just as she should be doing in her separate shower. But Ilsa didn't want to be separate. She wanted the steam of the hot water between them, the feel of Nathan's hands on her body. She wanted his mouth on her neck and his strong shoulders under her fingers. Before she could talk herself out of it, she tightened the towel around her and walked into his room, moving straight into the bathroom.

She could see the outline of Nathan under the water spray. She'd been in his bathroom enough to know his shower was big enough to fit a dozen people. Dropping her towel on the floor, she opened the glass door and stepped into the steam. Nathan stood with his back against the spray of water, watching as she entered the space. His gaze was heavy with lust as he took in her naked form.

"It doesn't look injured," she said, pointing at his swollen cock.

"It's still tender," he gritted out as she ran a hand down his chest, only to stop above his pelvis.

"Too tender for me?" She gave him a wicked smile as her nails skimmed along the root of him.

Leaning down, he rested his forehead against hers. "What you do to me, Petal...The way you make me feel."

"How do I make you feel?"

Their breath mingled together in the space between them, mixing with the steam of the hot water. His lips descended over hers in a searing kiss. His tongue traced the line of her lips, begging for entry. Her hands roamed his back, sliding under the water for purchase on his skin. As his kiss moved down her throat, she tilted her head back to give him better access. Ilsa ground herself against his hard cock. It'd be so easy to pull her leg up, to have him slide in.

Ilsa breathed out. "I don't want to hurt you. You're not healed enough, are you?"

"I might not be able to fuck you yet, but that doesn't mean I can't take care of you." Nathan pulled back, a wicked grin on his face.

To be taken care of. In the carnal sense, that sounded amazing. She refused to think of the higher implications of such a statement. She just wanted his hands on her body. Ilsa's back hit the cold tiles, sending shivers down her body. Her skin was aflame with his gaze. He stepped closer.

"You came in here to tease me. You know I can't do anything, but you came in here with your perfect curves, and your bitable ass, and those fucking divots."

"The what?" Ilsa's eyes widened.

Nathan dropped to his knees, grabbing her waist and holding her still. "These divots, right here. I want to run my tongue over them. See how my hands fit." He moved his palms down until his pinky rested in the dip where her hip bone stopped and her thigh began. The spot she'd worked out trying to erase. The spot that was airbrushed out of print ads. His thumb traced a circle on her pelvic bone. "Look how I fit you."

His eyes traveled up her body to her face. "Did you know I was going to fit you? Did you ever think about it?"

"This is dangerous," she breathed out. "You make me feel things."

His hands moved between her legs to her core. Cupping her mound, he looked at her face. Little drops of water clung to his long lashes as he stared at her. His eyes not wavering from hers, he kissed her thigh, his lips grazing the small birthmark she had on her right leg.

"Tell me," he commanded. His hands left her body.

"Touch me, Nate. Please touch me," Ilsa begged.

"Tell me how I make you feel, and I will. Tell me what you want, and I'll give it to you."

"I want your hands on me. I want your mouth...."

His hand wrapped around her ankle, moving up her leg. As he moved up, he pulled her legs apart. "What do you want my mouth to do, Petal?"

"Kiss me."

"You want my mouth to fuck you?"

Never did she imagine those dirty words coming out of his gentleman's mouth. "Yes."

At her words, his mouth closed over her center, sucking her clit into his mouth. Her legs buckled from the feelings overwhelming her. Taking one leg in his hand, he lifted her knee and put it over his shoulder. She leaned against the cold tile wall as he sucked on her, his tongue moving over her clit. His fingers joined in, plunging in and out of her pussy. She dug her fingers into his hair, pushing his face into her as the orgasm built higher and higher inside her. He crooked his fingers inside her, hitting her most sensitive spot, driving her deeper.

Sparks exploded behind Ilsa's eyelids as the climax hit her. She cried out, her screams of pleasure echoing around the bathroom. As she came down, her nails dug into his back, leaving little half-moon indents on his skin.

Once she could open her eyes, she gazed down at him as he watched her.

"I've waited so long to have you like this, Petal. How many times have I wanted to make you feel good." He pressed a kiss on her birthmark, his nose nuzzling her hip bone. "That was better than I ever imagined. You're better than I imagined."

Getting up, he moved under the spray of water, rinsing himself off. Ilsa wasn't sure if her legs could work after the orgasm she had. He smirked at her.

"Take your time in here. I'll get some stuff together for you."

"You don't need me to..." she motioned to his hard cock.

He shook his head. "If I let you touch me, I won't want you to stop, and I promised you dinner."

He pressed another kiss to her lips, leaving her in the steamy shower before she could grab for him.

Wrapped in a towel, Ilsa emerged from the bathroom to find Nathan standing in his room clad only in black boxer briefs. His short brown hair was already half dry and deliciously rumpled.

The towel on top of her head was heavy. His towels weren't from the bargain bin at Target like hers.

In his hand was a black dress on a hanger. "Last time my sister was here, I let her go shopping with a friend, and she bought some stuff. I'm pretty sure she left a few things here. You two are similar sizes, I think. She's tall too. She said it was an LA dress, not a hometown dress."

Ilsa held the velvet dress in front of her. It wasn't her normal style. It had a corseted waist with long bishop sleeves. Luckily it was a longer length, so she wouldn't be flashing people. One of the reasons she liked to make her own clothes was because most short dresses on the market were so short it looked like she was wearing a shirt. If she made her own, she could have the hem hit exactly where she liked it.

Holding the dress against her body, she looked herself over in the full-length mirror. "I think it's going to fit me weird. My hips are too wide, and my boobs are too small."

Nathan stepped behind her, his front against her back. Reaching over her shoulder. Nathan took the dress from her hand and tossed it on the bed. He set his hand on her hips, pulling her into him. She could feel how hard he was becoming from their contact and let out a shuddering breath. With his hands still on her hips, his thumbs rubbed a circle. "These hips?" Ilsa nodded as he ground himself into her, gripping harder. "I love these hips. They're exactly the right size for my hands."

Sparks from his touch were igniting inside her, darting to her core.

His hands moved up her body, tracing the edge of her breasts. Her hands laced around his neck as his head bent down to press a kiss to her bare shoulder. "As for those boobs, well, they're the perfect size for my mouth." His teeth nipped at her skin, and she let out a gasp.

"Nate, we have to get going, or we'll—" Nathan sucked the skin of her shoulder in his mouth. Her knees weakened, and she rested her body against him. He pulled her towel away, letting it fall to the floor.

Running his hand over her bare body, he hummed with pleasure. "You're right. I know. I just wanted to touch you one more time before dinner."

He pressed a chaste kiss on her head before leaving her alone in the bedroom with an aching core, no underwear, and a borrowed dress. The dress fit better than she thought it would, but it wasn't her style. The stitching was poor, and the hemline was trendy five years before. Still, it wasn't covered in soy sauce and wasabi.

Before placing her phone back in her bag, she saw the icon for a single email waiting in her inbox. Ilsa read the message a few times before letting out a cry of joy.

Nathan stopped in the hall, turning to face her. "Are you okay?"

"I have a second meeting. With Thomas Gallegos regarding the investment," she said, her eyes lit up with joy.

"That's good?" Nathan asked.

"Very good. Ms. Davis is unavailable, but Mr. Gallegos invited me to a lunch meeting tomorrow to discuss the company."

Ilsa wrapped her arms around Nathan's middle, burying her face in his chest. "It's all coming together. It's really happening, Nate!"

Nathan ran a hand down her back. "We definitely need dinner to celebrate."

With his hand on the small of her back, he led her to his car. He opened the car door and waited for her to climb in, closing the door after her. The black dress rode up on her thighs, but she thought Nathan would appreciate the view as they drove across town.

Chapter Fifteen

Embroidery
Ilsa

SEATED IN A SMALL alcove away from most of the other diners, Nathan let Ilsa order the food. Once the waiter was gone, she leaned forward.

Ilsa frowned at him. "Look, I don't know what's going on with us, but before we go further, I only think it's fair that I tell you I don't want kids."

"Well, that's jumping the gun a little, don't ya think? We just ordered the entrée."

She shook her head at him, a wry smile on her face.

"I mean, ever. I don't ever want to have kids. You seem like a guy who does. And I realized we never talked about it before, but I'm not having kids. In fact, I'm trying to find a doctor to get my tubes tied, but that's proving difficult."

The smile faded off his face as he considered her. "You're serious. Never ever? You don't want to have kids?"

"No. I don't. Is that a problem?" Ilsa asked.

"No, not necessarily. I've just never met a woman who isn't interested in being a mom. Back where I grew up, that's what women did. They got married and had babies." His brow furrowed.

"I'm more than just an incubator, Nate. I have goals and aspirations. I have a plan for my life, and having a child does not fit into my vision. The world is populated enough without adding another baby. Besides, I'm pretty sure I'd be a terrible mother. Passing on all the fucked-up stuff my mother gave me."

"For what it's worth, I think you'd do well in whatever you did. Parenting or other."

"I love kids. I will be an amazing auntie when Eloise and Keller have kids. But that's the fun stuff. The parties, the fun clothes, the spoiling them with cake pops. I'm not signing up for two-in-the-morning feedings, chapped nipples, and vomit-smelling cars."

Nathan nodded his head. "My sister has a kid. I don't get home to see them as often as I want, but I enjoy being an uncle. My nephew is smart. He's at the top of the fifth grade at his academy."

"Academy? How can your sister afford that? You said your family doesn't have—Oh." Ilsa felt her chest soften with the revelation. "You pay his tuition."

Nathan shrugged. "It's the least I can do. My parents raised me. Ashleigh got pregnant when she was seventeen. The dad is a deadbeat. I got them a little place and helped pay for Kaiden's school. I offered to move them out here, but Ash refused. His grandparents are better than their son, and my parents would never leave. The best I could do was move them into a better house in their town."

"You're a good man, Nathan Ayers."

A flush of pink dotted his cheeks at the compliment. Ilsa realized he likely didn't hear words like that often.

"I'm assuming, because you brought up the kids thing, that we can talk about what's going on here?" Nathan asked. "Between us?"

Ilsa wrinkled her nose. "Do we have to? Can't this just be fun?"

A shadow passed over Nathan's face, and she knew instantly that was the wrong thing to say.

"Is that what you want? Something casual, something fun?" When Nathan clenched his jaw, a small scar on the left side of his jaw grew white. Had Ilsa ever noticed that scar before? She had to urge to run a finger over the jagged pale line.

Opening her mouth to say that it was, Ilsa then closed it. No, she didn't want to be casual with Nathan. How she was feeling wasn't casual. It was scary, consuming her thoughts at work; it distracted her in conversations. Most of her relationships since she started dating were casual. She didn't know how to do anything else.

Casual meant there were no expectations of the other person. It meant Ilsa would never have to rely on the man for anything the way her mother did. She would never find herself kicked out of a house in the middle of the night with a child in tow. She's never had to go to bars to find the newest meal ticket. Casual meant she wouldn't be surprised when things inevitably took the wrong turn, as they always did.

Casual was safer. She knew this. But also knew that what she was feeling wasn't casual.

"I don't know what I want," she hesitated, seeing the disappointment on his face. "Let me finish?"

She took a deep breath. Talking about feelings was never easy for her. In pageants, they tell you to be "flexible and gracious" in every situation. To turn a difficult encounter into the best possible outcome. While there were plenty of times she was far from flexible and gracious, she still struggled with explaining to others why she felt the way she did. She wasn't even sure she understood how she felt most of the time.

"All I know is I want to be around you and spend time with you. I want to kiss you, like all the time, want to kiss you."

Nathan smiled at that admission.

"But I don't know what that means for us," she admitted. "Are you my boyfriend? That feels weird, right? *Boyfriend.* Like I'm in high school."

Nathan reached forward and took her hand, running his thumb over the back in a small circle. She could feel the callouses on his fingers from his years of playing instruments.

"How about we just say you're my Illy, my Petal." Nathan brought her hand up between them, pushing down her dress sleeve until he exposed her wrist. Ducking his head down, he kissed the tender skin inside her wrist. His eyes darted up to look at hers. Her breath caught. It was the same look he had given her in the shower hours before. A glance of longing, of need. Straightening up, he pulled her sleeve back over her wrist.

"And I can be whatever you want me to be," he said.

"You're giving me a lot of power here, Nate. I don't know if you should trust me. I already broke your gorgeous dick. What else will you allow me to break?" Ilsa asked with a smirk.

"My dick, my heart... Break away, Petal." He grimaced. "I take that back. Let's not repeat the kiwi incident ever again, please."

"But your heart?" she teased.

Nathan opened his mouth to say something, then shook his head as if he thought better of it.

Taking Ilsa's hand, Nathan squeezed her fingers before kissing her knuckles. Her face warmed. He had that effect on her. She wanted to object, but his touch made her want things she'd never dared to want before. A place to call home at the end of the day. A familiar face waiting for her. Someone to listen to her troubles, someone she could rely on. Pulling her hand from his, she tucked her hands back into her lap.

She was so distracted by the tingle running down her arm she didn't notice the man until he was at her side.

He was her height or maybe an inch shorter, with a balding hairline of dirty blond hair and a pudgy-looking face. She wasn't sure how he ended up walking by their table. It wasn't in a private room but was far enough away from the rest of the diners, so Nathan had privacy.

Ilsa watched as Nathan prepped his face for a quick conversation with a fan. It happened often enough. Instead, the man looked at Ilsa.

"Ilsa? Ilsa Kruger, from Sonora High?" he asked.

Blinking a few times at the man, she tried to place him. "Um, yeah. How did you...?"

"Peter, Peter Pickett. We had a few classes together." The man rocked back on his heels. "I heard you lived out here. We missed you at the reunion last year."

"Oh, was that last year?" Ilsa struggled to put a friendly smile on. High school wasn't a fun time for her. She had few friends from the area she wanted to keep in contact with. "I'm not the reunion type."

"We missed you there," he repeated.

Nathan cleared his throat from across the table.

"Oh, right, Nathan, this is Peter. We had *math class* together?" the words were a question more than a statement of fact.

"English. Not that it matters much. I'd recognize you anywhere, Mr. Ayers." Peter reached forward and took Nathan's hand off the table, shaking it fervently. She could see the lines around his eyes tensing up, but Nathan smiled.

"Good to meet you, too. Now, if you'll excuse us, we were having dinner."

"Let me buy you a drink, both of you," Peter offered.

Ilsa gave him a strained smile. "Now is not a good time, Peter."

Peter's smile wavered, but he seemed to shake it off. "No, of course. I'll leave you two be. Ilsabeth, I'd love to catch up and reminisce about the old fighting scorpion days." He made a gesture with his hand to imitate an attacking scorpion tail.

"Oh, well, why don't you email me, and we can get coffee sometime." She reached into her bag and retrieved a business card. Across the table, Nathan frowned.

"I'll do that. Ilsabeth, it's good to see you. Mr. Ayers, great job on the Grammy win."

They waited until Peter was out of sight before Nathan turned to Ilsa. "I can't take you anywhere. How many boyfriends are going to come out of the woodwork?"

Ilsa picked up a piece of edamame, pointing it at him. "That guy is as far from an ex-boyfriend as a man could get."

"So, who was he?"

Ilsa shrugged. "I don't remember, really. An old classmate? I'm terrible with names and haven't talked to my high school friends in years, let alone a random from my school."

"Well, he sure remembers you." Nathan glanced again at the spot where Pater disappeared.

Ilsa laughed. "I guess I'm unforgettable," she said, taking a bite of the edamame with zeal. The waiter came around, setting down their plates of sashimi and maki.

Nathan's face cleared slightly, taking a roll between his fingers. "I guess you're right. It's weird, though, right? What are the chances some guy from your high school would show up here?"

"This isn't some exclusive club, Nate. It's a well-known restaurant in a big city."

"Are you really going to meet him for coffee?" Nathan asked, frowning.

Ilsa shrugged. "Doubtful. I barely have time to come visit you."

Nathan laughed. "Good to know I take priority over one of your fellow fighting snakes."

"Scorpions. And, of course, you do. You don't pretend to be an arachnid in the middle of a high-end restaurant."

"Well, I'll save that for the bedroom."

Ilsa wrinkled her nose. "No, please don't."

Leaning closer, he hissed before breaking into an enormous grin that stretched his face.

Despite herself, Ilsa laughed.

Chapter Sixteen

Asymmetrical
Ilsa

A FTER DELIBERATING ALL NIGHT on what to wear to the lunch meeting with Thomas Gallegos, Ilsa decided on a simple but classic navy dress of her design, paired with some funky accessories and her lucky nude pumps. While she found the red-soled shoes over-hyped, wearing them was a status symbol, and she knew men like Thomas Gallegos were all about the appearance of status and prestige. Her mother may have taught her all sorts of fucked up things in her life, but she wasn't wrong about dressing for the job you want. If you project luxury and confidence, others will assume you always had it.

When she arrived at the restaurant, the hostess brought Ilsa into a private dining room in the back. Mr. Gallegos stood to shake her hand and motioned to the chair across from him. The hostess closed the door behind her, leaving them alone.

"Miss Kruger, so happy you could join me."

Ilsa smiled, straightening her shoulders. "I'm happy to have an opportunity to talk with you about my company, Mr. Gallegos."

"Thomas, please." He gave her a sharp, blinding smile. His forehead didn't move with the grin.

"Thomas, of course."

"I took the liberty of ordering some wine. I hope that's okay?"

Ilsa wasn't in the habit of drinking in the middle of the day, particularly with potential business associates, but to refuse felt rude. "Of course. I'd be delighted."

He poured her a healthy glass of white wine and motioned for her to take a sip. She knew nothing about wine but judging from his expression, it must be expensive.

"Good, right? It's my favorite here. It's from a vineyard I like to visit in the Russian River Valley. Have you ever been?"

Ilsa set the stemmed glassware on the white tablecloth. "No, I can't say I have."

"Now, some people like Sonoma, but me? I like grapes produced elsewhere."

Ilsa's cheeks burned from the fake smile she put on while he prattled on about grapes. After a few minutes, he paused, and Ilsa grabbed her bag to make her pitch.

"I have some new projections for the last sales quarter I wanted to share with you," she started.

He waved a dismissive hand, shaking his head. "Let's not talk about all that boring business. I want to get to know you. You were a model, correct? In Phoenix? Before moving to LA?"

"I did some minor print and runway work. Mostly local stuff. One national advert. Nothing that impressive, I assure you."

"Still, you did well for yourself. You moved out here, and in five short years, you've made a name for yourself with some heavy hitters. Impressive."

"I work hard."

"And you know what it takes to get ahead, do you not?"

The hairs on the back of her neck stood at the drop in his voice at the last question. He watched her with a gleam in his eyes.

"As I said, I work hard."

Gallegos seemed unnerved by her assertion. Sitting back, he crossed one leg over the other, resting one hand on his ankle. He wore designer sneakers instead of dress shoes. It was such an LA thing to do.

"Lucky break, getting all that national exposure with the Prevalent Notion styling. Being featured in publications, being seen with the band."

"Some might say that, yes." While it was a lucky break, she worked her ass off on tour, staying up late each night sewing and restructuring pieces for the band, all while creating her new line for her store.

"Particularly being seen around town with that Nathan Ayers. In fact, I saw a picture of the two of you looking very cozy only a few days ago. What's the story there?"

"Are you asking if I'm dating Nathan Ayers?" Ilsa tried to fight down the derision in her throat. The business was full of people who liked to push you to see where your breaking points were. He was no different from catty women who vied for camera time in her youth. Taking a steadying breath, Ilsa gave him a placid smile. "I'm sorry. I'm not seeing how that is relevant to my company."

"Well, your company, as you called it, your brand, is affected by the persona you put out. The company you keep, shall we say?"

Ilsa sat back, waiting for him to make a point.

"If you were seen dating a celebrity, it would be a positive factor for a while. You'd get some notoriety for your brand. But should you not be, well," he put his hands out in a *who-knows* gesture.

"Whether I have a relationship with Nathan shouldn't impact this conversation."

"But it does. So, I'll ask you again. Are you in a relationship with Nathan Ayers, and are you willing to use the press to promote your brand?"

A thick heat climbed through her chest at his words. She could never put Nathan through that. When she arrived in LA, it was with a single purpose that would not involve using a man's name to gain her success. She hadn't come this far to make the same mistakes her mother did.

"I will not use any relationship I may have with Mr. Ayers to promote my business. My clothes, my designs, will speak for themselves."

Clasping his hands in front of him, he leaned back, a snide smile playing on his face. "Well, they're not saying much. Your viability as a business in this town is about appearances. For every up-and-coming ex-model turned designer in this town, there are five more to take your place. So tell me, what makes you different? Why do you deserve it over each of them?"

Ilsa repeated her business strategies—the projections, the plans she had. Gallegos cut her off.

"I'm not talking about that. Any putz with a business degree can help with that. I'm talking about you. What are *you* going to do to ensure your business becomes successful?"

"I already told you."

Gallegos cut her off with a dismissive wave of his hand. Leaning closer, he laid a hand on her knee. "Let's not play games here, Miss Kruger. You're a beautiful woman; you have something you want from my company and me."

Ilsa stilled, her eyes darting down to his hand on her leg. The pressure felt like a brand on her skin, a warning. It wasn't moving, but she knew the way this played out. He wasn't the first man thirty years her senior to place a hand on her knee or brush a lock of hair from her face. To arrange her, fingers brushing against her breasts in a way that could be played off as accidental. Ilsa crossed her legs the other way, angling them away from his hand.

His smile widened at her movement as he motioned to the wineglass. "Have a drink, loosen up. We're just talking here."

Ilsa picked up the wineglass and brought it to her lips but didn't drink. He watched her movements with a predatory gaze.

"Mr. Gallegos. I think we have different definitions of what it takes to succeed in this town."

"No, I don't think we do. You knew exactly what you were doing being pictured with Nathan Ayers. You're hungry. You want to be successful. Some people might not like how you're going about it, but me? I admire it."

"I told you, my friendship with Nathan Ayers has nothing to do with my business."

"And that's all I'm asking for—a little *friendship*. We can help each other out. I've helped a lot of young ladies in your position. I'm very discreet, I promise."

Ilsa swallowed the bile rising in her throat. "Mr. Gallegos, I have to insist that we maintain a professional relationship only."

Frowning, he shook his head as if disappointed in an impertinent child.

"Well, I am sorry we won't be able to work together in the future." He set a card on the table before brushing invisible lint from his pressed suit. "Here's my personal number. In case you change your mind. Enjoy the rest of the lunch. It's on me."

Ilsa listened for the click of the door opening and counted to fifty before she gathered her items to leave. Leaving his business card on the table, Ilsa stalked out, walking past a sheepish-looking hostess waiting outside the door. Her hand shaking, she pulled her phone out of her purse to call Nathan. Staring down at the small rectangle in her hand, she studied her wavering reflection on the phone screen. She couldn't tell Nathan. As easy as it would be to call him, what would that help in the long run?

She was smart and driven. Nathan didn't need to help her solve this. She could figure this out on her own.

Chapter Seventeen

Piping 
ILSA

WHAT ILSA WANTED TO do more than anything, after kneeing Thomas Gallegos in the balls, was to go home and hide under a pile of blankets. The entire exchange left her feeling dirty.

No matter how many times she found herself in this situation, there was nothing to be done about the sickening feeling that followed. She knew her worth as a businesswoman. She knew her morals. There was no way she was going to cow to his demands. She would find another way to get funding for the business. They were making enough to run it as is, and if she had to put off the extended line until next season, then so be it. She refused to sell herself out.

Your mother would.

She blinked the thought away. Reason number fifty, she wouldn't be calling Thomas Gallegos back. Her phone buzzed in her purse, and she pulled it out to see two text messages from Nathan.

Nate: *My last girlfriend said women hate oral. You wanna prove her wrong?*

Nate: *How did the lunch meeting go? Are you flush with cash now?*

She shoved her phone back into her purse. She couldn't tell Nathan what had happened. He would get mad. He'd try to rush out in some misguided sense of chivalry to defend her. A move like that would only weaken her in the eyes of other potential investors. How would it look to have her rock star boyfriend, if she could even call him that, threaten asshole venture capitalists? No, she wouldn't be telling Nathan. There was nothing to tell.

Walking back into the store, only to see a red-faced man with a silk camisole clenched in his hand, screaming at her young sales associate.

"This place is a rip-off. What kind of bullshit is this?"

"Is there a problem here?" Ilsa asked.

The sales associate, Deja, looked at Ilsa with fear in her eyes. The man was standing far too close to the small nineteen-year-old. Ilsa set her hand on Deja's shoulder and pushed her gently away, stepping into the teenager's spot. Giving her a small nod, Deja stepped back. "This gentleman here is unhappy with the prices of the clothes."

Ilsa was familiar with these kinds of men. The ones who shout to get their way, throwing their bodies around in a show of power they couldn't wield in any other portion of their lives.

"I'll say I'm unhappy. My wife says she wants one of these little—" he shook the camisole in his hand, his face twisted up in a grimace. "Slippery little shirts, but you want ninety dollars for a piece of fabric with a string? It's bullshit."

"Sir, all the pieces in this shop are hand created—"

"Created by amateurs is right. I bet I could make this at my dining room table for five bucks."

"Then you are more than welcome to try."

"No, my wife wanted one of these shirts, and I'm going to get her one, and you are going to go behind your little cash register and give me a discount."

"Or what?" Ilsa laughed at the man, calling his bluff. "You're out of your depths here. Do you have any idea who I am? You think you can come into *my* business and threaten me?"

The man stepped back, his posture slackening at her words. "I didn't know this was your busi—"

After her lunch with Gallegos, the last shred of her patience snapped, and she raised her voice to match his. "It shouldn't matter if it is my business or not. Is this the way you treat people? Like servants to do your will? Look at you." Flipping her hand in his direction, she looked him up and down with disdain. "Five-year-old work pants from the bargain bin and a shirt that even the discount stores don't carry. You come into this business and harass *my* employees about *my* prices as if you have the slightest clue what quality looks like, let alone costs?"

"Well—" he fumbled for words. He straightened up, getting a second wind. "You need to assist me. I'm the customer."

"I'm not doing shit for you. I will not be condescended to by a man with a patchy chin beard. Now get out of my shop before I call the police."

Squaring her shoulders, she crossed her arms across her chest and stared him down. After glaring for a long minute, the man muttered a curse under his breath and turned on his heels to walk away.

"And if your wife wants to know why she didn't get her shirt, send her in. I'll tell her all about it," she called out after him as he reached the door.

The man paused for a minute before pushing the door open with one hand and flipping her off with the other. The manic beat of the blood in her ears drowned out the slam of the storefront door closing. Taking a steady breath, she turned to face Deja, standing behind the counter, staring at Ilsa with wide brown eyes.

"You okay?" Ilsa asked her.

Deja nodded. "He was scary. I thought he might hit me."

"No, a guy like that is all bluster. They think being loud is the same as being right." Ilsa laid a hand on Deja's shoulder, rubbing it. "Why don't you take a break."

"I just took a thirty."

"Take another one. Go get yourself an iced coffee or something. Actually, here." Ilsa grabbed a twenty out of the cash register. "Get one on me, okay?"

"Ilsa, I couldn't," Deja said, running a hand over her long black hair.

"I insist." Ilsa made a shooing motion with her hand until Deja left. After replacing the twenty in the register so the till was balanced, Ilsa turned the music up. With no one around, the small store felt empty.

When Deja walked in twenty minutes later, holding two iced coffees in her hands, Ilsa was still looking over the numbers, the pounding in her head only increasing. The sales had been increasing, and she hoped that they'd break the previous quarter's projections, but that still didn't give her the money she needed to expand.

"You okay?"

Ilsa snapped her laptop shut, clearing her face of any obvious anxiety. "Yeah, of course."

She couldn't tell her employee that they were floundering. Deja narrowed her eyes but didn't question further. "Here, I got you one too. I know you said you weren't freaked, but I figured you might be."

"Why would I be freaked?" Ilsa's voice rose high. Deja wrinkled her forehead. "Because that loser yelled at us?"

Ilsa had forgotten about the irate customer. "Oh, right, him? Yeah. He was a little intense, wasn't he?"

Gathering up the stack of mail in one hand, Ilsa took the coffee from Deja and retreated into the office. She didn't want to see a single person for the rest of the day.

Chapter Eighteen

NATHAN

T HAT NIGHT, NATHAN WAS halfway through his workout when his phone chimed a text. He hoped it wasn't Shelby again. He still hadn't responded to her, but at least her check-ins were decreasing. It was cowardly, but what could he say to his ex-girlfriend?

Stop trying to booty-call me? I'm having sex with someone else?

Luckily, this time, his favorite picture of Ilsa lit up the screen. It was taken while they were on tour. She's sitting on the edge of the stage in Nashville while techs are behind her, building the set. A few minutes before, he'd watched as a security guard tried hitting on her and was promptly shut down. At that moment, he'd had his first inkling that his feelings for Ilsa weren't platonic. He'd had a surge of jealousy when the guard hit on her. Then elation when she shut him down. He'd had female friends before. Hell, he'd spent years with Eloise and never once was annoyed when she was hit on, not that Eloise would've noticed. She was oblivious to Keller being head over heels for her, but that was a different story. After the security guard slunk away, his tail between his legs, Nathan sat beside her, nudging her with his shoulder.

"You broke that guy's heart." He smirked, jerking his head toward the lovelorn security guard.

"Nah, he'll survive. You know what he said, though?" She lowered her voice to make a poor impression of a manly voice. "Are you a sunset? Because I'd love to watch you go down."

Before Nathan could even understand the joke, Ilsa laughed. "Got to give him some credit. That one's especially terrible."

"I've heard worse," Nathan said. "Once, a fan came up to me and said I got an A in school. I want to F you."

Ilsa laughed. "Okay, that one is terrible too."

She reached into his jean pocket, pulling out his phone. Stilling himself, he didn't want to move as her fingers brushed against his thigh. "Let's get a picture. You and me. The terrible pickup line duo."

As she swiped to his camera, he watched her face, the way her smile was a little higher on her right side, and the brightness in her hazel eyes. He couldn't tell her no. She could've asked him for anything at that moment, and he would've said yes. Pressing her cheek next to his, she held the phone out, taking a selfie.

He saved the photo under his favorites when she had to leave to help Theo with a last-minute clothing mishap. One alongside his mom and one of and sisters. The one of his nephew. The picture of him and the band as they were toasting their first gold record years before. Only fifteen pictures were under his favorites, and then it was sixteen.

He looked at the picture for a moment. He'd suspect she was avoiding him if he didn't know better. After what Nathan considered a breakthrough in their relationship, he was prepared to find Ilsa at his house when she left work that day.

She didn't respond to his messages, even after he sent several throughout the day checking in. He felt like a lovesick teenager waiting for her attention. At seven that night, she texted she had a long day and would try to talk the next day.

He had a sinking suspicion the meeting didn't go well, but he didn't want to over-whelm Ilsa. He'd hoped she'd come to him for comfort but wouldn't force her. Here it was, three days later, and he was still clinging to the scraps of texts from her.

     Ilsa: *I just got back from Australia. You know I love going down under.*
Nathan: *I hope this is your version of "u up."*

Ilsa: *wyd?*

Three little dots danced on the screen, and then a second message.

Ilsa: *what are you wearing?*

Nathan smiled down at his phone. Holding the phone out, he sent her a quick picture of himself, shirtless and still sweaty from his workout. A moment later, Ilsa texted again.

Ilsa: *you're gonna kill a girl over here...*

Nathan: *your turn.*

The three bubbles popped up for a long minute and then disappeared. He set his phone down on the weight bench and got up to grab a towel from the side table. When he returned, a picture filled up the screen. Ilsa was at her desk, her hair pinned up in a high bun, clad only in a pink see-through bra. He could see the darkness of her small office behind her.

He hesitated. Sexting was something he'd done more times than he could count. He did it with Shelby when she was shooting on location in Vancouver. He had a few socialites and b-list celebrities slip into his DMs before. It was fun, no strings, and filled the void when he didn't have the chance to pick up a woman.

But this was Ilsa. He knew her. The look on her face right before he kissed her and the sound of her moans as she came against his tongue. He could dirty talk with her, but the real thing sounded much more tempting.

Nathan: *I'm coming over.*

His phone rang.

"Nate, I'm still at the store."

Nathan pulled a shirt over his head and toed his shoes on. "Then I'll come there."

"You can't."

"Why? Because you're busy? Make time, Ilsa. I'm coming."

He hung up on her, shoving his phone in his pocket as he walked out the door to his car.

LA traffic was as bad as it claims to be. It was forty minutes later when he arrived at the shop. It was plenty of time for Ilsa to change her mind, but just as he knew Ilsa was trying to keep her distance, he also knew she'd wait for him.

The pull between them grew stronger each day. Being apart had only strengthened his resolve to be with her.

The door to the shop was locked, but he saw her SUV was still in her parking spot. He knocked on the door a few times, the silver-frosted glass reflecting his image. He should've showered, or at least shaved, before heading over. It was too late now. At least his tired eyes were hidden behind a pair of overpriced sunglasses he got from the gifting suite at the Kids Choice Award last year.

The outline of a person appeared on the other side of the glass. He didn't need to see through it to know it was Ilsa. He'd know her figure anywhere. The jingle of the lock sounded, and then Ilsa was in the doorway, her arm braced against the doorframe. She wore a simple green dress, and she'd taken her hair down so it flowed around her shoulders.

"You ever heard of sexting? That wasn't an invitation to come over."

"Wasn't it?" Nathan stepped back, shoving his hands in his pockets. It was her choice to let him in, but damn if he wasn't bursting to touch her.

Gripping the door, she rested her head on the frame and blew out a loud breath. "Okay. Maybe a little. But I thought you'd send me a picture of that gorgeous dick. Then we'd both take care of ourselves and go back to work."

"You thought wrong. I don't want pictures. I want the real thing."

Ilsa looked him over before stepping aside to let him in. Nodding to his shades, she smiled. "Didn't know that seats come with glasses."

He smirked at her. The image of her poised over him, his tongue deep inside her. He felt himself get hard.

Not yet, boy. Give me a few minutes.

"You closed?" he asked.

Ilsa nodded. "About an hour ago. Deja had a family emergency, so I was on the floor all day. I'm just now getting to the closing duties."

He followed her to the office at the back of the store. In the office's corner was a two-seater couch and a crumpled blanket wadded in the corner. She'd obviously spent many restless nights here, burning the midnight oil. A wooden desk held her old laptop with piles of papers on all sides.

She deserved an office with a view of the city in a high rise somewhere. Not this shoebox of an office with a second-hand desk and an old leather sofa. Taking a seat on the couch, he touched the blanket. It was warm. Had she been sleeping?

Ilsa looked from the blanket to him and shook her head slightly. Right, a conversation for later.

"How did the meeting go?" he asked.

"Oh, it's not going to work out." A shadow crossed Ilsa's face, a pain that caused his stomach to clench.

She was lying. Nathan could see that clearly, but about what he didn't know. She sat at her desk, turning in the swivel chair until it faced him. The office was small enough that he could've reached out to touch her knee if he wanted to.

"What does that mean? Did he try something with you?" Nathan asked, deciding not to let it go.

Ilsa glanced up, blinking several times in shock. "No, of course not. We just had different priorities."

Ilsa turned away from him, grabbing a stack of papers. "Look, I have a million things to do, so maybe we can get together anot—"

Standing, he cut her off, grabbing the back of the chair to turn her to face him. "I'm not going anywhere."

Ilsa frowned at him. "Nate, come on."

He pulled her to her feet, his hand dropping to her hand, lacing it with his own. "No,

I have this time with you, and I want to spend it well."

She hesitated before the rigidity in her shoulders loosened. "Spend it doing what?"

With her hand in his, he brought it around his neck, pulling her close. She followed his movements until there was little between them.

"You know exactly what I want to do." Then he kissed her, his mouth urgent on hers. He had no idea before this day how much his skin ached for the feel of her against his body.

She pulled on his shirt, lifting it over his head. His fingers found the hem of her dress, bunching it above her waist. She found the front of his pants and pulled the button free, unzipping him until his pants fell to the floor. She backed him to the couch, pushing his bare chest until he sat down with his pants around his ankles. Standing in front of him, she pinned him down with her eyes as she grasped her dress, pulling it over her head.

Standing above him, clad in her bra and underwear, she stepped between his legs. Never breaking her gaze, she slowly lowered herself to sit astride him. The heat from her pussy shot straight to his dick. With only thin fabric between them, it'd be so simple to slip into her.

"I've missed your hands on my body," she said, gasping as his finger traced down her side to grip her hips, pulling her closer. His cock jumped as she ground against him. His hands tangled in her hair as he pulled her face to his to kiss her. Her nipples were hard through her thin bra. Reaching behind her back, he unclasped her bra in a single movement.

"That was so hot." Ilsa pulled away and looked down at him, letting her bra fall away to free her breasts.

"I'm just getting started." He said before capturing her nipple with his teeth, and pulling her into his mouth. She arched her back, giving him more access.

Pulling away, he grasped the hair at her nape until she looked at him.

"Do you remember the day we met?" Nathan's fingers grazed her shoulder as he pushed a lock of hair back.

"Yes," Ilsa was breathy.

"Do you ever think about that day?"

Ilsa nodded as if transfixed by the touch of his fingers against her bare skin.

"What do you think about it?"

Ilsa's voice was shaky. "I liked it."

"Do you think about it being you and me? When you close your eyes at night when you touch yourself, whose hands are you imagining?"

"Yours," Ilsa's voice was air.

"The way I would drag my lips down your neck? The feel of my hands on your hips as I pump my cock inside you. Do you picture how it would feel to have me fill you up?"

Ilsa nodded.

"Tell me." His voice was a command. He wasn't normally this demanding, but he needed to hear her say the words. He needed to know she was thinking of him as he did her. He needed to know she needed him.

"After I saw you with Shelby, I thought about you. I wished it was me. I wanted to be the one on your lap."

She squirmed on his lap, her wet pussy soaking his boxers.

"Did you like what you saw?"

"Yes. I liked how you pulled her hair to suck on her neck."

"Like this." He reached forward and sucked her skin into his mouth, pulling her hair enough to sting a little.

"Yes," she moaned.

"What else did you want?"

"Nathan, please!" She reached between them to palm his hard dick. He grabbed her hand, pulling it behind her back.

"Not yet. Tell me what else."

Ilsa moved over him. If she moved anymore, he'd come in his pants like a schoolboy. He grabbed her hips, stilling her.

"Tell me."

Her hands covered his on her hips. "This. You picked her up by the hips and moved her above you. I wanted that."

This is what he needed to hear. These words, her moans above him. "The second I saw you standing there, I wanted it to be you. Every night since, I've wanted it to be you."

"I want to, but we can't have our first time at my office. You deserve better than that." Ilsa said.

"Me? Isn't it supposed to be the other way around? Shouldn't I be protecting your delicate sensibilities?" he asked, sucking the skin of her bare shoulder into his mouth.

"Delicate is the last thing I'd call myself," Ilsa said. She pulled away to look at him. "You know that, right?"

"You can be vulnerable here, Illy. It's me. I won't let you be hurt. I want to take care of you."

As if shocked, Ilsa stilled. "What?"

He ran a hand up her side to cup her cheek. "I want to take care of you."

Ilsa pulled away, climbing off his lap. She pulled her discarded dress over her head, the hem barely covering the apex of her thighs. She flexed her jaw, her teeth clenched.

"Nate, you should probably go. I have a lot more work to do."

Nathan sat back on the couch, his empty arms at his sides and a stiff cock standing at attention. "Wait, what?"

Turning away from him, Ilsa gathered up the clothes strewn over her office. Her voice shaky, she shook out his shirt, snapping it violently.

"Illy. What's wrong?"

Ilsa turned back to face him. "Nothing. I have a lot going on, and I can't concentrate when you're around, so...."

"Was it something I said?"

Ilsa turned to face him, dumping his clothes on his naked lap. "What? No. Of course not. You're great. You're perfect." Her voice cracked on the last word. Pursing her lips together, she took a step back. The line of her throat moved as she gulped down words. "But I need you to leave."

"I don't understand."

Ilsa closed her eyes and pointed at the door. "It's not for you to understand. I'm asking you. Please leave."

She stalked out of the office, leaving him alone.

Nathan knew Ilsa enough to see she'd hit a breaking point. Pain bloomed in his chest as he pulled on his pants and shoes. He didn't bother with his shirt.

Getting to the door, Ilsa held it open, her face looking away from him.

He paused in the doorway. Something had snapped inside Ilsa. What it was, he wasn't sure. He'd give her the time to drive home to stew on her feelings, but he wasn't letting the issue go. He stepped into her body, flattening her to the side of the open door, one foot in the shop and one foot out. Bringing his hand to her nape, he pulled her face in for a searing kiss. She tensed before melting into his kiss, pulling his body close to hers. Her hair was soft against his fingers as he moved her head. After breaking the kiss, he pressed his lips into her throat and whispered. "Come home with me. I'll make it good. We'll be so good."

Her nails dug into his back as she ground her hips into him. It was like he saw a light flash behind his eyes at the feeling. No, there were lights. The flash of a professional camera. They pulled away, jerking their heads toward the paparazzi camera trained on them in the doorway.

"Shit," Ilsa said under her breath, stepping away from Nathan.

Nathan waved a hand at the paparazzi like he was an errant fly. "Get out of here."

The man lowered the camera and gave Nathan a big grin. "Already got what I came for, buddy." The man climbed into an old gold sedan and turned the car on before Nathan could react. It wasn't the first time paparazzi had followed him, but the other times it was with other celebrities like Shelby. They knew what they were getting into. Ilsa didn't.

Nathan whirled around to check on Ilsa. The door to the shop closed. He tried the handle, pulling several times before realizing Ilsa had locked him out.

"Illy, Let me in. He's gone now."

He could see her shadow through the door. "No. Go home. We can talk later."

"Come on, don't do this. We can talk now. Come on."

He watched as a woman walked down the street with a pug in a turquoise-colored bag and a phone in hand. Her eyes darted from Nathan to the storefront as she passed. The woman wasn't five steps from him when she whispered into her phone, "You'll never believe who I just saw yelling through a door like a crazy man."

There was silence on the other side of the door, and the glass was empty of her shadow. Nathan could wait there all night, but knowing how stubborn Ilsa was, she was waiting for him to leave, calling his bluff. He could wait her out. He had all night. But he knew it was hopeless. He just had to catch her somewhere else.

Chapter Nineteen

EMBELLISHMENT
ILSA

WHEN ILSA WAS BORN, her father was nineteen years old. John Kruger was a handsome sophomore at Arizona State University who spent thirty percent of his time studying to be pre-law. The other seventy percent was devoted to beer, babes, and bongs. That was how he met an eighteen-year-old freshman, Mitzie Sprink. John was handsome, tan, blond, tall, and strong. He was his fraternity's reigning keg stand champion and could pick Mitzie up with one hand.

Three months into what could only loosely be called a relationship, Mitzie missed a period, then another. John was raised Catholic and insisted she keep the baby, telling her he'd take care of them. Four years later, John moved away, leaving Mitzie with a three-year-old to raise. He sent dwindling child support checks every month but left his obligation at that.

Being a single mother at 22, Mitzie set off to find Ilsa a new father.

There were countless days when Ilsa would sit on her mother's bed, watching as Mitzie curled her Clairol light ash blonde hair. Mitzie would tell Ilsa about the new man in her life as she applied the blackest black mascara to her bottom lashes and blotted her Revlon pink lipstick.

Every time, the scene would remain the same: her mother getting herself ready for a date, the low-cut tops and tight skirts, the jangles of her bracelets on her bone-thin wrists, and the spritz of CK One on her throat. And every time, the same words.

"This guy is different; he's going to take care of us. I know it."

Each time Ilsa would watch her beautiful mother paint her face, and months later, she'd watch as the Great Lash mascara tracked down her cheeks.

Of course, there were nights when she wished she had a father who stuck around and a mother who took the time to get to know her daughter.

She'd see her school friends' mothers, a little full around the middle, wearing high-waisted jeans and floral print tops. The women her mother would accuse of "letting themselves go," and Ilsa would long for the taste of the afternoon snacks with silly names like "ants on a log" or "pigs in a blanket" and the way the mothers would set the plate down and remind them to help themselves. Her fridge at home was stacks of Slimfast and 100-calorie Snackwells.

These mothers with their too-large cameras before dances and whistling cheers at the end of the school play. The kind of mother with bumper stickers boasting about their honor student. Not that Ilsa ever got on the honor roll.

She'd visit a friend to swim in their pool and watch as their father grilled hamburgers in loud Tommy Bahama shirts bulging at the buttons and wonder what it felt like to have a father who called her things like "kiddo." She'd wonder what it'd feel like to have someone to care for.

After years of being told that this new man would take care of their family, Ilsa realized the truth about her mother. There was a canyon between believing someone would take care of you and someone who could truly love you.

Ilsa never had the heart to hate her mother for the life she'd given her. But she vowed never to allow a man to "take care of her." Her mother constructed herself a gilded cage only to find it was pillars of salt, running to nothing when the rains came.

She should have known Nathan would follow her home. His confident knock sounded before she dropped her purse on the table. Leaning her head against the door, she wondered if he'd leave if she were quiet enough.

"I can hear you breathing," Nathan called through the thin door. "You might as well let me in."

Tapping out a quick rhythm on the plywood door with her long designer-shaped nails, she wondered how long Nathan's patience would last. If she even wanted Nathan to hang around. Hadn't she known this was going to happen? Didn't she change into the mesh and velvet-flocked lingerie set before she sent him that first picture?

"Nathan, I'm tired. Please, can we…"

"We're not done talking. Open the door, Illy. There're no cameras around. It's just you and me."

Screwing her eyes shut, she could picture him on the other side of the door. He would have mussed hair from where her nails went through it, a wrinkled shirt from the floor of her office, and full lips from his mouth on hers. His green eyes would look over her as if he knew everything and still wanted her. She knew what would happen if she opened the door. They both did. This dangerous game had reached its peak.

"I can hear your thinking in there, and you need to stop. Open the door, so we can talk."

With a shaky hand, she turned the deadbolt on the door, trying like hell to keep her face blank.

"You don't want to 'just talk.'" She bracketed the door with her arm, barring his entrance.

He had the audacity of smiling at her statement. "Of course not."

Stepping forward into her body, he placed a hand on the door and pushed it open further. She had no choice but to step back, or his body would've collided with hers. Flattening against the door, he stepped into her apartment, turning to face her. His foot came between her feet, and he leaned down until his nose grazed her cheek, his lips pressed to her ear. "We both know I want a whole hell of a lot more from you."

Before she could respond, he was pushing off her, stalking into the bedroom/living room/office of her studio.

She'd been so busy with work it had been days since she'd cleaned, and clothes were scattered around the room. It took little for a 400-square-foot studio to look cluttered, and she'd been pushing the limits of tidiness for weeks. She was thankful she'd been too busy to eat at home, or else there would've been a mountain of dirty dishes.

Walking behind him, she grabbed a pile of discarded shirts off her lone kitchen chair so he could sit. Tossing them on top of the bed, she turned to look at him.

"You want some tea?" she asked. Before Nate could answer, she walked to the kitchen, filling a kettle with water from the tap. She could feel his eyes on her back as she went through the motions, her skin prickling with awareness.

He wanted answers. He deserved answers. But what could she tell him? She had lost the strength to push him away long before tonight. In the past few days, she'd tried to busy herself with work, hoping her desire to be near him would go away.

But having him near her in her office broke down all her resolve. Despite the partners she'd had before, she'd never yearned for a man the way she did Nathan. She wanted his body against hers, to possess every inch of him. She belonged to him, and she needed him to belong to her.

It would be more than sex with Nathan. He would want all of her. Parts that she knew were too broken to give. If she allowed herself to fall for this man, she would fail him. And to fail him would be the greatest sin of all.

Even though he hadn't responded, she plopped two tea bags into mismatched cups from her cabinet. Glancing at the tea box, she wondered briefly if her tea was expired. Can tea expire? The last time she made tea from that box was a year before when a college friend left the container. He was getting stale tea, whether or not he liked it.

"Illy, are we going to talk about this?"

Rummaging in her drawer, she found her plastic bag filled with sugar packets and soy sauce from takeout orders through the years. Ripping open three sugar packets, she dumped them in Nathan's mug.

"Not until we have our tea."

The kettle whistled on the stove, and she poured the hot water over the tea bag and waited for the water to change color.

"This is ridiculous. Would you look at me?" he asked.

Bracing her hands on each side of her, she gripped the small kitchen counter and counted to ten. She heard the chair scrape against the linoleum floor, and then his hand was on her back. A warm pressure that burned through the thin linen of her dress. Closing her eyes, she savored the feel of him at her back. The press of his hand against her skin and the sensation of his body so close to hers.

"Nathan, we shouldn't." Ilsa turned to face him, stepping away from his embrace.

His hand dropped away, and he shook his head at her. "Why are you holding back? I know you feel the same way I do. I know you want this as much as I do. So why are you playing games with me?"

Ilsa shook her head. "I don't know, okay? Yes, I want you. More than I should! More than I want anyone else, but it's not that simple."

"You can't keep pushing me away like this. I'm not some fuck boy or a pop star you can play with, Ilsa. If you want to play these games with some other man, be my guest. But you will not play with me like this. I deserve better."

"You do." Ilsa nodded. "That's what I've been saying. You deserve better. I'm fucked up. A complete mess."

Nathan's face softened at the words. Winding his arm around her waist, he pulled her into his body. His powerful arms wrapped her up. She could feel the strength in his arms and the softness of his stomach as she nestled into the clean musky scent of his throat.

"You're my mess," he said into her hair, his head leaning against hers. Pulling away, he looked down at her. His green eyes were so earnest she had the urge to cry. "Why don't you let me decide what I want instead of you deciding for me?"

Ilsa took a deep breath. "Nathan, I'm not like you. I'm going to screw this all up. I know it."

"Or it will be amazing." Nathan's gaze held such promise. He cupped her cheek, the heat of his palm warming her face. It'd be so easy to believe him. To fall into him and forget the heartache she knew was coming. She couldn't do it.

Ilsa stepped back, walking to the bed where she sat on her leather jacket. With her eyes downcast to the swirls of her rug, she took a deep breath. "My mom had a lot of boyfriends through the years. And you know what she told me each time a new one came around? *This guy is going to take care of us.* I believed her for years, but I can't anymore. Each time all those words left was a husk of a woman who grew older each year."

"I'm not like those men," he argued.

Ilsa stared him down, her hazel eyes flashing. "I know you don't think you are. But some of those men were good guys. They never meant to hurt my mother and me, but they did just the same."

Nathan opened his mouth and then closed it, watching her how one might watch a predatory animal about to strike. "I don't know how to convince you."

Ilsa pursed her lips, fighting back the lump traveling up her throat. "There isn't anything you can say. I'm not meant for someone like you."

Nathan's face softened, and he kneeled in front of her, his body between her knees. Brushing her hair away from her face, he rested his fingers at the base of her neck, holding her steady as he spoke.

"You need time to realize? That's fine. But I'm making you this vow now. I'm not leaving. I'm here as long as you need me. There's no power in my words. All I have are my actions. I will be here for you. Every day. When you need me."

A vow.

No one had ever made a vow to her before. Nathan was honorable, and she knew he believed every word he said.

In her hometown, there was a school tradition that students would paint a wooden mural outside the entrance to the school. At night, students would sneak in with buckets of paintbrushes and spray cans and paint funny jokes and their names. No one knew what the original sign said, only that it held layers upon layers of sloppy paint. In the desert heat, the pain would flake off in places, little wisps of soft color that cracked in your hands. The paint would crumble against your skin if you ran your hand over the surface.

There was no telling how many layers she'd created between herself and others, but being with Nathan, feeling his skin slick against hers, the veneer became brittle in his hands.

She closed her eyes and tried one last time to get him to see reason—give him one last chance to run from her.

"I know what you think you mean when you tell me that, Nate. But I can't hear it. Not from you. I couldn't handle the disappointment when this all falls apart."

"It won't fall apart. I believe in us. I know how I feel."

The confidence in his voice washed over her. She gulped at the earnestness of his touch. It was too much for her.

Ilsa put up a hand to stop him. "Please, don't say anything. I don't have the strength to resist you, to resist what this is between us. I want it. I do. All I ask is don't say you'll take care of me. I couldn't bear it to hear those words from you."

Ilsa could see he didn't like the request, but she must've convinced him because he nodded at her. "Okay. I won't say those words. But that doesn't mean how I feel has changed one bit. This—us? This is it for me. You know that, right?"

Ilsa placed a hand on his shoulder, reveling in the tense muscles under her hands. "I know."

She couldn't meet his eyes, so she watched her fingers move down his front, tracing a line down his torso with a long fingernail. She reached under his shirt to pull his tee up, exposing his solid stomach and toned chest. She rejoiced at the feel of his skin under her hands. This she could do. This was enough. The feel of him was all she wanted.

As she reached for the hem of his shirt, he placed a hand over hers. "I need to hear you say it."

"You're mine," she said, taking his mouth with hers.

The dimple on his cheek deepened at her words. "Damn right, I am."

"I'm not going to say I'm yours," she said, shaking her head. "I can't."

Nathan's mouth ticked up in a little smile. "I know you can't. I don't need to hear that you're mine. Just don't belong to anyone else."

Lust ran through her body, but there was something more.

Recognition.

Awareness.

He knew her. He'd pushed her exactly as far as she could and then said the only words that would get through—stripping her bare.

Picking her feet off the floor, she wrapped her legs around his waist, bringing him into the center of her. Pulling him down on top of her.

Bracing his arms on each side of her, he pressed the length of his body against her. Bringing her hands to his face, she rubbed her thumb over his lower lip. "Nate, I hope you know if I could belong to anyone, it would be you."

He took those words from her mouth, closing the gap to kiss her.

Chapter Twenty

Velvet
Nathan

How could he have known she would be this soft? Despite the hours he'd spent envisioning her body flush against his, nothing could've prepared him for the lushness of her skin against his hands.

His lips firm on hers, he sucked her lower lips into his mouth, teasing the delicate flesh against his teeth. Ilsa wrapped her legs tighter around his hips, grinding herself against his cock. Her dress had ridden up, and it would've been easy to pull his pants down and sink into her quickly. But he wouldn't do that. He had all night with Ilsa, and he would savor every second.

Breaking their kiss, he moved down her body until he got to the hem of her dress. Ilsa helped him pull the dress over her head, leaving her clad in a sheer bra and thong. Her rosy nipples stood at attention through the thin pink fabric. His fingers traced down her soft stomach to the edge of her mesh thong.

"This underwear is driving me crazy." His hand moved to cover her mound, hot against his palm.

"I wore it for you," she breathed out, moving against his hand for more contact.

His mouth traveled down her body to suck at her breasts. Arching her back, she grasped behind her to unclasp her bra. Her breasts came free, and he wasted no time, bringing one pink nipple into his mouth. Her hips moved against his growing cock as he twirled his tongue around her pert nipple. He could've spent hours marveling at the kiss, the curve of her stomach, and the little divots below her hips. Moving over her body, he kissed each side of her hips, where the indents were the perfect size for his thumbs. The sounds she made as he sucked one rosy nipple against his tongue. Digging her nails into his back, she threw her head back and moaned. As he moved his mouth to her other breast, his fingers grasped the thin straps of her thong and pulled it down to expose her wet center. Looking up at her, he dipped one finger inside her heat and watched as the sensation came over Ilsa's face.

Sliding down her body, he kneeled on the floor. Grabbing her thighs, he pulled her down the bed until her legs hung on each side of him, and he was faced with her wet cunt.

"Tonight, this is mine. Do you understand?" Nathan asked, expecting no answer. He ran his finger over her slit, his eyes wide with desire and admiration for this woman.

Ilsa nodded as she lifted her hips for purchase, her fingers digging into the blanket on her sides. Placing a hand on her stomach, he stilled her. "I'll be the one directing how this will go."

Kissing down her inner thigh, he hitched his hand around the back of her knee, placing it over his shoulder, repeating with the other side.

"I need," Ilsa whined.

Blowing a stream of air on her wetness, he ran a finger over her, watching her face as the sensation washed over her.

"I'm going to lick your pussy until you come on my tongue."

"Yes," she breathed out, moving against his hand.

His tongue lashed her tender skin, swirling around her clit. Thrusting a finger inside her, he hit the spot he knew would make her cry out. A second finger joined as he sucked her clit into his mouth. On the side of his head, her legs shook with the beginnings of a climax bearing down on her. Her juices ran down his chin, and he sucked harder, listening to her shouts of pleasure. Behind his head, she crossed her ankles, trapping him against her. He struggled to breathe in anything but her scent. The feel of her on his tongue sent heat rushing through his body.

If he were going to die, this would be a sweet way to go.

Coming down from her high, Ilsa's legs relaxed their grip on the sides of his head, falling off his shoulders limply. Wasting no time, he moved up her body, taking her mouth in his. Her hands came up to grab at the hair on the nape of his neck.

"Take off your clothes," she demanded.

He gave her a wicked smile. "I'm the one giving orders around here."

Kneeling over her, Nathan pulled his shirt over his head, flinging it to the floor. His pants and boxers soon followed. Grasping around in his discarded pants, he found a condom and rolled it down his length.

Ilsa reached up, pulling him down on top of her until it was nothing but slick heat between their bodies.

He grasped her chin, forcing her to look at him. "I'm going to take this pussy. I'm going to wreck you, and you're going to love every moment."

"Take it. Take me."

With her words, he sank into her. His hands gripped her hips, pulling her flush with him. His thumbs fit into those perfect indents in her flesh, just right for holding on tight as he buried his cock deep inside her. She fit perfectly. He'd known she would. Those nights alone when he'd grasped the root of his cock and stroked himself thinking of her were nothing compared to this exhilaration.

"You like that? Your pussy wants more, doesn't it?" With her warmth all around him, he thrust deep inside, eliciting a low moan from her throat.

"More," she begged, arching her back as he thrust inside her. Reaching between them, his finger circled her clit, letting her pleasure rise. He could feel the walls of her pussy contract around him, and he knew she was close.

"Look at me. You look at me when I make you come."

Her green eyes flashed open to meet his. A line in her brow furrowed as he moved inside her, forcing them both closer to where they needed to be. Her hands were on the small of his back, her nails etching into his skin as she pulled him closer. He hoped they'd break the skin. He wanted it to scar. Then he'd always remember the feel of her tight around him. And the look in her eyes as he brought her to that edge and let her fall.

Her cry was a soft breath as she shuddered beneath him. He came after, holding out until she was spent. Collapsing on top of her, his head rested on her bare breast. The scent of sex and her delicate clean skin filled him up.

"That was..." she murmured.

"Yeah." He lifted his head to look at her. "Same."

An unabashed smile widened on her face. This wasn't the smile she gave the cameras or the one she used when making small talk. It was toothy and full and made her look so young.

A lump formed in Nathan's throat. He wanted to see that smile every single day until his last.

He loved her. There would never be another woman like Ilsa for him.

"When can we go again?" she asked, running a hand down his back to grip his ass in both hands. "I need you again."

Waking up the next morning, Nathan was cold. His large body normally produced a lot of heat, so he was rarely cold in LA. Cracking an eye open, he looked over to find Ilsa still sleeping beside him, with all the blankets wrapped around her body like a chrysalis. Blinking a few times, he watched her sleep. Well, half of her face, at least. The upper part of her face was poking out of the blanket cocoon, and her blonde hair was in a messy clump above her head. Her breath was slow and steady, her full upper lip resting on the edge of the blanket.

So, this is what it would feel like to wake up beside Ilsa. Him cold from her blatant blanket thievery and her beautiful from sleep. His chest felt tight at the sight of her sleeping beside him. She was his. He wouldn't say it, not yet. He knew her well enough to know it would make her run as far away as she could. But he was going to show her how good it could be between them. Reaching over, he brushed a strand of hair from her forehead, smoothing it down on the pillow beside her. She didn't move.

Rolling out of her bed, he found his discarded boxers on the floor and pulled them on, moving to the kitchen five steps away. Ilsa didn't move as he filled her prehistoric coffee pot with water. Opening her fridge, he found oat milk creamer, a block of cheese, and an expired bag of spinach behind a twelve-pack of sparkling water. He made a mental note to arrange for grocery delivery for her.

Leaning against the counter, he listened as the coffee maker groaned and dripped. With his legs stretched out in front of him, his feet reached the other side of the narrow kitchen aisle. He guessed if he opened the small oven door, there wouldn't be more than an inch between the top and the cabinet on the other side. He needed to help her find a new place. Or have her move in with him. He wasn't opposed to that.

On the counter, his phone buzzed with a text from Keller asking where he was. Cursing under his breath, he typed out a response that he'd be there as soon as possible. He knew one reason they were successful was Theo's musical genius, but damn if sometimes he didn't want to tell him to chill out. After staying up half the night, his body against Ilsa's, he wanted to spend the morning wrapped in her embrace and sleeping. Then some morning sex. In the shower. Then he was going to feed her breakfast and take her back to his place where they'd have more sex in the living room, or the kitchen, or the patio. He wasn't picky. He had plans to christen every surface in his house with her. So when he looked around, she'd be all he could see.

He opened the cabinet and found a single clean cup and two wine glasses. In the sink were three coffee cups with various levels of murky water. He dumped the water out of two of them, washing them with the thin sponge and discount orange-scented soap.

Sniffing the creamer, he deemed it good enough before pouring a splash into each cup of coffee. Turning the corner, he found Ilsa in the middle of the bed, the blankets still bunched around her. Setting the mugs on the small table beside the bed, he sat beside her and placed a hand on a lumpy shoulder.

"Illy, I made you coffee."

One hazel eye opened as she took Nathan in. Nathan pulled the blankets away from her face. Blinking at him a few times, she woke.

"Did you unplug the coffee maker when you were done? Sometimes it smokes if it's plugged in too long."

Sighing, Nathan handed Ilsa her mug of coffee before returning to the kitchen to remove the coffee maker from the counter, leaving the pot on the stovetop.

With the coffee maker under one arm, he returned to the studio room. "I'm buying you a new coffee maker today."

Ilsa opened her mouth, no doubt to argue, but all that came out was a large yawn.

"Don't argue with me. I don't want to hear it. I'm not letting your stubborn ass catch on fire over a thirty-dollar coffee maker."

Narrowing her eyes at him, she took a sip of coffee. "It only smokes a little."

"I said I don't want to hear it. I've got plans for us, and I won't let you argue about this."

He could tell she didn't like to hear this but said nothing.

Setting the broken coffee maker down next to his shoes, he sat beside Ilsa on the bed, his coffee in his hands. The drink wasn't nearly as sweet as he normally liked, but he couldn't find any sugar.

"What are your plans today?" Steering the conversation away from the dangerous future talk seemed his best course of action.

"No concrete plans. I'm still in limbo with the funding, so there isn't much I can do for the expansion until I get more investors."

He felt a pang in his chest at her dejected tone. "You sure you don't want me to make any calls? I might know someone."

Ilsa shook her head, the crease deepening. "Definitely not. I have to do this myself."

The impulse to intercede clawed at his chest, but the tense set of her jaw stopped him.

"I actually have to get going soon. I forgot Theo needs us to rerecord a track. He wasn't happy with the tempo on one of the songs and wants to try it a different way."

"Oh, well." The coffee mug in her hands froze halfway to her mouth, a line forming between her brows. He wanted to kiss that line away.

"Come with me. It won't take too long. We only have the studio for an hour this morning. If we have to rerecord, it'll be later this week."

Hesitation warred over her face before she chugged the rest of her coffee, then shoved the mug back into his hands. "Give me twenty to get ready."

Settled into a sofa at the recording studio, she handed Nathan her phone, where an article was pulled up. "I thought I worked hard, but celebrity reporters are the hardest out there, look." A picture at the top showed her and Nathan kissing in front of her shop. The photo was grainy enough in the low light, but with the fancy script of the business sign *Ilsa Kruger* above them, there was little room to argue who was in the picture.

A Prevalent Romance: Mystery lady revealed.

by Trinity Flay

Los Angeles, California

Reports of Prevalent Notion bassist Nathan Ayers in a new relationship seem to be confirmed. Photographer Chet Baker recently spotted the musician in a very intimate position with none other than up-and-coming fashion designer Ilsa Kruger. Kruger worked as a stylist for Prevalent Notion's Hellion Tour last year. Reports close to the couple state Kruger is close with not only the band but singer-songwriter Eloise Dunning-Grant, wife to Prevalent Notion's drummer Keller Grant. They were recently photographed attending Dunning-Grant's album release party, and an anonymous source said they were very cozy indeed.

A request for information from Ayers's publicist was denied, but we at AllCeleb can't help but speculate. Rumors buzzed around a new love interest for Ayers after an unidentified woman brought him to Cedars-Sinai for undisclosed treatment. Could this be the same woman?

See below for a slide show of Ayers's past relationships, including actress Shelby Waters and the daughter of movie producer Tania Kerr.

If you have information regarding this story or have any other celebrity news, please email us at our tip line at gotcha@allcele bs.com.

"This is bullshit." Ilsa cursed. "I'm going to hunt down that reporter myself."

Nathan wrapped his arms around her waist, bringing her flush with his body. She smelled of rosewater. "Illy, it's not worth it. You know it'll only throw more fuel on the fire. Give them five minutes, and they'll write about something else."

Ilsa flexed her fist. She looked ready to punch something.

"You want me to call my publicist? I can put out a statement."

"And say what, Nate?"

Nathan pulled away to look down at her. "Whatever you want me to say."

Ilsa pulled her lower lip between her teeth, the line between her brows deepening. "No, you're right. They'll move on to something tomorrow. It's just this is exactly what I was nervous about. I don't want to build my brand on being your..." she trailed off, looking away.

Nathan bit back the laugh that was forming in his throat. "My what, Illy?"

She narrowed her eyes. "Nothing. Something. I don't know." She threw up her arms in frustration.

After the night they had, he wasn't nervous about her not wanting him. What she said the night before was the support he needed to overcome her fear of labels and romantic words.

... if I could belong to anyone, it would be you."

That was enough for him today. Ilsa was his, even if she didn't want to admit it yet.

Bending down, he pressed a quick kiss to her lips, savoring the taste of the spearmint gum she'd been chewing.

"I'll grab us a drink. You want water?"

Ilsa nodded, and Nathan left to grab two waters from the vending machine in the hall. Returning, he saw Ilsa and Theo talking, her shoulders rigid. They couldn't see him, but he could see the irritated cross of her arms and Theo nervously running his hands through his golden hair.

Ilsa moved to walk through the door, and Theo put his arm out to stop her. "We need to talk."

Stepping back, Ilsa raised a brow, waiting on Theo to continue.

Theo dropped his arm from the doorway to scrub a hand over his face. "Look, I know you don't like me—"

"I like you fine."

Laughing, he shook his head. "You don't have to like me. It's okay. I didn't have much of a family growing up. It was…" he paused, and a shadow descended over his face. "Anyway, Nathan and Keller are my brothers. I would do anything for them."

"I'm sure Keller would disagree," Ilsa quipped.

Nodding, Theo continued. "I screwed up with Eloise and Keller. I know you might not see it that way, but these guys are the only family I've ever had. Despite all the fucked-up antics I pulled, Nathan's been there for me. So, if you're jerking him around, if you're not serious about him, you need to be clear."

"I would never hurt Nathan."

"You don't have to try. Nathan is the most genuine person I've ever known. He's no bullshit. You don't have to try to hurt him. You just have to want something different. So, if you're playing around on him, if you're not serious, you need to be clear about that now."

"I'm not going to talk about my relationship with you, of all people."

Nathan knew the insult had to stick. Theo had done a lot of fucked up things in his past, but the rift he caused between him and Keller the year before almost destroyed the band. It was only through Eloise forgiving him and Theo working his ass off at redemption that they'd gotten to the shaky point they were at now.

"Look, I know I've been a shitty friend. I need to do a lot of work to earn back the respect of Eloise and Keller. But that's on me. Nathan, he's a good one, and as his friend and brother, I have to look out for him. I won't tell you not to date him. We both know I have a terrible track record in the dating world. But be careful. He's not like me or any of these guys out here."

Nathan wanted to rage at his bandmate, but he couldn't find the words. Did no one trust in his feelings? All around him were people who thought they were protecting him, but all they were doing was getting in his way.

Ilsa narrowed her eyes. "I know that. You think I don't know Nathan? You think I don't care?"

Theo stepped closer to her, his voice lower. "I think you are a lot like me, and you don't see a great thing right in front of you because you're too stupid to notice it."

"I know exactly what's in front of me."

Theo studied her for a moment before stepping back. "Good, don't forget it."

Theo never talked about what his life was like before he moved to LA, only that he showed up one day with only a guitar and insane talent. In moments like this, Nathan wondered what he'd left behind. In all the years they played together, Theo was a closed book regarding women. Even Safiya, the year before, had been more publicity and sex than a genuine relationship.

Standing back, he watched as his girl and best friend glared at each other. With her hands shoved in the pockets of her one-piece shirt-shorts thingie. He didn't know the name, only that getting it off in a hurry looked annoying. She looked so fierce, defending herself and Nathan to Theo. He hoped she would come to see how good they could be instead of pushing him away.

Ilsa, telling him he wasn't allowed to take care of her. Telling him, she was going to hurt him. When it was the opposite. He heard her story about her mother. He could picture her on her mother's bed, hoping for a better life and the disappointment each time it didn't work out. Of course, she would be fragile. Of course, she would build up walls to protect herself.

He knew to be with her, to earn her trust would take time, and for her, he was willing to give it. As long as she wanted him.

Ilsa was the fragile one. He had the privilege of being loved by his family; he knew what it felt like to be happy, and he knew he could give it to Ilsa. If she would only allow it.

Chapter Twenty-One

P ROPERLY SEXED UP AND refreshed, she settled into the chair at her local coffee shop down the road from her apartment. After going to the recording studio, Nathan treated her to lunch, then three orgasms at his house. She fell asleep in his massive bed and didn't wake until the next day. She couldn't remember the last time she'd taken the day off work, but being with Nathan made her forget her troubles. At least until her phone chimed with another notification.

While Nathan had bought a fancy new coffee maker for her place, she didn't have the heart to tell him she didn't know how to operate it. There were too many buttons. And she might have dropped a big piece of pad thai on the instructions while eating over the sink the night before. So, she was back to slinking around coffee shops for her daily caffeine intake. She could look up the instruction later. Everything was online anyway.

All day she'd tried to put her conversation with Theo out of her mind. She knew better than most about having loyalty to those who have been there in your darkest days. He knew Theo was only worried. As much as she didn't want to admit it, his words scared her.

The thought of Nathan getting hurt made her chest ache. She'd rather cut herself than let him be scratched.

Ilsa typed out a response to a local lifestyle magazine requesting a few pieces they could use in an upcoming photo shoot. As great as the exposure was, it didn't pay her bills. She believed in the clothes she made, and they seemed to get good press, but if she didn't find another investor soon, she'd be auctioning off that fancy coffee maker to pay rent. Her eyes darted to her lavender oat milk latte. Maybe getting a ten-dollar coffee hadn't been the smartest choice.

Nathan texted her that his meeting with the band's manager was about to finish, and he invited her to dinner at any restaurant she wanted. She let him know she'd rather have dinner at his place, and he sent her a winky emoji and a pick-up line.

Nathan: *The word of the day is legs. Let's go back to my place and spread the word.*

Ilsa set down her fork, raising a brow at her empty plate. "Okay, seriously, where did you learn to cook like that?"

When she was picturing dinner at his place, she imagined takeout or a frozen pizza. Instead, Nathan made melt-in-your-mouth biscuits and fried chicken with coleslaw.

The corner of Nathan's mouth ticked up with a smile. "My momma had me helping in the kitchen from when I was knee-high. She told me her father never let her brothers in the kitchen growing up, and now they're useless as a screen door on a submarine. Told me that wasn't gonna happen to me."

His accent came out more when he talked about his home. In public, he worked hard to tone down the twang, but when he was with her, especially when he was talking about his family, his "i's" flattened out.

"Well, she must have taught you right because that was incredible. Those rolls home-made?"

Nathan put a hand over his heart. "Those were my Granny's famous biscuits, and she would spin in her grave if I ever used store-bought for a girl I liked."

Ilsa narrowed her eyes. "Didn't you say the other day that your Granny lived two houses down from your parents?"

Nathan smiled. "Yeah, but she'd be fixing to whoop me, that's for sure."

Pushing the plate into the middle of the table, she teased him, "So you like me?"

Standing up, he walked around the table to stand above her. Bending down, he pressed a kiss to her lips. She could taste the sugar and bitterness of his homemade sweet tea. "Ilsa, you are driving me wild. You know that?"

Reaching up, she took his cheek in her hand. "How crazy?"

His fingers dove into her hair, bringing her mouth to his. His grasp was firm on her head. His tongue swirled against hers. The caress of his fingers against her scalp caused her to moan into his mouth. He deepened the kiss, bringing his hands down to pull her up from her chair. Without breaking his kiss, his arms wrapped around her waist, picking her up and setting her down on the edge of the table. Blood pounded in her ears as he stepped between her open thighs. Wrapping her legs around his waist, she pulled him into her center. The bulge in his pants rubbed deliciously against her clit. She'd worn a dress for exactly this reason. Fingers skimmed the outside of her thighs, pushing her dress around her waist. The need to feel him overwhelmed her.

They'd had sex more in the past two days than she had in years. Still, she needed more. She wanted his hands on her breasts as he held her down, and she wanted his teeth on her shoulder as he entered her from behind.

Running her hands down his back, she pulled the back of his shirt up, revealing the cords of muscles in his lower back. Dipping lower, she grabbed two handfuls of his ass, pulling his bulge closer to her aching clit. Squirming against him, she sucked his lip into her mouth, biting down on the flesh of his lower lip. Groaning, his grip on her waist tightened. She wondered if she'd have an imprint of his thumb on her stomach the next day.

Pulling away, he brushed a hair off her face. "The things I want to do you to you. I want to fuck you right here on this table until you're screaming so loud the neighbors call the police."

Smiling wickedly, she leaned into his touch. "It's LA. People are going to mind their business."

"No one is neighborly around here," he quipped.

Reaching down between their bodies, she gripped the bulge of his hardening cock, rubbing it through his pants. "Works for me. What if I want to make you scream?"

"Baby, you keep touching me like that, you could make me do anything."

Power thrummed through her. Her fingers danced over his stomach, reaching the front of his pants. Dipping her hands down the front, she palmed his erection, grasping the tip with one hand.

Groaning, Nathan's head fell forward, resting on her shoulder. He hadn't shaved yet, and his scruff bristled against the softness of her skin. Stroking down the length of him, she pulled out his cock. The tip was wet, and she swiped a single droplet from him, sucking the taste from her finger.

"That's it."

With no warning, he picked her up around her waist. Her legs still wrapped around his hips, he walked her down the hall to his bedroom. His cock moved against the thin fabric of her silk underwear, jostling her closer to an orgasm with each step. She could have come from the friction alone.

In the bedroom, he tossed her down on the edge of the bed and stepped away from her. "Strip," he demanded.

Kneeling in the center of the bed, Ilsa gripped the hem of her dress, pulling it over her head in one motion. She moved until she was bare for him. His eyes never left hers as he stood at the foot of the bed, naked with his cock in his hand. Nathan seemed to appraise her as he stroked his fist down his length.

"What am I going to do to you?" he asked, his voice husky.

Leaning forward on her hands and knees, she crawled cat-like across the bed to him. "What do you want to do to me?"

At that moment, she would have complied with any request only to have him touch her again.

With his free hand, he gripped her chin, pulling her face up to look at him. His fingers were tight on her throat. His thumb rested on her pulse.

"Your heart's racing," he said, a wicked smile crossing his mouth. "Do I excite you?"

"Yes."

Pulling her to her knees, his mouth found hers, and his tongue lashed against hers. The kiss was hard, bordering on painful, but she wanted more. Wrapping her arms around his waist, she grabbed his bare ass, marveling at the firm skin as she ground her aching center into his cock.

They fell back on the bed, limbs tangling. Nathan braced himself over her as he moved down her body. His mouth found her aching clit, and he sucked while moving his fingers in and out of her channel. Edging her closer to an orgasm, his fingers touched her exactly where she needed them. She began to cry out, and his hand slid away.

"No. When you come, it's going to be on my cock. Do you understand?"

She nodded at him.

"Now turn over, grab the headboard and close your eyes."

She'd never heard him so demanding before. She complied, the wood firm against her hands. Grabbing her waist, he pulled her up to her knees in the middle of the bed with her hands outstretched.

She couldn't see what he was doing, but she felt him, the nip of his teeth at her shoulder, the tease of his fingers on her upper thighs.

He reached around her and pinched her nipples. She groaned at the feeling, her hands dropping slightly.

"Put them back. Don't you move your hands from the headboard," he demanded.

She moved her hands up to grip the bars tight, her knuckles growing white.

He moved down her body, kissing and nipping at her flesh. Without being able to see what he was doing, she had no idea where his next kiss was going to land. His hands were rough on her waist as he gripped them. She felt his mouth on her ass cheek. He kissed her, and then there was the sting of his hand striking the full flesh.

"Oh!" She called out. She'd been spanked before, but the sensation he created was something completely different. She arched into him.

"You liked that, didn't you?" he asked, his body leaning down to cover hers, pinning her.

"Yes."

"Ask me to do it again."

She writhed against him, rubbing her bare ass on his dick. "I want you inside me. I want it again."

"Be a good girl, and I'll let you have it."

She ground her ass harder against him, and he hissed.

"I've never been a good girl."

His body moved from hers, and her hands slipped down so she could turn to look at him.

"I told you to keep your hands on the wall. You do what I tell you to."

Her hands back up, he ran his fingers down her spine. His demanding tone sent sparks throughout her body.

She had no words, only the feel of his hands over her skin and the anticipation of his touch. On the headboard, her knuckles were white from gripping so hard, and she knew she would be sore the next day, but she didn't care.

Rubbing her thighs together for friction, she waited for his next touch. She heard the crinkle of a condom, then the bed compressed behind her, and the heat from his body radiated against her. With one hand gently on her hip, he parted her folds with deft fingers.

"You're so wet for my cock." His body covered hers. He slid into her, his thickness fitting her exactly right. Behind her, he began to move, picking up speed and hitting her in the spots that drove her over the edge.

"Good girl, taking my cock," he ground out as he moved inside her. "You feel so good."

She gasped at the feeling of fullness, her hands moving down to brace herself.

"What did I tell you? Keep your hands up."

Biting her lip, she glanced back at him as he continued moving inside her. "I'm not a good girl."

His hand came down against her ass cheek again, the sting going straight to her clit. She arched her back, her hands still braced behind her. Her other cheek got the same treatment.

He grabbed her hands, pulling them back onto the headboard. "You're my good girl, and I'm going to fuck you until you know it."

He drove deeper inside her, one hand on her hip and the other reaching down to palm her breast. With a few tweaks of her nipple, she felt herself convulse around him.

"That's it, come all over me. I'll catch you. I got you."

As the orgasm hit her, her arms and legs lost all strength, turning to mush. True to Nathan's word, he wrapped his arms around her waist, keeping her upright against him. The jolt of his orgasm sent the last wave of climax through her, and she collapsed on the bed.

His strong arms lowered her to the bed, where her arms and legs splayed like a starfish. Rolling to his side, he rested beside her, his hand on her lower back. Turning to face him, she laid a hand on his unshaven cheek. "You flattened me."

His forehead creased. "Flattened?"

She flopped her arms and legs out haphazardly. "Yeah, you and your gorgeous dick flattened me. I can't move."

He leaned over to press a kiss to her lips. "I'll be a steamroller any day for you."

Running her thumb over his lower lip, she marveled at how supple it was. She wanted this feeling again and again. At her touch, his eyes drifted shut, a small smile playing at the corner of his lips.

"Promise?" she asked.

Her heart clenched at the simple word.

Opening his green eyes to study her, Nathan's face grew serious. He took her face in his hands, bringing her to him in a sweet kiss that blossomed in her chest.

"For you, I'll promise anything."

Words escaped her. She had no terms of endearment to give him nor any love declarations. All she had was her body beside him, and she hoped that was enough for the time.

As his breathing leveled out beside her, the dark twinges of doubt crept in. When she was with Nathan, the way he made her feel, the ache in her chest when he laid his hand on her cheek, was exquisite. When he said those sweet words, her heart wanted to believe them. She tried to let him in. But as she edged closer to trusting in him, her mind returned to the small apartment, watching as her mother cried over another broken promise. Another cut into the person her mother was. Another piece of stolen time, never to be recovered.

Chapter Twenty-Two

Muslin 
Nathan

W HEN HIS ALARM WENT off at four-thirty the next morning, Ilsa grumbled in her sleep, wrapped his favorite blanket tighter around herself, and rolled away. There was a comfort in seeing that she was the same blanket hog at his home as she was in her own. Showering, he replayed the night before in his mind. The way she reacted to his touch, the vulnerability in her eyes as she kissed him. There was a warm tingly feeling all over his body, thinking about how comfortable Ilsa looked in his bed. How comfortable she would be in his life.

After a series of phone interviews with radio stations on the east coast, he started making breakfast for them. The night before, she'd mentioned she had to be at her shop at nine to do inventory. He watched as she set three different alarms on her phone with various labels like ***don't hit snooze*** and ***get your ass out of bed, or you'll look like a swamp monster.***

Eying the clock, he pushed the scrambled eggs around in the pan. Wearing his blue UK Wildcats T-shirt, Ilsa emerged in the doorway with rumpled hair and an uncertain look on her face.

"Get over here." Nathan motioned with a spatula.

Shuffling over, Ilsa wrapped her arms around his waist. Bending down, he pressed a kiss to the top of her head, breathing in the rosewater scent of her.

"You hungry?"

She nodded against his chest.

"Good. Go sit down, and I'll fix you up."

Turning back, he grabbed the coffeepot and filled her mug to the top, adding a splash of oat milk creamer he had Alexis pick up on her last grocery run.

Nathan handed her coffee in his favorite mug from the diner in his hometown. She took a long sip of the coffee, watching him over the rim of her mug.

She inspected the oversized white ceramic mug with a cartoon cardinal in a chef hat brandishing a spatula and a plate of pancakes, the name Linda's Café in fancy script. "Cute."

"Someday, I'll take you there and get you a big helping of their world-famous fried apple waffles."

She raised a brow. "World famous?"

"Only world I want to live in." Swallowing the last of his sweet tea, he turned away to set the glass in the sink.

When he turned back to her, he slid a plate of breakfast in front of her. Nothing fancy, just scrambled eggs and cheese on a piece of toast. As much as it killed him not to have meat on the plate, he forgot to ask Alexis to pick up sausage links. His personal trainer will be happy about the omission.

"You made me breakfast?" she asked, her brows wrinkled.

"Well, yeah. It's breakfast time." He glanced at his dirty blender in the sink. He was supposed to slim down for the upcoming press photos. "Did you want a smoothie instead? It's not the same as a good breakfast to me, but Tamara said I gotta lose this paunch I got going."

Ilsa frowned. "You do not have a paunch. She's full of shit."

He rubbed his belly. He knew his stomach was softer than Keller and Theo's, but he didn't let that bother him. "I got a little one."

Setting her fork down, she pushed off from the breakfast nook to walk to him. She wrapped her arms around his waist and buried her face in his chest. "Trust me when I say you don't. Compared to the dehydrated bros walking around LA, maybe, but even if you have a paunch, I love it. It's sexy. I don't want that softness to go away."

Warmth flooded through him at the comment. He didn't know how much he needed to hear those words until Ilsa said them. Where he was from, men didn't complain about their bodies. But also, where he was from, he wasn't surrounded by people who worked out five hours a day every day, living on kale and cashew sour cream. "Thanks."

Pulling away, she looked up at him. "Trust me when I say there is nothing you can do for a perfect body. I chased that for years when I was modeling and doing pageants. There was always a girl with bigger boobs or a curvier waist, one who didn't have such broad shoulders or shinier hair. I like the way your body feels next to mine. The feel of your skin and the way your hands touch me. I love your body."

I love you.

The words were right there on the tip of his tongue, but he couldn't say them. Ilsa didn't seem to notice his hesitation. Slapping his ass, she stepped away, walking back to her plate of food.

"Plus, if you lost a bunch of weight, that fine ass might shrink, and I love your bubble butt even if it is in those terrible shorts again. Seriously? A denim print? Who does that?"

He gave her a fake pained expression as she topped her piece of toast with a piece of scrambled egg. What did he do to deserve a woman like her, even if she made fun of his favorite shorts? Once she finished her breakfast, he took her plate from her and set it in the sink. Seeing her cup of coffee was getting low, he topped her off, pouring a splash of creamer in and stirring it before giving it back. Ilsa watched his motions with an inscrutable look on her face.

"You refilled my coffee."

"Yeah, did you not want more?" He furrowed his brow.

She looked from the coffee to him. "No, I always want more coffee." She shook her head as if to dislodge a thought. "I should get going, though. Can't neglect the store much longer."

He flipped the towel over his shoulder, a habit he picked up from his father while cleaning the kitchen. "Maybe when you're done at work, you could come over, and I could *flatten* you again?" he asked.

"I'd love to be flattened by you." A coy smile lit up her face. "Do you want me to stay over?"

He wanted her to stay forever. He sat in the tall chair beside her, angling his legs to face her.

"Yeah, absolutely."

She grinned before her face fell. "Oh damn. I can't stay tonight. I'm having dinner with Eloise. With our crazy schedules, tonight was the only time we could get together before she leaves on her publicity tour."

Nathan trained his face not to show disappointment. "Of course. Where are you going?"

Ilsa scrunched up her face. "Um, I think Lou wanted to go to that Mexican restaurant down the road from their house. The chain that smothers everything in cheese. I swear she has the worst taste in Mexican food."

"What would be good taste?"

Ilsa shrugged. "I don't know. I just know that her pasty Pacific Northwest ass couldn't tell a mole from pozole."

Nathan nodded noncommittally. He was sure his Appalachian ass wouldn't know much more than Eloise. Plus, who didn't like more cheese?

Ilsa finished the rest of her coffee and set it down on the counter. Turning to face him, she took his hand in hers, tracing a scar on the back of his hand with her thumb. "But I'll come over after dinner. Though don't expect fancy underwear anymore. I've run out of matching sets in the few days we've been together."

"Wait, really?" he asked.

Ilsa wrinkled her brow. "Yeah. Most women have maybe four bras and about thirty pairs of underwear. You think they always match under there? No. We save the matching sets for when they know they'll be getting some."

"I don't give a damn about what you wear under your clothes as long as I get to take them all off you at the end of the night."

Leaning forward, she rested her forehead against his. "Deal."

He considered taking a nap after she left. He'd gotten up early for those east coast calls. But his body was humming with energy from having Ilsa near. Instead, he made his trainer proud and put in a workout. Two hours later, he was sweaty, smelly, and no less fraught with how he felt about Ilsa. When he did things for her, he saw her creased brows—the surprise on her face that she was being cared for.

While he understood her hesitation, he could work through it with her. To show her he was different than the men her mother used to bring home. Whether that's refilling her coffee mug or something more. Wiping the sweat off his face with a towel, he picked up his phone, turned off his workout music, and called Alexis to make arrangements for him.

After checking that task off his list, he took a quick shower, cleaning the stink of a hard workout off his skin. Ilsa told him once she liked how he smelled after a workout, but he doubted that was true. Getting out of the shower, he looked at his reflection in the mirror. His hair was getting a little longer than he normally kept it. He wondered if Ilsa liked it longer or shorter. Placing a hand on his stomach, he felt the softness give. He'd always been muscled but never had that definition to his stomach. Under his hand, his stomach rumbled for food. The breakfast smoothie was not cutting it. He talked to people who swore they could live on tiny portions and liquid fasts, but he never made it through before breaking down and having a cheeseburger. At twenty-seven, he was ambivalent about the shape he was in. He ate far more vegetables than he was used to growing up. He cut out a lot of dairy and ate whole grain bread now, though that was still an outlier in the area's keto fads.

And Ilsa liked his body.

Pulling on an old Bill Monroe T-shirt and a pair of jeans, he ran a hand through his hair. Not much he had to do there. The band was getting together later to film a segment for a talk show at noon. But he had an hour before the studio sent the car to get him, then another hour while the car navigated LA traffic to get to the studio. Now he had nothing but downtime and his relentless thoughts.

Retiring to the porch with a glass of sweet tea, he lounged on a chair, his long legs in front of him. Scrolling through his phone, he sent a quick text to Ilsa.

Nathan: *Girl, you make me want to dive into the sea. That Pus-sea.*

To which she responded with a wink emoji and a skull. He knew she was busy at work, though she'd been cagey about why her investment fell through. While she'd explained that it didn't work, he had a bad feeling there was more to the story.

He wished she would take his help. There was no way she'd accept a direct investment from him or any of their friends, but she had to be reasonable. She was making a name for herself, but she knew just as much as he did that those connections were everything in this town. If she let him use his name to make introductions, he might get her the money she needed for her line.

At the studio, Nathan studied his reflection in the makeup chair. The stylist in front of him was combing blue goop into his hair with a surgeon's precision. The stylist moved in front of him, and with her face inches from his, he shut his eyes. It felt awkward to keep them open. Plus, the motion of her running her hands through his hair was soothing, and he got up early that morning after a vigorous workout the night before. So, he sat back, closed his eyes and allowed himself to relax.

He felt the brush of a hand on his wrist. Nathan opened his eyes to see a dainty wrist with its telltale birthmark on the inside. Glancing up, he saw the strawberry-blonde hair and blue eyes of his ex-girlfriend.

"Shelby." He tried to keep the surprise out of the sentence, but it still tinged his voice. He coughed, covering his mouth. "What are you doing here?"

"I just finished a promo bit with Olly. I'm on for the Friday show promoting *The*

Raspberry Agent." Her eyes glimmered with the news. Nathan recalled her getting the part of the raspberry farmer from rural Oregon, turned CIA super-spy. At the time, he was concerned about her working with the action star Buck Dieter. But now, the idea that he could be jealous of another man with Shelby was laughable.

"Right, I saw the photos from the premiere. You looked great. I've heard good things about the movie."

She waved his comment away. "The movie is garbage. We all know it. Buck is still chasing the high from the Delphi trilogy, but it'll be a blockbuster and bring in a ton of residuals over the years."

He'd forgotten how snide Shelby could be.

Glancing at the stylist who was discreetly putting away her tools beside them, Shelby leaned over. "You can go now. I need to talk with Mr. Ayers."

The stylist's eyes grew wide, and she opened her mouth to say something.

"Now, please," Shelby snapped.

He was fighting the urge to roll his eyes at her rudeness. He made a mental note to get the stylist's name and to send her a personal apology after Shelby left.

With the area cleared of anyone else, Shelby stood in front of him, her legs crossed at the ankles as she leaned against the makeup table. Her hair was perfectly styled with shiny waves that framed her heart-shaped face. Nathan knew she didn't trust the show's stylists and had her own that traveled with her for every appearance.

"Natey, you haven't been responding to my messages."

Blinking, it took him a minute to remember what the last message he got from her was. Oh. That's right.

"Shelb. As nice as those, urm, pictures, were, I..."

She sighed heavily, leaning closer to him. "They are more than nice. You know damn well how much my tits cost me."

"Right, despite how great they are, I'm involved with someone."

Shelby straightened to her full height. "Someone? Who? I would've heard unless... No." Shaking her head, she clicked her teeth together. "You can't be telling me that smear piece in AllCeleb was true? Nathan, you're a rock star. You should be back with me instead of some nobody. I mean, she worked for the band. She worked for you."

Groaning, Nathan pushed off from the director's chair, making it scuttle backward behind him. Stepping toward her, he looked down at this girl he'd thought he cared about. Had she always been so much shorter than him? Had she always been this small-minded?

No, she used to be nicer, sweet even.

"Ilsa isn't a nobody. And I won't hear you saying anything against her."

"Yeah, okay," Shelby mocked.

Scrubbing a hand over his face, he wondered if Shelby was even worth the conversation. When they dated, he'd liked her a lot, but this diva behavior was ridiculous. "And for god's sake, Shelby, you have millions of little girls who look up to you. I don't know what that asshole boyfriend of yours did to you, but you are better than this. You are talented, smart, and beautiful. You're just not the woman I want to be with."

She scoffed. "It's not you. It's me?"

"You dumped me, Shelby. Unceremoniously, might I add. Not the other way around. You'll find a good guy soon. All you have to do is be the kind, beautiful girl from Pacific, Missouri, that I knew."

Folding her arms across her chest she glowered at him. "You're different."

Stepping back from her, he shoved his hands in his pockets. "Love does crazy things to a man."

Her face softened as she looked up at him. "You love her?"

He nodded. He shouldn't have said that to Shelby, especially before telling Ilsa. Not that Ilsa wanted to hear those words yet.

Pushing off the makeup table's edge, she stretched her arms. "Then I'll try to be slightly less bitter."

He accepted her hug, a warm thing that sent zero lusty thoughts to his brain. Pulling away, he looked down at her. "And no more boob pictures, okay? Save it for someone who can appreciate them."

Cupping his face in her hands, she smiled at him. "Okay, deal."

Behind them, a PA called for Shelby to say that her car was waiting on her.

He waited until Shelby had left the area to grab his phone off the table. The top text was from Ilsa.

Alexis appeared beside him, handing him the double chocolate mint coffee he ordered.

"I got the appointment scheduled. The car should be ready by four today. Desiree Johansen from The Riff magazine called again, asking for an interview, and the creative team at the label wanted to go over the layout of the album art with you guys. I checked with George and Beatriz on the availability of the guys, and all three of you have time on Thursday at two."

Nathan nodded at her. He was hesitant when he hired Alexis that he needed his own assistant. Eloise had done the job for all three of them for years, but he was surprised by how nice it was to have Alexis around. He wondered how Eloise did it by herself for so long. Now all three of them had separate personal assistants who coordinated their lives.

"No, to the interview with Desiree. She has some vendetta against Keller, I think they might have hooked up once, and now her articles are mean. I don't trust her. Thanks for arranging the rest. You're the best."

Alexis smiled at him, the flush of pink on her cheeks contrasting with her freckles. She had come to LA to work behind the scenes as a music engineer. He knew he'd have to let her go on eventually. But until that day, he was going to help her get hands-on experience with the music industry while she did her job.

"Oh, I know it's last minute, but I was hoping I could work remotely tomorrow. It's my anniversary with my boyfriend, and I wanted to take him to the Santa Monica Inn tonight."

Nathan shook his head. "No."

Biting her lip, she nodded at him. "Okay, that's fine."

Placing a hand on her shoulder, he shook his head. "No, you're not staying at the Santa Monica Inn. Pick whichever five-star hotel you want and put it on my card. My treat. Room service, spa, dinner out, whatever you two need. Make it two nights. Just be back by one on Thursday."

Alexis nodded, her smile brightening. "Are you serious?"

Nathan nodded. "Completely. You work your ass off for me. You deserve it."

Alexis glanced at her phone. "You have two minutes before they expect you for sound checks."

Nathan let her know he'd be there and let her get back to her to-do list. As she left, Keller walked in, chatting with Theo. With a nod, he let them know he'd join them in a minute.

It was showtime.

Chapter Twenty-Three

BLIND STITCH
ILSA

A LL MORNING LONG, ILSA felt a tingling through her skin like the phantom of
Nathan's hands on her body. She missed him. Never had she missed a person
before. She didn't miss the mother she left in Phoenix, and she refused to miss the father
she hardly knew. Neither did she miss the boyfriends who had come and gone through
the years. She never stayed long enough to allow herself to know them enough.

But she missed Nathan. She fought the urge to call him dozens of times throughout
the morning. Her hand itched to set down her pencil and pick up her phone. She started
doing something reserved for the direst of circumstances to keep herself from calling him.
Trinh walked into the office, glancing around at the reorganization efforts with a raised
brow.

"What's the matter?"

Ilsa looked up where she was sitting crossed-legged on the floor, the metal filing cabinet
in front of her and a stack of financial forms in one hand.

"Nothing."

"Ilsa, you're cleaning."

"And?"

Trinh sighed, taking the papers from her hand. "And you never clean."

Ilsa scoffed. "That is so not true. I cleaned the office like…" she trailed off as she tried
to wrack her brain to remember the last time she'd cleaned. There were days she came in
and found her office cleaned, but her doing it? Unlikely.

"If you're spun up enough to clean, there must be something going on. So, spill."

Snagging the papers in Trinh's hand, she shoved them into the folder she took them
out of. "I don't need your negativity right now."

Throwing her head back, Trinh laughed a bawdy noise. "That's rich. You are so full of
shit right now."

Scrambling to her feet, Ilsa towered over Trinh's five-one frame. "I'm getting a smoothie. Mind your business and the store while I'm gone."

Trinh laughed again, mock saluting Ilsa. "Sure thing, boss."

Resisting the urge to make another snide comment, Ilsa made her way to the door, stopping to fish her ringing phone from her purse. It was an unknown number. For a moment, she considered not answering, but with her business, she couldn't afford to ignore calls.

"Ilsa Kruger."

"Miss Kruger, this is Dante from Harbor Auto. I'm calling to let you know your SUV will take a little longer than estimated, but it should be ready by three-thirty."

Ilsa wrinkled her brow as she walked through the door to look at the parking lot. "That's impossible. My car is—" She stopped short. Her car was gone. "My car's been stolen."

There was a long silence on the other end, "Ma'am. Do you own a silver SUV?"

"Yes, but it's not in the parking lot."

"Because it's in our shop. An Alexis Vickers dropped it off this morning."

Ilsa cursed under her breath. Nathan's assistant. Somehow, he must have taken her car to have the AC repaired. Ilsa didn't have the time or money to deal with this, but it'd already been done.

"Okay, do you guys take credit cards?" Rubbing a hand over the line between her brows, she considered her credit limits. "Or multiple credit cards, I might have to put it on a few. I'm a little maxed out right now and—"

"The bill has already been paid in full."

"What?"

"Yes, according to our records, Mr. Nathan Ayers paid." The man on the other end laughed. "Hey, like the rock star! Weird."

Slumping against the concrete wall, she could feel the rough surface digging into her back. Squinching her eyes shut, she managed a nonchalant noise. "Right. Weird. Thank you. I'll find a ride to your shop around five if that works for you."

The man on the end let her know they'd be open until six and to have a nice day. Hanging up, she clenched the phone in her hand, willing the frustration to dissipate.

It was exactly the kind of "favor" that could be held over her head. Deep down, she knew Nathan would never be the kind of man who'd pay for something only to expect a return on investment. But the sensation remained the same. Guilt. Shame for being in a vulnerable position. Anger that he didn't follow her wishes. The desperation of knowing nothing she could do would make them even.

Ilsa had a flash of her mother chiding Ilsa for back-talking one of Mitzie's boyfriends.

Who do you think is putting those clothes on your back and food in your mouth? We are in his debt, and never forget that.

She promised herself. She swore she would never be that woman.

She started writing a text, then deleted the thread, calling instead. Nathan picked up after two rings.

"How's your cold air?"

"Nathan, I told you not to do things like this."

"No," he drawled out a long *o*. "You told me not to *say* I would take care of you. I haven't since. This is different."

"This is worse. You understand how this is worse, right? That was my car. I am responsible for my own car. If I choose to ride around in a sweltering hot car, that's my choice."

"Did you need AC?"

"Yes."

"And did you have the money to fix it before the hottest part of summer?"

"Probably not," she reluctantly agreed.

"So, what's the issue?"

"The issue is..." she trailed off. She couldn't explain that issue to him. He'd never understand that this was exactly what her mother wanted for her. It was more than being independent or having a sense of pride. She couldn't rely on a man. Deep down, Ilsa knew Nathan was nothing like those men her mother dated. But where was the line? When in that fight would she lose her autonomy? It was little gifts now. Then it was relying on him to help with rent. Then where would she be when it all went to shit?

"The issue is that it's my choice. You can't take my stuff and have it fixed because you think it's your right."

"Ilsa, take the gift. Please don't make it into something it's not. It's not my right, but it's my privilege to help you. I would have done the same for any friend."

"But I'm not just your friend. I'm your..." she trailed off. She wouldn't say, girlfriend.

"My what?" She could hear the humor in his voice.

"Nothing. Something. My point is that it's different when you sleep with someone."

"Agreed. All the more reasons to help you. How is this different from you bringing over teriyaki when I was down and out?"

Ilsa groaned at him. "If you don't understand the difference between those two things, we are in a world of trouble, Nate."

There was a long stretch of silence on the other end, muffled shouting of people on a television set working in the background. "We'll talk later. Take the gift. It's not like you can remove the AC fluid now."

"Fine. But I want to pay you back."

"Not a chance. But I want to see you after dinner with Eloise. I've been moonlighting as a weatherman, and I'm forecasting you'll be getting a few inches tonight."

Ilsa pursed her lips to keep the smile from her face. Even if he couldn't see her, somehow, he'd know.

"We'll see. I might still be mad at you."

Nathan laughed. "Nonsense. No one can stay mad at me. I'm adorable."

How true that was. Despite the irritation over him taking her car, she couldn't muster the anger she wanted to feel. He took the fight out of her. "We'll see how I feel after a few margaritas."

"And then Sakina said that maybe we could collaborate on her next album, which, come on, just having her listen to my music was incredible, but...." Eloise trailed off. "Oh, no. I've spent the last half hour boring you over all the great things with me and haven't asked you a single question about yourself. I'm terrible."

Ilsa feigned a smile. Listening to her friend's triumphs was nice. "It's been five minutes, tops."

"Still, tell me how things are going. I've been so busy that I haven't got the full story about that firm. Griffin and Daniels?"

"Gallegos and Davis. And it was a disaster. I had one terrible meeting with Thomas Gallegos, and all I got was a creepy come-on and dry salad."

Eloise shook her head in disgust, "Are you kidding me? What happened?"

Ilsa relayed the story with as little emotion as she could muster. It felt good to let the story out, even if it wouldn't do anything concrete to help her.

Setting down her glass with force, Eloise narrowed her eyes. "What a grade-A-level prick. I would've kneed him the balls."

Ilsa laughed. "No, you wouldn't have."

"You're right. I wouldn't have. But I would've thought about it." Eloise frowned, considering her words. "Did you tell Nathan?"

Ilsa shook her head, "I can handle it. I don't want to worry Nate over something silly like this."

Reaching out, Eloise took Ilsa's hand. "It's not silly. You should tell him."

Eloise set her oversized margarita glass down on the bright green tablecloth. "It's not just the business meeting that's bothering you, though, I can tell. What else is going on?"

"Nothing, I'm fine." Ilsa fingered the stem of the glass. The green cactus-shaped glassware was cold on her fingers.

"No, you're not. I can tell. And don't give me the crap about work because I know things are exactly where you want them to be right now."

Ilsa traced the edge of her glass until the crystal goblet let out a telltale song. She studied the neon green liquid. It had to be from a mix, not even real lime juice, and triple sec. Nothing was this fluorescent color in nature. "It's nothi..."

"Nathan. It's Nathan, isn't it? What did he do? Do you need me to talk to him? I'll do it. He'll listen to me."

"Stop," Ilsa cracked a small smile at her friend's fierce loyalty. "He hasn't done anything. It's me."

All afternoon long, she'd wrestled with the doubts plaguing her. Any other woman would be thrilled to have a handsome and rich man make the arrangements to fix her car and pay for it. So why couldn't she let it go?

Ilsa hesitated. She had never really talked about her family with others. Everyone had their problems. What was the point? But she knew Eloise hadn't been gifted with the shiny nuclear family any more than Ilsa was.

"Nathan has no idea what it feels like to grow up and never be appreciated. I mean, have you met his parents."

Eloise nodded. "Yeah, they're pretty impressive."

"Nathan deserves that. Someone without all this bullshit around him. Someone who has their shit together, who could devote their life to him."

"Nathan doesn't want a fan. He has plenty of those. He wants you."

"And when I'm not enough? When I screw everything up? When he meets my mother and finds out exactly how not together my family is and wants to bail? What if he thinks I'm going to end up just like her? If I let him in, if I let him take care of me, what if I *do* end up just like her? She had goals and dreams once. And then she had me, and they all fell apart. Who's to say the same won't happen to me if I let him take care of me?"

Reaching across the plastic tablecloth, Eloise took her hand, squeezing it. Her oversized diamond ring twinkled in the neon light of the Pacifico sign.

"Trust me. I know what you're saying all too well. But you can't honestly think you'll end up like your mother just because she raised you? You got out. I got out. We are not our dead-end mothers."

Drawing her hand back, Ilsa slid her fingers around the edge of the table. "I know that, in some way, but still. I can't help but wonder."

Eloise frowned, a small line forming on the edge of her lips, her tiny, freckled nose wrinkling up as she considered Ilsa. Eloise frowned as she crossed her legs. "Last year, Ana talked me into coming up for Viking Fest. It's this little holiday weekend in May in my hometown. Anyway, we ran into my mom on Front Street while we were there. The parade was finished, it was midday, and she came stumbling out of the Skol House. I hadn't even told her I was in town, and there she was."

"Was she drunk?"

"Oh yeah, sloshed. I'm used to it from her. I haven't relied on her for anything since my brother passed. But still, not how I wanted Keller to meet Dana."

She felt her heart clench. Ilsa's mother might demand all the wrong things, but at least she put on a good face for the public.

"My point is, he didn't care because he loves me. Because despite what our parents have told us, we can expect more of the people we care about. We are capable of more. We got out. You and me both. We left those towns behind and, with it, all the baggage they tried to pile on. Trusting Keller was the hardest thing I ever had to do. I can tell Nathan cares about you. How do you feel for him?"

With a shaky breath, Ilsa looked away from her friend. It would be too hard to look into her big blue eyes and say the words.

"I like him. I mean, look at him. Who wouldn't be attracted to that? And the sex is phenomenal. Like out of this world, roller-coaster cresting and waves crashing cliche great. But more than his charm and his positive attitude and amazing arms—and they are amazing—he's good to me. In a way, I never thought I'd want."

"It's scary to want someone, to give yourself over truly."

"I've spent my whole life building this life for myself. What if I allow myself to care for Nathan but lose myself in the process?"

"That won't happen," Eloise interjected.

Looking at Eloise. Ilsa was struck by the resolute hold of her chin. "How do you know?"

"Honestly? Because I won't let it. And neither would Nathan. All those parts of yourself that you're scared you'll lose? That is what he loves about you: your tenacity, your no-bullshit attitude. You wouldn't be you without those qualities. So why do you think that loving someone would take it away? If someone loves you for who you truly are, they don't want you to change a single thing."

"I don't want kids. What if, down the line, he does? I'm not some Suzy homemaker type. I never will be."

"Does Nathan know that?" Eloise asked.

Ilsa nodded. "Yeah, I told him pretty early on. It doesn't seem fair not to."

"If he wanted that type of woman, he could have one. I'm not trying to bring attention to his legions of fans, but seriously, do you think there aren't five women in this restaurant who wouldn't love to have his baby right now? It doesn't matter. He loves you."

"You don't know that."

Eloise stifled a laugh, and Ilsa narrowed her eyes. "What's so funny?"

Eloise laughed harder, fanning her face. Tears were coming from her blue eyes. "Sorry, it's not funny, it's just..." she let out another loud guffaw.

"What?"

Eloise took a minute to calm herself down. "What you just said. *You don't know, but* I said the same thing to *Nathan* about Keller. And I was wrong. He knew. Nathan might be a little trusting, sure. He might have a soft spot for people. But one thing Nathan is not, is indecisive. He loves you. I bet he's been half in love with you for a year now. It's you who needs to figure out what you want."

Tipping her margarita glass up, she drained the bottom of the sweet mixture down her throat. Across the restaurant, a waiter caught her eye, and she gave him a thumbs-up while pointing at her empty glass. The waiter hustled over, and before he could open his mouth, Ilsa handed him the empty glass. "Another one? Thank you."

The waiter looked at Eloise, and she shook her head. "I'm fine. Thanks."

Once the waiter left, Eloise turned to Ilsa, frowning. "Is this your answer, then?"

The waiter returned with a new margarita. Ilsa knew she would have a pounding headache from the sugar and cheap tequila the next day, but she didn't care.

"You need to figure yourself out."

Ilsa set the drink on the table. "You sound like Theo, lecturing me about how I don't deserve Nathan."

Eloise wrinkled her nose. "I'm looking out for you. Nathan's a big boy. He can take care of himself. I'm not worried about him."

"Well, I'm fine. Change of subject, please. Are you still willing to model for me? It could help to have someone with your good press representing us."

Narrowing her eyes at her, Eloise nodded. "You know I will. And I'm not letting this go. Ceasefire tonight, but figure your shit out soon."

Ilsa raised her glass for Eloise to clink. With a begrudging smile, Eloise brought her drink up to cheers.

"To figuring out shit tomorrow," she said. Bringing her drink up to her mouth, she licked the salt rim, letting the flavor explode on her tongue.

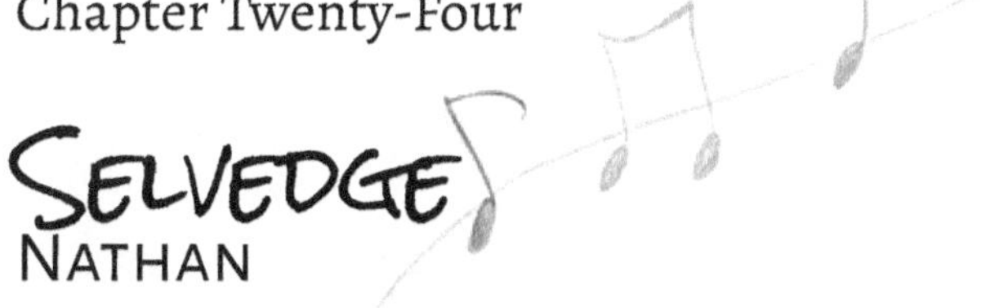

Chapter Twenty-Four

Selvedge
Nathan

T HE BEEPING OF HIS phone woke him up. The night before, Ilsa showed up at his doorstep, margarita drunk and giggling, Eloise propping her up against the door frame. Ilsa's car was left at the restaurant to be retrieved later.

Before the door closed behind Eloise, she'd already tried to take his pants off. Nathan stopped her before she got to his zipper. No matter how much he missed her, it was obvious she was in no place to be intimate. She was currently snoring beside him, tangled in his favorite blanket, her underwear still on and her hair plastered to her forehead.

The phone beeped again, and Nathan fumbled on his bedside table. His manager had sent him an article with the words. *"This u?"*

Cursing under his breath, he climbed out of bed, pulling on a pair of athletic shorts off the floor. Padding to the kitchen, he sat at the counter to read the article without the chance of Ilsa looking over his shoulder. He knew he had nothing to hide, but he was never fast with conversation in the mornings.

Shathan Flame Rekindled?
By Trinity Flay
Los Angeles
Only days after news broke that Prevalent Notion bassist Nathan Ayers was spotted lip-locked with up-and-coming fashion designer Ilsa Kruger, new photos are coming in of him getting cozy with none other than his former flame, Shelby Waters.
Waters and Ayers dated on again, off again for a little under a year. Fans were shocked over reports that Water dumped Ayers for director Sam Leahy. The relationship between the actress and the director didn't last long, and from a recent insider tip, the once hot and heavy couple may have found their way back to

each other.

An anonymous source said they were quite cozy backstage at the Olly Robinson Show, where they were both promoting their various projects, Waters's Raspberry Farmer and Ayers's new album release with Prevalent Notion.

Could love once again be in the cards for these two? And if so, what happened with Ilsa Kruger?*If you have information regarding this story or have any other celebrity news, please email us at our tip line at gotcha@allcelebs.com.*

Nathan stared at the photo on his phone. It was grainy, obviously taken backstage at the show on a phone, with the brightness turned up. He didn't remember anyone being around when he was talking to Shelby, but people were always milling around backstage. It was possible one of the many people working backstage or a guest of a guest could've taken the picture. It didn't matter who took the photo. What mattered was how it looked, and it didn't look good.

Shelby was holding Nathan's face in her hands as she looked up at him in what could only be described as a loving look. If he hadn't been there, he would've assumed they had just shared a passionate kiss. Scrubbing a hand over his rough whiskered face, he called Tamara.

"Hey, dumbass," she barked without a hello. "What's the scoop?"

He groaned. "No scoop. Just two old friends were talking. Ilsa and I are a thing, not that I want to give that info to the paps."

"I'll handle it." Tamara had a rough voice, but she got shit done for the band. When they lost their previous manager the year before, he worried that Tamara with her hippie dresses and red frame glasses wouldn't be up for the job, but she exceeded their expectations. She was a bulldog when she needed to be but took care of them in a way Arnie never did.

"Thanks, Tam."

"You tell that girl of yours before she hears about it from someone else." One of the first things Tamara did when she started was to take Eloise out to dinner as a thanks for keeping the band together for so long. She was a good one.

"I will."

She hung up on him before he could say anything more. Squinting at the picture more, he tried to formulate a response. He was still staring at his phone when Ilsa stumbled down the hall. Her hair was pulled off her face, and his old Allison Krauss and Union Station T-shirt was falling off her shoulder. He had the impulse to bite that swath of creamy skin between her shoulder and neck.

Lucky one, indeed.

She walked up to him, wrapping her arms around his middle and rubbing her face in his bare chest. Her flushed skin was warm to the touch, and he reveled in the feel of her sleepy body against his in the kitchen, the sweet banality of having her with him in the morning, all rumbled hair and old T-shirts. She looked up at him, little mascara flecks under her eyes. Bending down, he held her face in his hands and gave her a soft kiss, tracing a crease on her cheek from the pillow with his thumb. She closed her eyes and leaned forward, resting her forehead on his collarbone and pressing a kiss to his bare chest.

Pulling away, she glanced at the counter behind them. "Is there coffee?" she croaked as she settled onto the high-back stool and buried her face in her hands.

Getting up, Nathan set his phone face down on the counter. "There will be in five minutes."

Busying himself with brewing a pot of coffee, he wracked his brain, trying to figure out what to say. He wanted to think that Ilsa would believe nothing was going on, but she was such a skeptic by nature he wasn't sure.

When he turned back to face her with a steaming cup in his hand, he was no closer to an idea. Luckily, with Ilsa's head buried in her arms and a slight greenish hue to her skin, she didn't look ready to have an important conversation.

Setting down his favorite mug with coffee and a plate with toast and mashed banana next to her, he leaned down and pressed a kiss to her head.

"What is this?" Ilsa asked with disgust.

Gripping his second favorite mug, he looked to see that she was pointing at the plate of toast.

"Toast and banana. My momma always made that for me when I wasn't feeling too good."

Wrinkling her nose, she inspected the toast. "It looks gross."

"Didn't your momma make you something special when you were sick?"

Darkness flashed behind her eyes, gone almost before she could catch it. He cursed himself inwardly. That was a dumb question. He knew the answer. "Sure, Mitzie made me 'special juice' with Benadryl and Tylenol so I could sleep and not bother her with my complaining."

She used air quotes as she talked.

No wonder she didn't want people taking care of her if that was the kind of care she got growing up. He wanted to apologize, but he knew she wouldn't like it. She didn't want his pity.

"Well, I won't do that." Pushing the plate closer to her, he took on a firm tone. "Eat your toast."

Picking up a corner of the toast, she groaned. "I don't think I can. Pretty sure I ate some bad food last night. I might have food poisoning."

His mug stopped, poised halfway to his mouth as he studied her. Setting the mug back down on the counter, he opened his mouth to say something, then closed it.

"What?" she asked.

"Do you think," he grimaced as he spoke. "That maybe the gallon of margaritas you had with Eloise might be more to blame?"

Her brow furrowed, and her eyes darted around as if she was counting in her head. "Maybe, a little. But I'm telling you, something was off with that salsa."

Stifling his laugh, he nodded at her. "If you say so."

She raised the toast to her mouth and took a tentative nibble off the edge. Raising a brow as if to say it was passable, she took another larger bite. His phone buzzed in his pocket, and he hoped it wasn't Shelby again. Pulling it out, he saw the picture of his father at a Wildcats basketball game a few years before.

Holding up his phone, he showed Ilsa the screen. "It's my dad. I have to get this. Eat all your toast before you drink another cup of coffee."

After pressing a kiss to her bare shoulder as he walked past, he made his way to his balcony as she grumbled about *bossy grumps.*

On the privacy of his large balcony, he sat in the chair as he answered. "Hey, Pops."

"Well, yello there, Nathan. Didn't think you'd answer." The warm voice of his father sounded on the other end. "What with your new girlfriend taking up your time."

Nathan rolled his eyes at the good-natured ribbing.

"I picked up, didn't I?"

"So, you did. So, you did. I was about to trim the hydrangea bushes, but they'll keep. It's too darn hot to be outside doing yard work, anyway. Now I have an excuse when your momma asks why I didn't finish my honey-do list."

Nathan smiled. He could picture the large chalkboard in their hallway and the ever-changing lists his mother would write out for tasks to be completed. The tasks changed through the years, from music lessons for Nathan to picking up school supplies to paying the bills, but the chalkboard with its hand-painted blue flowers adorning the top never moved. Glancing around his large home, it felt so cold. There were few personal touches to the place. It was professionally decorated and gorgeous, but it didn't feel like a home. His eyes caught on Ilsa's sweater from the night before, draped haphazardly on the back of his dining room chair. That felt like home.

"Blame it on me. She'll forgive you."

His father barked out a laugh. "Blame you? Not likely. Though you know, she needs to hear from you. I don't know if I'll tell her we talked 'til later. She'll want to whip my hide."

"I miss her too. I miss all of you."

"Well, good cause that's why I'm calling. Kaiden has some big graduation thing at that fancy school you pay for. Now I don't see what all the fuss is about. When I was in fifth grade, all we did at the end of the year was moving on up to sixth grade, but I guess nowadays they do a big thing, and Ashleigh wants you to come out for it."

"Of course I will. When is it? I'll have Alexis put it in my schedule."

"Your schedule." His father hooted with laughter on the other end. "You too big for your britches to write it down yourself?"

Nathan stifled the sigh he had. He loved his father but had no idea about the pressure of being a successful musician. "Give me the dates, Pops."

His father rattled off a date in a few weeks.

"You better get tickets soon. You know they get expensive if you wait."

Nathan refrained from explaining to his father that he didn't have to worry about the cost of air travel anymore.

"I'll do that."

"Good, use all that fancy music money you got and fly out here. Your momma misses you, and so does your sister. Bring that oddball girlfriend of yours."

Nathan smiled at the description and that his father wouldn't say he missed Nathan. Though he knew he did.

"I'll see if she can. She's got a busy schedule too."

"She got one of those fancy assistants to get her coffee and write down dates?"

"No, she doesn't."

"Good, smart girl. I can tell."

"You haven't even met her yet."

"I can tell. You know, I got a sense for this stuff. I knew the moment I met your mother she was the one. Might-a taken her a bit to catch up, but I got her in the end."

"Okay, I'll ask her."

"Oh, darn. Your mother just pulled up. I got to get, son. Your momma is dragging me to one of those charity events. Some murder mystery theater thing for the parks and rec department."

Nathan could picture his father grumbling the whole time he was there to save face, but inside loving the entire experience. Tobias Ayers was wrapped around his wife's finger. And he loved every minute of it.

"... Let me know when your flight is, and I'll come to get you and your friend from the airport."

Nathan blinked a few times, realizing he had missed part of what his dad had said. "Right, I will. Love you, Pops. Give Momma a kiss for me, will you?"

"I'm going to give her a lot more than that tonight." His father chuckled.

Groaning at his father's over-share, Nathan bid his father goodbye. Setting the phone down, he gazed out over his small backyard.

Nathan wished for something like what his parents had. He knew what love looked like. His parents were an example of it every day. He knew love wasn't big gestures and flowers. It was showing up for each other, listening about their day over a meal. It's making sure your wife's oil never had to be changed and picking up your husband's prescriptions from the pharmacy. It was picking out their favorite brand of ice cream at the store and turning up the volume when their favorite song came on the radio.

He thought of how Ilsa had taken him to the hospital and how she doted on him afterward. The way she always texted him before she went to bed at night and saved all her dirty pick-up lines for him. Was that love?

Returning to the kitchen, he found Ilsa settled on his couch with a fresh cup of coffee. The banana toast plate was picked clean.

"Did my *gross* food help?"

"Marginally," She agreed, settling her cell phone on the table face down.

"Are you too sick to take a bath with me?" he asked.

She perked up. "I think I have the strength for that." She looked down at her body. "Do I look like a haunted house?"

Nathan felt this was a trick question, narrowing his eyes before responding. "No, why?"

Flashing him a devilish grin, she pulled the shirt over her head as she turned to make her way to the bedroom. "Because I'll make you scream when you come in me."

After handing her a silk robe he had bought a few days before and giving her strict instructions to sit and wait, Nathan filled the tub with hot water. Before getting his money, he was never much of a bath man. Either he had to bend his knees up to his chin, or his lower legs hung out of the bath at weird angles. This tub was specially built to accommodate his large frame. Pouring in some of that good smelly stuff that he had Alexis pick it up for him—she'd raised a brow but was silent about the request—he swirled the solution around until it created a nice layer of bubbles. Once the tub was filled to a good level, he beckoned Ilsa to get in.

Shucking the robe, Ilsa held his hand as she stepped into the soapy water. He watched as the water lapped around her body, the bubbles covering her mound, then her waist, and then her breasts. It was like a reverse strip tease. He'd never tire of seeing her like this.

Laying back against the leather headrest, she closed her eyes and let out a sigh that verged on the sound she made when she came. His cock stirred in his shorts at the noise.

Opening one eye, she looked at him. "Are you joining me?"

He didn't need to be asked twice. He pulled his shorts off and did a mediocre job of not spilling water all over his floor as he slid in behind her. Cleaning up water was a later issue.

Placing a hand on her shoulder, he tilted her head back to wet her hair.

"I can wash my own hair, you know," she mumbled, a small smile playing on her lips.

"I know but isn't this more fun? Now we can both get clean." Squirting some shampoo in his hand, he massaged it into her scalp. She sighed against him as he lathered her hair. "Lay back to rinse."

She obeyed him, sliding down his body until her hair was underwater.

"I need..."

"Conditioner?" he asked, holding up the matching bottle. "You think I wouldn't already have all your stuff here?"

She narrowed her eyes but looked at the bottle on the edge of the tub. "How did you know?"

"Illy, come on. What kind of man do you think I am that I can't figure out what products you use? I've been to your place. I've seen your cluttered shower."

Working the conditioner in her hair, she stopped him as he worked his way from the top of her head. "Just the bottom of the hair needs conditioner." She pointed to the throat. "From about here down, or my hair gets greasy in a day."

He obliged her, conditioning her hair in a swirl at the base of her neck so he could access the bare part of her shoulder.

Over the slickness of her wet shoulder, he moved his hand down her bare arm until it disappeared under the bubbles with her body.

"So, when were you going to tell me about Shelby?" Ilsa asked, her eyes closed as she leaned against his front. Her head rested on his shoulder. Nathan's hand stilled under the water.

"Um...now?"

Opening one eye, she squinted at him. "So, tell me."

He recounted what happened, leaving out the rude things Shelby said. "...it was just a tricky camera angle, nothing more."

"Okay." She relaxed back onto Nathan's chest. Her bare ass rubbed against his half-hard cock.

"Okay?" he asked. "Is that all you're going to say? Are you mad? Do you believe me?"

Ilsa sat up, water sluicing over her body as she tucked her legs closer to her body. Turning around to look at him, she frowned. "Do you think I would take a bath with you if I thought you were back together with your ex-girlfriend? That I'd be kissing you and grinding against that gorgeous cock if I did?"

"No?" he guessed. Sometimes he thought he had Ilsa all figured out, and then she'd pull this kind of mind trick.

"No." She trailed her finger over the water's surface, breaking the little bubble with her long nails. "Nate, you are many things, but a cheater isn't one of them. I know that. I know you. If you say nothing is going on, I believe you. I trust you."

"You know, me and Shelby, she didn't want to be with me seriously. I thought she did for a while, but I was wrong."

"She's the fool. She knows it too, but that's too bad. You're mine now."

He pulled her back against him, tilting her face to kiss her lips. His hands moved around her waist to pull her bare ass against his cock.

"How did I get so lucky with you?"

Pursing her lips, she seemed to consider his question. "It's your fake denim shorts. I couldn't resist."

He leaned forward, biting the section of the bare shoulder he was so fascinated with before. His teeth scraped the tender skin, leaving a red mark beside the top pink petal of her back tattoo. Scraping and sucking until his mouth scored her skin, he didn't care if he left a bruise. He wanted it. He wanted to mark her permanently until everyone could see she was his.

She sighed at the sensation, and he felt himself grow hard. But he could wait. This wasn't about sex. Not yet.

"You know I've never bathed with a man before."

"Never?"

She shook her head. "Once I had to do a photo shoot in the shower, wearing a swimsuit, but that was different."

He brushed a lock of wet hair off the back of her neck. His fingers moved down the green stem that covered her spinal column. "How was it different?"

She glanced back at him with a wicked smile. "For one, I didn't want to sleep with Antonio."

"Antonio?" he raised a brow.

"Oh, he was gorgeous. Six-five, built like a god, chiseled abs, and that V that goes right down to his dick that all the girls love and," Nathan could feel his throat thicken with the description. He knew she had men before him. She'd even told him, but hearing about it now, after knowing what she felt like beneath his hands, knowing what sounds she made as she came around his cock. It was too much.

"... and these thick black curls, and I'm sure his boyfriend just loved having him home every night."

"Boyfriend?" he asked, letting out a whoosh of air at the word.

"Yeah, most of those jacked-up dudes in the modeling world are gay. His boyfriend, Todd, was a sweetheart. They came out to visit me a year or so ago. They own a gym in Chandler now. They use all those crazy acronyms for stuff. WOD and MetCon and lord only knows what else."

"So, you didn't date him?" Nathan asked.

Ilsa shook her head. "No, truthfully, I don't know if I can say I've ever really dated anyone seriously. I don't do boyfriends. I mean, I have my fun now and then, but I don't know if I can say I've even had a 'boyfriend' before."

"Never? Not in high school?"

Ilsa shook her head. "No, I was too busy with the pageants and modeling to have time for guys. The most meaningful relationship I had was with this other model, Armand.

I lost my virginity to him when I was seventeen. But even that wasn't what I'd call a relationship. More like a mutual understanding that we were attracted to each other, and I wanted to try sex. I'm going to take a wild guess that your dating life was more typical."

"Clare Duncan, sixteen after Sadie Hawkins. We dated for three years. She dumped me when she started going to the University of Kentucky, and I was out here for college."

"Did you love her?" Ilsa wasn't sure why she asked that, but she had to know.

Nathan scratched his head. "Yeah, I thought I did. I mean, we dated through high school. At the time, I thought we would graduate and then get married. Have a few kids, all that."

"Do you still want that?" The sweet line between her brows furrowed as she waited for his answer.

"Marriage? Yeah, someday. But kids? No. If I had stayed in town, maybe I would've had kids with Clare, and it would have been fine, but I never pictured myself as a father. That's what you do back home. You get married and have kids. But I'm not back home. I'm here. I love being a musician with the traveling, the late nights, and the parties. You can't do that with kids."

"You don't think you'll want them later?" Ilsa asked.

"Nah."

Ilsa let out a shaky breath, smiling at him. "I hope this doesn't freak you out, and I swear I'm not trying to get ahead of myself, but I'm glad you agree with me. You wouldn't believe how many people think I'm wrong for not wanting kids."

"Plenty of people don't want kids."

Ilsa cocked her head to the side and pointed down at her crotch. "Yeah, but I have a uterus, so I must want to fill it up."

"I don't want that for you," he said, his voice soft.

"Why is a bare minimum statement like that so sexy right now?"

He tried not to let the words sting. He knew she was reacting not to him but to the world with that statement. "I don't want to be the minimum for you. I want to be everything." He paused, gathering his words. "You understand that, don't you?"

Reaching behind her, she ran her long nails through his hair. "I do. That's why you're so good for me."

He hoped against hope that her statement meant what he wanted it to mean.

"As long as you want me, I'll be good for you." Pushing her forward, he disentangled himself from behind her. "You stay here and soak. I'll be right back."

Leaving her in the water, he ran to get things ready for her in bed. He was going to show her what love felt like.

Chapter Twenty-Five

LACE
ILSA

WHEN NATHAN LEFT THE tub, Ilsa tipped her head back against the leather bath pillow. Alone with her thoughts, her mind returned to the blur of the morning, her dusty tongue and seeing the news article first thing when she opened her phone. Setting an alert to get news about Nathan might have been a mistake.

There was a momentary flash of jealousy and annoyance seeing the words. Despite not discussing their status, the moment she saw that picture of tiny Shelby Waters looking up at her Nathan with that soppy look, she knew she wanted to be the only one touching him like that. As casual as she tried to be, nothing had ever felt this way for her. She wanted every part of Nathan and needed him to want her too.

Despite his questionable hangover food choices, Nathan was a good man. She had never had a reason to trust a man to this degree. But listening to Nathan talk to his father on the phone, she knew he was a faithful man. There were countless articles about celebrities she knew to be untrue. She'd seen firsthand the way PR spins things. Theo was in a PR relationship, after all.

So, when he offered her a kiss, took her hand in his, and ran her a bath, she trusted in him. It was an odd feeling growing deep within her. Overhearing his conversation—he really should be better at shutting the door if he didn't want her to eavesdrop—she was struck with how sweet and funny and *normal* their conversation was. The way he told his father, 'love you, Pops,' without any shame. She tried to remember the last time she'd said that to Mitzie—likely not that long ago, but always with annoyance. It was an expectation—the adoration, the platitudes—but she couldn't remember the last time she talked with her mother and enjoyed hearing her voice.

She imagined, as she hadn't in years, what it would've felt like to grow up with a parent who could delight in their child. Someone who could make banana toast. Someone to miss her when she was away. Sitting up, she blinked back the wetness threatening the corner of her eyes. She was not going to cry over her mother, for God's sake. Cupping the scented water in her hands, she splashed it over her face. The perfumes in the soap would likely wreak havoc on her skin, but the rose scent was so nice she let it slide this one time.

When he returned holding a towel in his hand, he motioned for her to come out of the tub. Standing up in the tub, he walked to her, unfolding the large white towel and holding it wide for her to step into.

He wrapped it around her shoulders and rubbed the water off her body. The towel was warm to the touch. Taking one of her hands, he helped her step over the tub's rim. She started dripping water on his expensive marble flooring. Clad in only a towel around his hips, he moved down her body with a second towel, drying all the spots on her body until she was warm and dry.

"Do you have a towel warmer?" she asked.

Busying himself with her lower leg, he looked up from kneeling beneath her. "I put this in the dryer before I got in so it would be warm for you."

Holding the warmth against her cheek, she closed her eyes, a pang of something aching in her chest. Making her food, warming her towels, kissing her senseless. It was all too much. When she took a breath, she was surprised to find it was shaky. All her resolution was evaporating in the presence of this man. She couldn't hold on much longer, and she wanted to let go for the first time in her life. To allow herself to fall and maybe, for the first time in her life, trust that someone could catch her.

"No one's ever done that for me before. Today is a day of a lot of firsts." Her eyes were shut when she spoke gently. "I've never taken a bath with someone before. It's very intimate."

When she opened her eyes, she saw him kneeling on the floor, watching her. He was silent as if he knew that what she was saying wasn't just about the bath.

"It can be," he demurred.

Her body dry enough, she dropped the towel around her shoulders to the floor, where it soaked up the spilled water. Stepping into Nathan, she placed a hand on his shoulder. Standing above him, clad in only her stud earrings, she felt powerful and in control of the moment and where it would lead.

His hand gripped her ankle before running up the inside of her leg, stopping at her upper thigh. Leaning forward, he pressed a kiss to her hipbone, the divot he said he loved so much. The part of herself that took years to accept. Sucking her skin into his mouth, his fingers parted her, pressing against her clit. Sparks sizzled in her as his thumb pressed her clit and his large fingers slid into her wetness. Gripping his shoulders, she ground herself into his hand.

"You want more than my fingers, don't you?" he asked against her skin.

"Yes, I want your cock inside me."

He smiled as his free hand moved up her body, tweaking her rosy nipple until it stiffened at his touch.

"You're so beautiful. I love watching you bloom for me."

"Only for you." She gasped as his fingers began to move inside her, hitting her clit and walls perfectly.

Pulling away, he stood up. "I'm going to give you everything. Now hold on to me."

Before she could guess what was happening, he reached down to grab hold of her thighs, pulling her up around him. His hard length pressed against her as he moved to the wall, her back against the cold tile. "Hold on to the bar."

She squirmed against his hard cock, her hot pussy pulsing with need. "No man has ever been able to..."

"I'm not any man, Illy. I'm yours." His fingers dug into the fleshy part of her upper thighs, gripping her tight as he arranged himself. "And I'm strong enough to fuck that doubt right out of you. Now grab the bar."

She obeyed his command, her arms above her head, holding onto a pull-up bar he had installed in his bathroom. He slid on a condom, and then the ridge of his cock slid against her clit, sending sparks up her body. Her grip loosened on the bar, and Nathan chuckled.

"I haven't even made it in that pussy, and you're already giving up. Come on, Petal. Hold on tight."

Tightening the grip above her head, she arched her back. His hold around her legs held strong, and then he was inside her, filling her up. She gasped at the sensation, the way he hit all the spots inside that ached.

He clamped her legs around his waist and moved her up and down on his dick. Their bodies were slick with sweat as he fucked her. Every stroke he made took her closer and closer to orgasm. Her arms became tired, and she let go of the bar, pulling his face close for a searing kiss. His tongue moved with hers as he thrust in and out of her, never losing his momentum. It was as if he could read every cue her body made, answering them exactly how she needed. She had never had a man give her exactly what she craved like this.

"That's it, come for me. Come all over my cock," Nathan demanded as he continued to fuck her.

Between his dirty words and how he moved inside her, she tensed, stars forming behind her eyes. Crying out, she ground herself closer to him, needing more, wanting more, and reaching the very top.

A guttural sound erupted from his throat before he pulled out, ripped off the condom and came all over her stomach and breasts. Opening her eyes, she found him staring at her. With a shaky breath, she loosened her grip on his shoulders, running her fingers through the hair at the nape of his neck. Loosening her grip around his waist, her legs dropped down, and he lowered her to the floor. In her bare feet, she looked up at him. Cupping her face in the palm of his hand, he bent down to press a sweet kiss on her lips. It was an unnerving juxtaposition from the sweaty sex they just had.

"I can't believe you held me up like that," she joked.

Rubbing his thumb over her lower lip, he smiled. "Why do you think I lift? That's all I think about when I'm doing presses. I think about holding you up and being inside you."

Quirking a small smile, she stepped away. "Well, now that you made me all dirty again, what are you going to do?"

He looked down at her bare skin, the stickiness across her stomach and breasts. "I'll clean you right up."

Grabbing a wet cloth, he wiped her skin, getting to every nook until she was clean. Another first for her. She'd heard of aftercare from a man but had never experienced it. Maybe she never stuck around long enough after having sex, or maybe Nathan was the only man worth sticking around for.

"Now it's nap time," he declared.

At the sound of the word, her body felt tired. She was sleepy. She always was after a night of drinking too heavily. He walked her to his bed and pulled back the blankets on what was now her side. She'd never had a side of the bed before. Collapsing into it, she lay there as he pulled the blanket up around her. "You nap for a bit. I have to squeeze in a workout."

Stretching her arms over her head, she grinned at him. "Are you saying that wasn't enough cardio for you?"

"Not according to my trainer, no. You know I got to build up my stamina if we're going to repeat that performance soon." Climbing back on top of her, he kissed her, this time with a tenderness that burned through her. Cupping her face, he pulled away. "Sleep, and we'll talk when you wake up, okay?"

He kissed her forehead before leaving her in the comfort of his high thread count sheets. Satiated, she burrowed under the covers. A warm feeling flowed through her as she replayed the morning. Happiness—no, more than that. Contentment. She was content. What a startling thought.

She liked the feeling of Nathan making her mushy toast as a hangover cure and drawing her a bath. Of bringing him cheap teriyaki when he was hurt, and the thrill of texting him every night before she went to bed. She liked the slack look on his face as he slept beside her. She liked the feel of his hands on her body, and the sparkle in his eyes as he handed her coffee in the morning made exactly the way she liked it. It all felt so domestic, and for the first time in her life, she wanted that with a man. She wanted that with him.

She rolled back to the other side of the bed, pulling the blanket firmer around her. She tried to distract herself from her overwhelming thoughts by recalling the dance steps to her opening number for Miss Arizona ten years before. Soon, sleep washed over her worn body, and then darkness.

She wasn't sure when he joined her in the bed. Only when she rolled over to wrap more blanket around herself as he lay beside her. Opening one eye, he came into focus. Shirtless, he was propped up beside her, tapping away on his laptop. The scruff on his face was day old, and his hair had a wild rumpled look. His long muscular legs were crossed at the ankles.

"Hey." Sleep coated her throat as she spoke.

His face softened when he turned to her. "Afternoon."

Stretching her arms over her head, she yawned. "What are you doing?"

He set the laptop down on the floor and turned to put his arm around her shoulder, pulling her half onto his chest. "I was looking at flights back home."

Ilsa laid a hand on his chest, looking up at him. He had his hand tucked behind his head as he leaned against the headboard. "Missing your family?"

"A bit, sure. I miss them all the time. I want you to come to Kentucky with me," he said.

Raising her chin from his chest, she furrowed her brow. "Like Kentucky, Kentucky? Like where you grew up, Kentucky?"

The corner of his mouth tipped up. "Yes. That's what I mean. Kentucky. Pretty sure there's only the one.

"What's going on back home?"

"My nephew is graduating from fifth grade. My sister asked me to be there."

"And you want me there? Like with you to meet your family? That's a big step." She fought down the fear rising in her chest. No man had ever asked her to meet his family before. She didn't even know if she wanted to be that kind of person. To meet a family. "Well, when is it?"

"Next month."

"It's kind of far out in the future, isn't it?"

"It's not that far." His grin widened. "Are you scared to meet my family?"

"No," she said, a little too sharply.

"I think you're scared."

"I'm not scared. I just don't know if I want to plan for the future like that." Pulling her up close, he tucked a hair behind her ear.

"Hey. This is it for me—you, us. We don't know what next month is going to bring. But I do know I want you there with me. Now that I have you. Now that we have this. There is no other future for me."

Ilsa took a deep breath. His words stirred deep behind her ribs. How could he be so resolute? How could he know his feelings so well? All her life, she'd known nothing but doubt and shame around trusting someone else. Years of disappointment and erecting walls around herself to never have to give herself over. And yet here was Nathan, giving his heart to her to be destroyed. It was terrifying.

"Nate, I know what you're trying to say, but—"

"No," he interrupted her. "No, you don't. I love you. And I think you could love me if you tried. This isn't just fun we're having. This is us falling in love. You and me both."

So, he said the words. Those three little words had destroyed her mother's sense of reason and left her beholden to others. The words Ilsa never wanted to desire, and yet they echoed through her. They rippled from her chest and warmed her. "Nathan, you know I care for you."

"I'm all in, Ilsa. Let's lay it all out here. No miscommunication, no pretenses. Do you want to be with me?"

How was she supposed to answer that? Love was heartache and grand gestures, followed by eventual disappointment. Love was fancy dinners out and being shown off, then suddenly being alone in apartments with no air conditioning. Ilsa hesitated, unsure how to say the words. How could she give herself over to someone else so easily? She felt her resolve wilting under his soft touches.

"It's not that simple, Nathan."

He rubbed a circle on her shoulder with his thumb, his tone decided. "It is. Either you want to be with me, or you don't."

She felt her resolve wilting under his soft touches. Her normally strong voice wavered, "You know I want you, I want to be with you, but you don't understand. I have no idea how to love someone. How to let someone take care of me."

"Whatever you were taught about relationships, it was wrong. That wasn't love."

"It was all I knew, Nathan." The last of her fight left her. She couldn't struggle against the force of his resolve.

"Let me teach you. Let me be there for you. We can learn together. Let me love you, Illy."

Her eyes stung. She brought her hands to her face, finding them wet with tears. Looking at the shimmering wetness on her fingers, she whispered, "I can't say it back, you know that."

He nodded at her. "I don't expect you to. How I feel for you doesn't need you to feel the same way. I'll love you no matter how you feel for me."

She couldn't say it, not yet. But she could show Nathan she cared. Reaching up, she pulled his face down to hers for a kiss.

This was her affection.

This was all she could never say.

Beside the bed, her phone chimed with a message.

Chapter Twenty-Six

BASTE
ILSA

S HE WAS SKEPTICAL WHEN she got the email from the young socialite Greta Landis in New York. Sure, she made inquiries to acquaintances all over the country, but this was the biggest long shot.

Ilsa had only once spoken to the rich socialite at the actor Kaspar Lian's party the previous year. It was in the middle of Prevalent Notion's tour, and that night had been overshadowed by Theo and his girlfriend, Safiya Khan, getting into a screaming match in the middle of the party. He'd called her old, and she said he didn't know how to work a clit.

That Greta even remembered her was a stretch. And offering to fly her and Trinh out to New York for two days was a miracle. A free trip and a business meeting couldn't be ignored, no matter how unlikely the offer was to be legitimate. And Trinh deserved a break from the monotony of running the store while Ilsa was trying to manage the brand.

The Lochlan was a block from the Waldorf Astoria, a luxury hotel built by real estate and hotelier company Gerald Landis in 1916. Somehow surviving the great depression, two world wars, and terrible disco music, the secretive Landis family owned a majority share in the worldwide billion-dollar real estate and hospitality company. Greta Landis, the youngest and only daughter of Gerald's grandson, was known for her fabulous parties with celebrities, never wearing the same outfit twice, and walking the runway at New York Fashion week for experimental designer Eunjoo Park at eleven years old. What she was not known for was being a businesswoman.

After settling into their sumptuous room with its view of the city and a tub bigger than her bed at home, Ilsa met Trinh in the hotel lobby. Ilsa changed into one of her designs, of which she was particularly proud. The crepe mod style dress had a jewel neckline in the front, with a low back that showed off her spine tattoo. Pairing the dress with a trendy forest green heel was the only pop of color. She didn't have time to style her hair much before the meeting, pinning it up quickly in a side chignon. Her undercut was growing out and would need to be reshaped when she returned to LA, but that was only one item on her long to-do list.

As she emerged from the elevator, Trinh waved her over from the lobby bar, where she was currently nursing a stemmed glass of brown liquid.

Setting her purse down beside her, Ilsa raised a brow at the drink. "Since when do you drink whiskey?"

Trinh raised the glass and looked at the brown substance. "Since this is my first trip to New York and it seemed fitting to order a Manhattan."

"You don't even like brown liquor. You said it's for douchebags in wire-rimmed glasses and your uncles."

Trinh took a small sip and grimaced at the taste. "That's disgusting. Who would put that in their mouth?"

Ilsa refrained from making the dirty joke she would have made if Nathan had been there.

Trinh waved over the bartender. "Sir, this is not going to work for me."

Across the bar, the man took in Trinh's purple shock of hair against her all-black ensemble, finger tattoos, and nose piercing. Around them, the bar was filling up with business types in suits. Ilsa knew the dress code on the east coast was stricter than on the west coast, but it drove the point home seeing them in their edgy dresses and tattoos on display. In LA, wearing a suit every day meant you worked at a jewelry store. Here it was expected. Her low-back dress felt out of place.

The bartender looked from Trinh's leather corset top to the side of Ilsa's scalp, where her hair was a few inches long. "What might you like then? We don't serve Pabst."

They both knew the bartender was trying to insult them, but Trinh was made of sterner stuff. "Good never liked PBR. I'm a Lagunitas fan myself."

The bartender sighed loudly, and Ilsa took the opportunity to order both of them a glass of wine. Once he left to serve other customers, Ilsa turned to Trinh.

"I have no idea what we're doing here. It has to be more than a request for a custom dress, right?"

The bartender returned with two glasses of what he assured her was the best pinot grigio from the Finger Lake region.

"We're taking a meeting with a potential investor. You're going to put on your pageant girl charm and make this socialite give you all her money. And yes, maybe create a new dress for her in the process."

Ilsa took a sip of her wine as she gathered her thoughts. Setting the average-tasting wine down, she looked at her friend. "And if we don't? The bridge with Davis Gallegos has been burned. I haven't heard from anyone else. We're doing okay right now, but if we don't get an investor soon…"

Trinh gave Ilsa's hand a reassuring squeeze. "Hey, deep breath. We'll get through this. We might be flailing, but we're not failing."

"Pretty sure I'm doing a little of both." Picking up her wineglass, she slammed the drink, the cold liquid soothing the panicked laugh that threatened to escape her throat.

Trinh didn't remark, instead picking swallowing the rest of her drink as well. The bartender returned, his eyes darting from the empty glasses to the women in front of him. "You know, wine is meant to be savored."

Trinh handed her credit card to the man. "Thanks for the tip, Monsignor."

They were early for lunch, getting a table at a chic spot Ilsa had seen featured in a magazine only a month before. Ilsa bunched her hands under the table, fidgeting with her dress until Trinh grabbed her fist and smoothed it out.

"Stop it. You're going to break a nail. Look, there she is." Greta approached them. She was thinner than Ilsa remembered. She was a statuesque brunette with her long hair pulled tight into a high ponytail and sharp cheekbones accentuated with an expert highlighter.

Greta approached, kissing both Ilsa's cheeks before clasping their hands together. "Ilsa, it is so great to see you. You look as fabulous as ever. And who is this?" she turned to Trinh. Ilsa made the introductions and was pleased to see that Greta was gracious about Trinh being with her.

"Well, it is wonderful to see you, Ilsa, though I'm bummed to hear you didn't bring that piece of man candy you've been seeing." Greta sat gracefully down on the chair and did a small wave to the waiter, who appeared with a bottle of sparkling water and began pouring without a word.

"Nathan?" Ilsa asked.

"Obvsies! Who else? I love him. He is by far my favorite out of those guys. Everyone is all goo-goo over Theo or whatever but come on. He's *blond!* There's nothing wrong with being blonde if you're a girl but in my man? No way. Plus, Nathan seems to have a little extra to love on. Am I right?" Greta nudged Ilsa in the side with a bony elbow.

"I… um…" Ilsa struggled for words.

"I love a big man. Tell me the truth. Is he big everywhere?" her eyes glinted with meaning.

"Well, I..."

Ever the professional, Trinh rescued the line of questioning by steering the conversation to some Broadway actor photographed with Greta on page six. Greta shot Ilsa a sly smile but took the bait, talking at length about the prospects of her new friend.

"... and you know, all he wanted to ask were questions about my previous boyfriends. Then he got mad at me for telling him off. I don't care if his father owns three private islands. Is that even a flex? I can assure you I have no issue finding men to fuck. Mediocre dick is abundant. But finding the right guy is so hard!"

Trinh and Ilsa nodded along as if they understood. Settled in with a bottle of white wine that Greta insisted was *divine,* Ilsa began to relax. Talking to this hotel heiress was much less pressure than she thought it'd be.

At some point, Greta waved the waiter over and, in perfect French, ordered something for the table. Catching Ilsa's eyes, she smiled. "You'll have to try the Bonnotte de Noirmoutie. I'm assuming you eat carbs, right?"

Ilsa considered if the question was a backhanded compliment and decided to let it be. "I do."

"Good. My dietitian, Patrice, has me on a diet that confounds my friends, but potatoes are amazing, are they not? You'll love these."

Ilsa shot Trinh a look from the corner of her eye, but she had a much better poker face.

Setting down her wineglass, she narrowed her eyes at Ilsa. "Okay, enough fun talk. Let's get down to it. I love your clothes. I mean, that lavender number you put Eloise Dunning in for her show was simply breathtaking. Not to mention those great T-shirts. I heard you were looking for investors, and I want to know more."

"Oh? You do." Ilsa stumbled for words. "Right."

Reaching down, she pulled out her portfolio. It was the same one she'd presented to Davis Gallegos weeks before. Handing the folder over, Greta took it with a manicured hand. As she flipped through the pages, she was silent. Ilsa picked up her wineglass, took a large swallow, and held the glass in her hand just to have something, anything to do with her hands, while Greta looked through the pages.

For a few long minutes, Greta made small noises, *hmm* and *huh,* while reading. Closing the folder, she frowned. "Well, it looks pretty good to me, but I'm no expert, so I'll have my money manager look into it. I'm sure she'll have some questions about the profit sharing with your employees, but I like the idea." She tapped the front with a long taupe nail. "I'm assuming this is for me to keep, yes?"

"Yeah... Yes." Ilsa said, struggling with words. She cleared her throat, pulling her shoulders back. "Yes, please keep that copy, and if they have questions, Trinh or I will be happy to answer them for you."

"Wonderful. Now. Tell me. Is that really Theo's eye color, or does he wear contacts?"

Back at the hotel, Ilsa flopped onto the bed. Greta had invited Ilsa and Trinh to a party in another borough, but Ilsa declined. Trinh checked in before she left, telling her to stop worrying and to remind her to eat dinner. She knew she should be excited about the prospect of this partnership. Still, she worried after failing so spectacularly with Davis Gallegos.

Checking her phone, she saw a text from Nathan

Nathan: *I'm mad at your heart because it's pumping inside you, and I'm not.*

Just as she was about to spiral out, he sent her exactly what she needed. Smiling to herself, she clicked on his picture to call him.

He picked up after a single ring as if he was holding his phone in his hand. "How's New York? You kicking names and taking ass?"

Ilsa shook her head. "I wouldn't go that far. I met with Greta Landis for a lunch meeting. Do you remember her? She was at that party last year, you know, the one where Theo went ballistic."

Nathan let out a small noise that said, yes, he remembered. Ilsa left that alone. That was a dark night, almost ending in the breakup of both Keller and Eloise's marriage as well as the band.

"Anyway, she said she liked some designs I'd made so far and that she's been keeping an eye on me. It's nice to hear, but I don't know if it'll go anywhere. I mean, she's only twenty-three. I'm not sure I want to base my company's future on the whims of someone so young." She toed off her shoes, pulling her legs onto the bed.

"That's only four years younger than you. Should you be ageist?"

"I'm just saying, I can't trust that an heiress in her early twenties will invest in my company. Anyway, I've been thinking about numbers all day, and I don't want to discuss that. Distract me. What are you doing tomorrow?"

Nathan groaned. "Theo is dragging me out tomorrow for another early morning run."

She tsked. "Poor guy. He's a sadist."

On the other end, Nathan laughed. A warm feeling ran through her at the sound. "What about you?"

"Trinh wants to see some sights and be a tourist for a day. Maybe get a nice dinner for just the two of us. Though with how tight things are, it might be more like a hot dog from one of those carts. We have an early flight the day after tomorrow, so it shouldn't be too late of a night."

Her phone chimed, and when she pulled away, she saw a transfer of five hundred dollars in her mobile banking app from Nathan. Frowning, she wondered why she even mentioned her money troubles when she knew he'd do exactly what he did.

"Nate, stop it. I'm sending it back. I don't want your money. A hot dog is fine."

"No, treat yourself and Trinh to a nice dinner on me. It's more for her than you. She deserves a treat after taking care of you when I can't. Don't act like you haven't been a nervous wreck all day."

She rolled her eyes at his comment. "What did I tell you about that phrase?"

She could picture him putting his hands up in mock surrender. "If you don't take it, I'll send it to her and make her take you out. Actually, maybe I will do that instead."

"Fine, I'll take it, but I'm paying you back."

"I'll put it on your tab."

Rolling over, she buried her face in the pillow. "That's worse."

"What are you wearing?" he asked her.

Picking her head up from the pillow, she glanced down at her dress. "My crepe backless drop waist with the jewel neckline."

"I don't know what those words mean, but if you're wondering what I'm wearing...."

"No! Not the shorts. Nathan, I can't."

"Illy, Illy, Illy." He changed his tone every time he said her nickname from stern to humored. "You need to broaden your horizons on fashion. I know you have a little experience but these shorts—"

Ilsa laughed. "Stop. I can't hear it."

His voice got more serious. "I miss you. I know it's only been a day, but knowing you're so far away sucks. I'm used to having you near."

Tucking her hand under her cheek, she placed the phone beside her. "I know. I never expected it, but it feels odd to be far from you."

The vulnerable statement sent pressure to her chest. She'd prided herself for years on being an independent woman, and now that one sexy rock star gives her the best dick of her life, she gets mushy. She wanted to take the words back but couldn't. Wouldn't. These would be her baby steps. Allow herself to miss him when she's gone. To trust him when they're apart.

"Will you send me a picture of you and Trinh enjoying your fancy dinner tomorrow? Maybe wear something sexy?" he asked.

"Okay, I can do that for you."

"Illy, I love you."

A lump formed in her throat. Nathan was eroding all the barriers she'd built.

She couldn't speak because what could she say? In the silence of her hotel room, with no one around to see the vulnerability on her face, she felt as fragile as an iridescent bubble before it popped. One more word and everything could be gone.

Chapter Twenty-Seven

Notion
Nathan

THEO WAS RUNNING LIKE he was training for a marathon. He'd added three more miles to their morning run. Nathan wanted to support his friend on his health kick, but a man has limits.

Finally, they sat in their usual spot at Dot's diner and waited for Dot to bring their orders over. Setting down the silver creamer pitcher, Theo leaned against the table closer to Nathan. "So, how is Ilsa doing with all that Thomas Gallegos stuff?"

Nathan wrinkled his brow. It seemed odd that Theo would ask about Ilsa's funding, but he was trying to turn a new leaf, after all, so he should be grateful.

"She's disappointed, of course, but she's got a few other people she's been talking to. I had her taken to the airport a few days ago. She met with a potential investor in New York."

Theo nodded. "Nice, that's great. I'm glad she's not letting a creep like Thomas Gallegos get to her. I've met the guy once at a party, and he seems like the type."

"The type?" Nathan set down the spoon he used to stir his coffee to study Theo. Dot set their food in front of them, reminded Nathan not to tip his chair back again, and left.

Shoving a piece of turkey bacon in his mouth, Theo chewed as he talked. "Yeah, you know, the type to ask for sexual favors for funding."

"I'm sorry, what?" Nathan asked, fear trickling down his spine.

"Shit, did you not know?"

Theo pinched his forehead, "Fuck, man. I thought she told you. I really did. I heard Eloise...."

Nathan didn't have time to deal with Theo's slip of the tongue. For the first time in his life, Nathan had no appetite. He fished his wallet out of this pocket and threw down a fifty. Pushing away from the table, he stood, "I got to go."

"Wait," Theo called out to his back. "Man, I'm sorry!"

Nathan parked his truck on the street in front of the high rise, not caring about ticketing or getting towed. It'd be one more fight he would wage that day. Stalking into the lobby, he bypassed the large security desk, pausing to look up Gallegos Davis in the directory beside the elevator.

A thin young man with a shock of neon green hair sat behind the desk, his eyes growing wide at seeing Nathan in the doorway.

"Where is Thomas Gallegos?"

The man stood, his hands wringing in front of him. "Uh, Mr. Ayers. Can I call you Nathan? Mr. Gallegos is busy but—"

At the desk, Nathan set his large hands down on the cold marble and peered down at the receptionist. "If you don't tell me where I can find him, I will rip every door off its hinges on my way down this hall."

The man grew pale under his highlighted cheekbones and purple eyeliner. "Fourth door on the right. But he's on a call—"

Nathan strode away without listening to the rest. The man could be in the middle of a meeting with the president, and Nathan would still interrupt him.

The door was locked, but the flimsy knob was nothing compared to the anger boiling inside Nathan. Squaring his shoulders, he rammed the edge of the door until it flew open, wood splinters flying as the door crashed into the wall behind it. Thomas Gallegos sat behind a large glass desk, a phone poised next to his ear.

"Now, what is the meaning of this? Who do you—"

Nathan didn't let him finish.

"Are you Thomas Gallegos?"

"Yes, but I don't know who you think you are to be barging in on me."

Nathan rounded the desk and pulled the middle-aged man from his chair by the collar of his lavender shirt. The man was nine inches shorter than Nathan and likely fifty pounds lighter. His feeble hands grabbed Nathan's arms as his feet left the ground.

"Did you come on to, Ilsa? Try to get her to sleep with you for an investment?"

The man's eyes grew wide as recognition crossed his face. "Look, Mr. Ayers, I don't know what she told you, but she must have misunderstood something. I would never—"

Nathan dragged him backward, his toes skimming the ground until he was pushed against a wall with a loud *oof* coming out of his mouth. Nathan's hands were tight on the front of the man's shirt. He slammed the man into the wall a second time. A potted plant clattered beside them and fell to the ground with a loud crack, spilling dirt and greenery over the cream carpet. "What you're never going to do is talk to her again. You won't look at her. You won't think about her. You're going to stop badmouthing her around town. In fact, you're never going to say her name again."

"It was a misunderstanding. She's new to business relationships and—"

"I said stop talking about her." Nathan removed his hands from the man's shirt, letting him drop to the floor.

On his hands and knees, the man looked up at him, a sneer lacing his face. "I don't know what kind of backward place you're from, but this is not how we do business. Ms. Kruger may not have what it takes to gain investment from my company, but at least she wasn't some inbred hooligan punching doors when things don't go her way."

Nathan let the comment sting, glaring down at the man on the floor. In his periphery, he saw a few people standing in the broken doorway, watching them. The receptionist, a few twenty-something employees, and a middle-aged woman with hair pulled back as severely as possible.

"Thomas, what is the meaning of this?" The older woman asked, her eyes darting from Gallegos on the floor to Nathan above him.

"Nothing, Irene. Just a misunderstanding." Thomas stood on shaky knees, brushing little bits of dirt from his dress pants. "Mr. Ayers was about to leave."

The fight left him as he stared down at this man so much smaller than him. He'd said his piece and hoped that was enough to keep Ilsa safe from the asshole.

Brushing past the onlookers, he made his way down the hall to the waiting elevators. It had been years since he was in a fight, but he was fairly certain Thomas Gallegos wouldn't press charges. All that would do would be invite the press. Coverage of a rock star getting in a fight was a minor news story, but a middle-aged venture capitalist? Thomas Gallegos was a slimeball, but there was no way he'd want business partners to know he was thrown around his office like a rag doll.

"Send the bill for the door to my lawyer," Nathan called to the receptionist as he made his way to the stairwell.

Theo and Keller were waiting for him at the house when he returned, blood still pumping in his ears.

"What did you do?" Keller asked.

Pausing past them, he stomped into his kitchen to grab a beer from his fridge. Disregarding the harm it could cause his marble countertops, he popped the cap off with a fist slam. He could feel his bandmate's eyes on him as he chugged the beer. Theo was a little scared, and Keller was confused. Wiping his mouth with the back of his hand, he grabbed three more beers out of the fridge and offered them. Both men took one, holding it in their hands as a talisman to protect them.

"What did you do?" Keller repeated.

"I took care of it," Nathan replied.

"What does that mean?" Theo asked.

Nathan opened his second beer with less force, taking a large swallow before responding. "It means that man won't bother her again. It means I'm protecting the woman I love from a creep. I took care of it."

"Does Ilsa know?" Theo asked.

Nathan set the beer down on the counter and studied Theo. "No, but the better question is, how did you know? How the hell could you know about that before me?"

Theo looked sheepish. "I overheard Eloise telling Keller the other day and figured you already knew. You know, I'm trying to be a better friend, asking about other people instead of being a self-serving asshole."

Keller frowned. "And yet again, your big mouth got you in trouble, didn't it?"

It was a low blow but one Theo deserved. He had the decency to accept the insult. Theo looked at Nathan. "I really thought she told you."

"Well, she didn't," Nathan snapped. He brought the beer to his mouth only to realize it was empty. Damn. He couldn't imagine why Ilsa would keep something like this from him. The moment he found out, he had one focus—find the man who threatened her and neutralize the issue.

"You need to tell her," Keller said. "Trust me. You do not want her finding out the wrong way."

Nathan took a steadying breath. He wasn't a lightweight, but slamming two beers in five minutes would impact anyone. Setting the empty bottle down on the counter, he leaned against the marble. "You're right. But I can't do it over the phone. She'll be home tomorrow around lunchtime. I'll talk to her then."

"How do you think she'll react?" Theo asked.

For the first time since finding out, Nathan thought about the question. She probably would be mad. She didn't like people helping her, but what was the alternative? He loved her. This is what people who love someone do for each other. She'd have to understand.

"I don't know." He answered honestly.

Keller clapped him on the back. "Don't fuck it up. Keep your head on straight, and whatever happens, don't get drunk and take groupies back to your house."

Nathan narrowed his eyes at his friend. "That was you."

"Yeah, I speak from experience." Keller shook his head, glancing at Theo like *check this guy out.*

Nathan ran a hand over his face, the grime of a sweaty morning run and the dirt from Thomas Gallegos's office plants on his skin.

After the guys left, his skin still buzzed with nervous energy. He worked out, lifting in front of the mirror until his biceps quaked from exertion. Nothing was taking away the sensation of Thomas Gallegos's shirt in his fist.

How could Ilsa let that weasel touch her and not tell him? Did she not trust him? Did she not care enough? The last time he hit another man was when he found his sister's ex sleeping around on her. He defended his sister, and Ilsa deserved someone to defend her too. No matter what games she wanted to play, how she wanted it described—she was his. It was his duty as the man who loved her to defend her.

His heavy metal song paused for a second as a text came through.

Ilsa in some rainbow flower dress, the front was low cut, showing off exactly the right amount of cleavage. He could see the peek-a-boo of her pink heels. Trinh, tiny beside her, both smiling big for the camera.

Ilsa: *Dinner was amazing. I'll buy next time.*

Damn, he missed her. Staring at her face in the photo, the curl of her blonde hair around her face, the pink of her lips, and the brightness in her hazel eyes.

His thumb hovered over the image as if he could touch her through the screen. Swallowing the lump in his throat, he set his phone down on the bench beside him and picked up the barbells.

Chapter Twenty-Eight

DART

ILSA

A FTER GETTING THROUGH SECURITY, Ilsa found a quiet spot to sit and catch up on emails while Trinh went to the shop for a last-minute souvenir to bring back for her mother. Settling into the pleather terminal seat, she balanced her overpriced latte in the crook of her arm while she dug out her ringing phone. Davis Gallegos flashed on the screen. She couldn't imagine what reason the venture capitalist firm would call her. Thomas Gallegos seemed to make himself very clear on his expectations of her. Even if Irene Davis suddenly showed any interest, she couldn't imagine partnering with their firm, allowing his pockets to be lined despite his piggish ways. But curiosity got the best of her.

"This is Ilsa," she answered.

"Miss Kruger, it's Irene Davis. I'm glad I reached you."

Ilsa switched the call from her speaker to her ear. "Are you?"

"Well, yes. I heard you were visiting Greta Landis in New York. Rumors about her diversifying her investments have been circulating."

Ilsa wasn't going to give this woman any information. Who knows what she would do with it? "If I can be frank, Ms. Davis. During that initial meeting, you didn't seem very interested during the meeting. I assumed you had passed."

On the phone, Irene's crisp transatlantic accent was more prominent. "To be honest, during that meeting, I wasn't sure you were a good investment at the time. As you know, many young women have more impressive portfolios than yours, larger social media presences, and better backers. You know that socialite, Devlin Teague is starting a line, and she certainly is a more profitable investment at this point."

"I would disagree, but I also know you wouldn't be wasting your time calling me if you were only turning me down for the investment."

"You are a smart one. As I said, Thomas and I were unsure if you were a sound investment. But after hearing about how you handled yourself with Thomas, I am reconsidering."

Ilsa's palms slick against her plastic phone case. She cleared the blockage that formed in her throat. "Um. Did Mr. Gallegos say something? Because if I may, nothing happened between us, and I would never cross the boundary between professional and personal, and if he said—"

"Thomas didn't say a thing." Irene's voice lit up with humor. "It was that boyfriend of yours."

A chill washed down her spine at the words. "My... what?" she stumbled out.

"Nathan Ayers came and had a, what shall I call it? A talk? With Thomas yesterday."

Ilsa felt her heart sink. She hadn't told Nathan but vaguely remembered telling Eloise after her third syrupy margarita. Did Eloise tell Keller? Did the whole band know about Thomas Gallegos making a pass at her?

"I don't understand."

"Mr. Ayers came in and, to put it in no uncertain terms, scared the shit out of Thomas. Rightfully so. You certainly were not the first to be propositioned by him. I know I was in my day, but I must say, I wriggled out of his clutches more artfully than you." She gave a barking laugh. "Sometimes these men just need a little ego stroke before you take their job."

Fear rose in her. The image of Nathan barging in on a meeting at the office, yelling and pushing Thomas Gallegos around, flooded her mind. As much as she would've relished the sight of that scum getting his comeuppance, she would never want her name attached to such a display. "I never asked him to do that, believe me. I don't even know how he found out about it."

On the other end of the line, Irene tsked. "You should be grateful for Mr. Ayers. I wouldn't be calling you if it wasn't for him."

Anger thrummed through Ilsa at the statement. *Grateful? Indebted?* All the things she never wanted to be. Never wanted to feel. It didn't matter how hard she worked, the sleepless nights, the calloused and sliced fingers, and the bloodshot eyes.

Her hard work didn't mean shit in this land of nepotism and fame.

"So why are you calling me?" The politeness in her voice before faded away. What was the point? She could already see where this conversation was headed.

"I would like to offer you partial funding for your line at a higher rate of return for us, of course, with the assurance that you will remain in the press in association with Nathan Ayers."

Her voice was thin with exhaustion. "I can't give you that assurance. My personal relationships aren't part of my business dealings."

"Well, they should be. You've lived here long enough. It's all about who you know, and you, Miss Kruger, know quite a big fish. If you were smart, you'd use that to your advantage."

Not trying to keep the ice out of her tone, Ilsa gripped the phone in her hand until her thumb throbbed. "Ms. Davis, as much as I appreciate your offer, I will have to refuse. I can't have my personal relationship be the reason I will or will not receive funding for my business. My employees deserve better. I deserve better."

On the other end, Irene paused for a long moment. "Very well. I can appreciate your wanting to make your own way in this world, whether or not I agree. Woman to woman, I applaud you. But as I need to protect the integrity of my business, I cannot, in good faith, award you the investment without assurances of help from Mr. Ayers. We all have our keepers, and I am beholden to mine."

It took all she had not to hang up on the woman.

When Trinh returned with an *I heart NY* baseball hat sitting jauntily on her head, Ilsa was still staring at her phone. Glancing up at her friend, a wave of nausea rolled through her. Had she made a mistake? As promising as the meeting with Greta Landis was, there were no guarantees until the ink was dry. They still needed an investor, or the company would never expand past its lowly stage. She knew if she approached Nathan with the idea, he would agree. Of course, he would. And it'd be one more item in the growing mountain of inequity between them. All the things he was doing for her. Even if the episode with Gallegos wasn't publicized, people talked. In the industry, everyone knew everyone's business.

Would all that she'd worked for be attributed to his success? Being with Nathan meant she wouldn't be Ilsa Kruger, the designer. She'd be Nathan Ayers's girlfriend. She'd always be the second name listed in the press. Her identity would recede as his star power outshone her.

She could handle that as long as they kept business separate. But if he was the reason she got that funding, the future of her company may rely upon his wanting to stay with her.

She could never do that. People would know. And worst of all, she would never feel like she earned her place.

"You okay?" Trinh asked, sitting beside Ilsa.

Shaking her head, Ilsa handed Trinh the phone where the news alert had pushed a notification about a blind item.

Sit Here By Me; your source for anonymous gossip
Southern Charm only goes so far. We have some big ideas that a certain rock star dropped the awe-shucks act and picked up his fists last Friday when he threatened a prominent businessman in his own office. Was this a deal gone wrong? A lady love?

Trinh furrowed her brow. "What is this? I don't understand."

Leaning forward, Ilsa put her elbows on her knees and buried her face in her hands. Her long nails scraped her scalp as she tried to focus on how to get the words out. Huffing out a loud breath, Ilsa turned to look at Trinh.

"Thomas Gallegos came onto me at that lunch meeting. I turned him down, of course, but I guess Nathan found out somehow and confronted him yesterday. I just heard from Irene Davis about it."

Trinh handed the phone back with a confused look. "You didn't tell him yourself?"

Ilsa shook her head, glancing at the screen again. "He has this overwrought sense of chivalry. I knew he'd freak out. And I handled it... kind of."

"And freak out he did."

"According to Irene Davis, he '*scared the shit out of Thomas Gallegos.*'"

Trinh wrinkled her nose. "I don't know. The guy seemed like a bit of a creep to me. I'm sure there are a lot of people who'd want to do the same."

Ilsa shoved the phone back into her bag. "That's not the point. It was a business relationship. I can't be the girl whose boyfriend punches a guy for looking at me wrong. I worked my ass off to get that initial meeting, and now what? Word will spread, and no one will want to work with me because I'll be seen as unprofessional, or worse, all I'll get is shitty proposals. Like Irene Davis gave me. She said they'd only fund me if I agreed to continue my association with Nathan in the press."

"Of course, he would." Trinh shook her head, a smile on her face. "No question, is that all it was? You know he'd be happy to work with you."

Tensing her jaw, Ilsa spoke slowly. "I told her no."

Trinh blinked a few times, her neon purple eyeshadow crinkling in the corners. "What? Why?"

"They only want to fund my line because we're sleeping together. Because they obviously see no value in my product, only what his celebrity could bring to them."

Trinh sat beside Ilsa, taking her hand in hers. "That's not true—"

"It is," Ilsa interrupted. "Mr. Gallegos let me know that hundreds of people out there will do whatever it takes to get their products funded, and then Irene Davis says the same thing weeks later? If I agreed, what would that say about my product? That the only value it has was being made by a rock star's girlfriend? What about who I am? What about all my hard work?"

"It's okay to use the connections you have."

"This is more than that, and you know it. Thomas Gallegos wouldn't have met with me again if it wasn't for me being seen with Nathan. It has nothing to do with who I am as a designer and everything to do with how I look on Nathan's arm at an awards show."

Above their heads, their group was being called for boarding. Trinh stood, taking Ilsa's bag in one hand and holding it out to her.

"Give the guy a break. There are a lot of shitty men out there, but he's a good one."

Taking the bag from her, Ilsa hefted it over her shoulder. She wanted to believe Trinh, she wanted to believe *in* Nathan, but doubt was creeping in, sure as it had always been there.

When they arrived back at LAX, a driver was waiting at the doors with a sign for them. Ilsa knew Nathan had hired the driver or had Alexis call for the car. As the exhaustion from the swirling thoughts and the six-hour flight seeped into her bones, she couldn't fight it. Her car was left at Nathan's before she left New York, and she'd need to get it soon, anyway. If she had more energy, she'd have called a rideshare, but Trinh walked ahead, happy for the free ride.

The drive was quiet in the LA traffic, but it took almost two hours before Ilsa was deposited at Nathan's door. Before she could make it up the drive, the door was pulled open, and Nathan was there, all rumpled hair and day-old scruff. His green eyes were concerned as he looked her over.

Taking the bag from her hand, he held the door open and guided her into the house. Silently, she walked down the hall and into the bedroom, where she sat on the edge of the bed.

Nathan followed after her, setting her bag down on the floor.

Wiping her hand over her face, she turned to him. "I heard what happened."

He blinked a few times. "Okay, um..."

She put up her hand to stop him, the last of her energy draining away. "Nate, I can't have this conversation now. I'm going to wash my face and go to bed. We can talk tomorrow, not tonight."

Before he could say anything, she moved to the bathroom, where all her skincare products were lined up beside her toothbrush. Seeing the little bottles in a row filled her with a juxtaposition of comfort and fear. Was this domestic life what she wanted? To be pampered in his shadow? To never have her own success? Nausea rolled through her at the thought.

Her hands were heavy as she washed her face and did a short version of her nighttime routine. When she walked back into the bedroom, Nathan stood beside the bed, the corners of the blanket tucked down for her to get in. Wordlessly, she climbed between the sheets, the cool cotton smooth against her skin. Nathan bent down and pressed a kiss to her head.

"I love you, Illy."

Her chest hurt at the words. Swallowing down the pain, she turned over and closed her eyes.

Chapter Twenty-Nine

FROGGING
NATHAN

H E KNEW THE SECOND she arrived that she was livid. Below the dark circle around her eyes and the slow way she walked up the drive, there was tension in her gaze he'd never seen before. He knew she might be upset about the way he reacted, but she had to understand why he made the choice he did. What kind of man would he be to allow such disrespect to occur?

He watched as she walked out of his room wearing a new outfit. He'd gotten used to seeing her in his old T-shirts first thing in the morning. Her hair was wet from the shower and pulled up in a topknot. She looked like she was ready to go.

Holding the mug of coffee out to her, she took it, sitting at the large dining table instead of the breakfast nook where they could be close.

She took a large gulp of the coffee, and he could feel her gaze as he made his own. She was far away. Her legs crossed primly at the ankles as she sipped her coffee and waited for him to talk.

Rip it off like a band-aid. She can't be that mad.

Sitting on the stool across from her, he set his coffee mug on the counter. "So, you heard what happened."

"Irene Davis called me. Told me all about it. And even if I didn't, there was a blind item about you. It wasn't hard to connect the dots."

He studied her. Her jaw was tense, and her knuckles were white around the coffee mug. She really was mad, even after sleeping on it. "It wasn't how I wanted you to find out, but I'm glad I took care of it."

She huffed loudly, burying her head in her hands for a moment before running her fingers over her wet hair. "I never asked you to do that. I would never ask for that."

"You don't have to. This is what I'm here to do. He won't bother you again now."

She shook her head at him. "You are unbelievable. Do you understand how much you're screwing me?"

"Me? I'm protecting you. When a man talks to you like that, you call me. No one has the right..."

"No. You don't have the right. Listen here, Nathan. I do not need you fighting my battles for me. I am a grown woman. This is my future. You have no say in how I conduct my business."

"So, I should just sit by and allow some douchebag in a five-thousand-dollar suit to harass you?"

"Yes, you will because I can handle it. Was I mad? Yes, of course. But I have never needed a man to fight my battles, and I refuse to start now."

"I'm only trying to help you, Illy. Trying to protect you."

Ilsa scoffed. "Protect me? Please."

Nathan's mood soured. "What's wrong with protecting you? With trying to help you?"

"Were you protecting me, or were you protecting your ego? Is your issue with him manhandling me or how you think I belong to you and no one else can touch me?"

Nathan sputtered. "What? That's not..."

"I handled it, Nathan. It might not be the way you liked, but it was handled. I am the only one who can be outraged by what happens to my body and my life. Not you."

"I was trying to help. What's wrong with me looking out for you?"

"Maybe nothing today. But what about tomorrow? No one will take me seriously if I don't fight these battles myself. And when you're not around..."

"Where am I going to go?"

Ilsa opened her mouth and then snapped her jaw shut, the clack of her teeth sounding in the room. Sucking her lips into her mouth and squinched her eyes shut as if she was in pain.

Nathan lowered his voice and asked again. "Where do you think I'm going to go, Ilsa?"

When Ilsa opened her eyes, they were overflowing with tears. Glossy over her hazel irises, the sight took the breath from his chest. He'd never seen her cry in all the time they knew each other. She put out a hand to stop him from moving closer and tilted her head back to the ceiling. She stared until the tears receded and all that was left was the wet clump on her bottom lash line.

"Nathan, I know you're trying to help. But you have to let me do this myself."

Nathan shook his head, trying to wrap his head around what she was asking him. Why would she want to fight this battle alone when he was right there, loving and supporting her?

"But I can help you. I'm just trying to help you. That's what any good boyfriend would do."

"You are not any boyfriend. You are not some random guy, Nathan. That you can't understand the power dynamic here, that you can't see how this affects me, proves how incredibly naïve you are about this. You put off this persona like you're some hometown boy, like you still ride around in a pickup and drink cheap beer. When you don't. You are a rock star, Nathan. Stop acting like you're not. Stop acting like you're not a celebrity. If I were with you, truly with you, fame would be an added layer to our relationship. You act like it's just you and me. That we're the only ones who matter in this choice, but that's not true."

"You're overcomplicating things here."

Ilsa shook her head, the weight of the words heavy on her chest. "I'm not. I've worked my whole life for this level of success. In the years that I've struggled to get my company off the ground, you have no idea how scary it is for me to do all this work, only to be told that I won't achieve my dreams if I don't attach myself to someone else. You are wonderful, Nathan. You are the best man I have ever known. But you did not do this work. And I refuse to have your name cited as the reason I'm successful."

"No one is asking you to do that."

"But they'll say it just the same. I've lived here long enough to know it's true. How many influencers and half celebrities launch makeup lines, perfumes, purses, or whatever as they coast on the celebrity status of those around them? That may be fine for them, but that will never be me. I do it on my terms, or not at all."

"Even if it means you don't get the funding?"

"Yes. Even then."

The idea of her losing everything she worked for was heavy on his chest. Why wouldn't she accept this help? Why was she being so stubborn about this? All he wanted to do was help her; she was acting like being with him was causing the breakdown of her whole life. "Why can't you accept that I'm trying to help you? Why do you fight me on this instead of being grateful?"

Ilsa sucked in a breath. The moment he said the words, he knew they were wrong. But he was too angry now to take them back. She didn't need him or want him the way he wanted her. And she never would. It was a moment of truth.

"I know you're scared. You treat me as if I don't understand heartbreak? Because I didn't have a rough childhood, you assume I don't know what it feels like to be hurt? I'm hurting now. You act like it's the brave path to close yourself off from everyone who cares about you. But you're a coward. I love you, Illy. There has never been a day since I met you that I didn't love you in some small way. I'm not scared of loving you. But you can't say the same. You won't."

She stood from the table, pacing the floor before him. Her mouth would open as if she was about to say something then it would close.

When she finally spoke, it was with ice in her voice. "You tell me you love me. You say all these words as if they mean anything to me. When I needed you to trust that I could solve my own issues, you disregarded everything I told you I needed to soothe your precious ego. Don't act like what you did was for me. It was all you and your false sense of chivalry. If I can't trust you to believe me when I say don't get involved in my business, how can I trust you won't do this again?"

Nathan took a deep breath, her words hitting him. She was right. He knew she was. She never asked him to help her. He thought of all the conversations they had where she was clear about what she needed, and all the times he disregarded that.

She was close enough that if he reached out, he could've touched the softness of her shirt, but he knew she didn't want that. Her voice softer, she stopped pacing and stood with her arms crossed around her body.

"It doesn't matter how much I care for you. It doesn't matter if I might love you. I won't be my mother. I refuse to be with someone who expects me to be *grateful* for something I never asked for. Never once did I ask you to take care of me like that, Nathan. I never asked for the air conditioning or the food. And I sure as hell never asked you to go into a potential business partner's office and assault him. I won't listen to your fucked up justification. Because I know exactly how this ends. You never accept that I don't need you to fight my battles. And I won't be beholden to a man who holds so much power over me."

"What are you saying?" he asked, knowing her answer before she spoke.

"Right now, I can't see you," her voice cracked at the word, you.

"For how long?" he whispered. Fear clenched inside him at the thought of her never wanting to see him again.

She shook her head. "I don't know, a day, a week? There's a lot of work to do, and I can't have this hanging over me. I need time to think."

Every impulse in his body screamed at him not to let her go. But to not trust her now, after he'd so royally fucked up, would only drive her further away.

"Okay, I'll give you all the time you need."

Nodding at him, she turned away, emerging a few minutes later with her rolling suitcase and keys. Pausing at the doorway, she glanced back at him. Her eyes were red-rimmed, and her face was blotchy pink.

"I meant it when I said you are the best man I've ever known. Just give me a few days, okay?"

Walking to the door, he grabbed her suitcase and opened the door to get to her car. Putting her suitcase in her trunk, he turned back to look at her. She'd followed him out to the car and rested her hand on the roof, studying him. Holding the door open, he took his chance that she wouldn't push him away and leaned into her. She didn't step back, didn't push him away. This kiss was soft, full of sadness and regret. He could taste the salt from the tears in his mouth.

He wanted to push her up against the car and kiss her madly, make her want to stay, make her beg him for more. He knew he could do it. But she would regret it, and he could never live with himself if she regretted him. Finishing the soft kiss, he pulled away, cupping her cheek where she was crying anew.

"Let me know you got home okay."

She nodded before climbing into her car and starting it up.

He stood in the driveway as she pulled away. Seeing the fading dots of her taillights, he wondered how he screwed up everything he thought he knew about loving someone.

For too long, he stood there in his professionally landscaped yard, wearing his over-priced slippers, and waited for her text.

An hour later, his phone chimed with a single line.

Ilsa: *I'm home. Take care.*

He hoped it wasn't goodbye.

Chapter Thirty

THIMBLE
ILSA

L EAVING NATHAN'S HOUSE, THE tears stayed away until she rounded the corner. Once her car was out of sight of his home, she pulled over to the side of the road and put it in park. A sense of overwhelming vulnerability flowed through her. This man could destroy her. He could take every part of her well-constructed heart and shatter it.

If this was love, she wanted no part in it.

She remembered little of the drive home. When she arrived at her small studio, she collapsed into a bed that felt too large. She had plans to make, bridges to build, and a business to run the next morning, but until then, she would burrow under too-cold blankets and cry until she fell asleep.

She ignored the worried texts and calls from her friends until her phone died, and then it was the oppressive silence of her warring thoughts.

When she left Nathan's home, she was furious. More than she'd been in years. She prided herself on her strong will to keep up with every situation. She knew what kind of woman she was and what she wanted. Being with Nathan—falling in love with him—changed everything she held dear. She could see now that pushing him away was the wrong choice, but what was the alternative? How could she know he wouldn't undermine everything she worked for again?

The next day she charged her phone just enough to let the shop know she wouldn't be in for a few days before turning it off and opening a bottle of Nathan's favorite seven-dollar Moscato she had delivered for thirty-nine dollars. She thought of taking a bath with the bottle, drowning her sorrows in a sweet wine and bath bomb salve, but the last bath she took was with Nathan. Staring down at her small tub, she grimaced at the chipped pink porcelain. The shampoos and conditioners jammed into her rusted shower caddy in the corner, the three loofahs in various stages of unraveling, and the razor in desperate need of a new head. It all felt so empty.

She was empty.

Sitting on the edge of the toilet, she tipped the cup to drain into her mouth. The wine tasted of sugared grapes, of sweetness. She was reminded of how Nathan would hold her face in his and brush his lips against hers. Her lips puckering, she swallowed the syrupy liquid down before picking up the bottle from its spot between her retro pink sink and her makeshift towel rack. Glancing at the bottle, she saw it was half gone. A sommelier she dated briefly told her once that there were five glasses in each bottle. That man clearly never had his heart broken over a rock star before because she now knew the correct answer was two full coffee mugs.

Refilling her cup, she sipped the liquid slower, pondering whether the bath or a nap would be a better use of her wallowing time when there was a quick rap on her door. Setting her mug down on the edge of her crowded sink, between a perfume bottle and her toothpaste, she walked to the door. It didn't sound like Nathan's confident knock. Setting her hand on the door, she knew it wasn't Nathan. If it were, she would be able to sense him.

Pulling her robe tighter, she looked through the peephole and groaned. Of all the people she didn't want to see at this moment, this was worse than she anticipated.

"Hello, Mitzie," she chimed as she opened the door for her mother.

Her mother walked in, bringing in a cloud of Clinique Happy with her. Stopping in the bedroom/living room/office, Mitzie turned on her heels to look at Ilsa still in the doorway.

"Sweetie, you look terrible. Have you been falling asleep with your makeup on again? You know that ages you."

"Good to see you too." Closing the door, Ilsa kept a hand on the doorknob, hoping Mitzie would only stop by for a quick hello.

From Phoenix. Likely.

Mitzie frowned, coming forward to lay a hand on her daughter's cheek. "I only worry. Is that such a crime, wanting you to look your best?" She stepped back, clapping her hands together. "Now, do you have any diet coke? The airline only had Pepsi products, and I couldn't drink that. And then Doug didn't stop because he was already late for his chiropractic conference or something. I don't know..."

"I don't have any soda."

Mitzie adjusted the oversized bag on her bony shoulder. "Then we'll have to go out to lunch. From the smell of your breath and that half-empty bottle of wine in the bathroom, I guess you need me to drive?"

Ilsa opened her mouth to respond, but her mother cut her off.

"No excuses. I came all the way to see you, now get dressed. That robe is doing nothing for your figure."

Arriving at the over-hyped restaurant her mother insisted on, they waited an hour for a table on the patio in case "a celebrity might walk by."

Ilsa refrained from telling her mother she'd met her share of celebrities in the past year and felt hung out to dry from it.

Sipping an iced tea, no sugar, her mother insisted, Ilsa's lips puckered at the bitter taste. She'd become used to the sweet tea in Nathan's fridge. Across the table, Mitzie was perusing the menu while keeping one eye on the other diners in case one ended up being a reality star.

When the waiter came by, Mitzie ordered her $47 grilled vegetable salad, hold the dressing. Ilsa started ordering the ravioli before her mother interrupted.

"Dear, do you really want something so heavy for lunch?"

Ilsa narrowed her eyes at her mother. She was in California for three hours and already passing judgment.

"Yes. I do." Turning to the waiter, she repeated her order.

After the waiter took their menus, Mitzie tsked before picking up her drink. "No need to get huffy with me, Ilsabeth. It was only a suggestion."

Pinching the bridge of her nose between her fingers, she felt the dig of her long nails in her skin. She didn't care if it left little red marks. The sting was worth it to keep her grounded.

Mitzie flapped her napkin dramatically before laying it on her legs.

"Now, sweetie, what is happening with you and that handsome rock star? He looked quite smitten from the pictures I saw. Of course, you never call me, so how am I supposed to know..."

Ilsa considered lying to her mother, but the energy to make up a story was more than she could offer. "Nothing's going on. It didn't work out."

Mitzie's hand stilled on her dripping water glass. "Oh, no. What did you do?"

Ilsa scoffed. "What makes you think I did anything?"

"Okay," her mother dragged out the *oh* sound. "What didn't you do?"

"It didn't work out. It happens sometimes," Ilsa snipped.

Frowning, Mitzie placed a hand on top of Ilsa's. "I can help you get him back. Tell me about it, and we'll come up with a plan."

Sliding her hand back, Mitzie's square French tips scraped against her skin. "What if I don't want to? What if he was the one who screwed things up, and I don't want to be with him anymore?"

The lie was bitter in her mouth. She missed Nathan with a hunger she'd never known, and while he made a mistake, she knew she was equally to blame for this implosion.

"That's silly talk. Don't be ridiculous. He's a rock star, Ilsa. A rich rock star. Of course, you want him back. A man like that could take care of you for the rest of your life if you played your cards right."

"Mother." Her voice was sharp. She hadn't called her anything but Mitzie in almost fifteen years. Taking a deep breath, Ilsa's words were measured. "I was never with Nathan because he was famous or rich…"

"Well, of course not," Mitzie said with mock sincerity.

"No. Really. We aren't together because he potentially cost me a business deal by meddling in my affairs."

"Well, men like to be helpful, change tires, make business deals, etc."

"I didn't want that. This life I've built is mine. I have to protect it."

"Sounds like you're ruining it by being too independent if you ask me." Mitzie took a long drink of water as Ilsa slowly simmered across the table. "If only you'd called me. I could have given you some relationship advice, and you wouldn't find yourself in this mess."

"And why would I go to you, *Mitzie*?" she hissed her mother's name.

Mitzie blinked at her several times, shock coloring her cheeks at Ilsa's tone.

"Because I'm your mother. That's what daughters do."

"Is it? Because…"

Mitzie cut her off. "Ilsa, you don't understand now, but you'll see once you have a child of your own. I tried my best with you and the circumstances we were dealt."

Ilsa snorted, shaking her head. "You are delusional. And for the record, I'm not having kids. Ever. So, you can forget about that little dream of yours."

"Was I really such a terrible mother that you wouldn't want to have your own?"

Ilsa was used to this guilt trip. It was as familiar as her favorite pair of jeans. "Believe it or not, my decision not to have a child has very little to do with you. I've never wanted them and wouldn't be a good mother. Why subject a child to being unwanted?"

"And that's what you think you were, unwanted?"

Ilsa wavered. Saying the words out loud would be too real. She couldn't form them.

"I always wanted you. Why would I have spent so much time and energy on your interests if I didn't want you? I only pushed you into all that because I wanted more for you than I got. I knew you could do anything with that face."

"Anything with a man, you mean. And those were never my dreams or interests. The modeling, the pageants. It was never me."

Mitzie frowned. "Women didn't have the same options back then. I wasn't going back home with a baby in tow and listening to my mother's judgment. I did what I thought was best for us."

"Do you know, I have no idea how to be in a relationship because of what you taught me?"

Red filled her mother's cheeks as she sputtered a response. "Me? What would I have to do with this? I'm not responsible for your romantic failings, Ilsa. I tried my best with you, but I won't be held liable for you screwing up what could've been a great catch."

"A catch?" Ilsa snorted. "A catch. Yeah, that sounds about right. Because that's all you taught me to do. How to reel them in, how to hook them, and make them think it was their idea. Never how to stay. Never how to be on equal footing with a man. No, we have to reel in another good one, and who cares how they treat us? Who cares if they leave after a few months? We'll just get a new one."

Mitzie coughed delicately, pink blotches forming on the thin skin of her throat. "Well. If that's how you felt. I was just trying to find a good man to support us."

"We didn't need a good man to support us. I needed my mother to support me. For you to show me how to make it on my own. I needed you to love *me* for me and not for what I could give you. I needed..." Ilsa's words died in her throat, the tears choking her. She was in one of the most public restaurants in LA, crying into her twelve-dollar iced tea.

Mitzie pushed her white linen napkin over to Ilsa, who wiped her eyes, thankful she didn't put on mascara before they left.

"Now, that's enough, sweetie. We can't be crying here," Mitzie whispered.

Ilsa glanced at the street. She doubted anyone would recognize her, bare-faced and blotchy, but the paparazzi were known to hang out around the place. It would be her luck to be in the background of a photo looking like an abstract painting of red and yellow. Ilsa excused herself and went to the bathroom. In the reflection, she looked even worse—red-rimmed eyes and chapped lips. Wetting a towel, she dabbed her face with cold water, trying to pull some of the swelling from her skin. Glancing back at the mirror, she was now pink and slightly wet. No improvement.

Pulling her phone out, she scrolled to the last text from Nathan.

Stay safe. I'm here when you're ready.

Ready. Ilsa shook her head. Ready for what? To have her curated life ruined? To be broken again? To let him down when he realized she wasn't worth all the effort.

That's what it was. She knew it deep down. All her life, she'd seen how the men left her mother when they realized she wasn't worth the gifts and the attention. How could she ever expect a man like Nathan to love her when she'd never experienced it before? She had no idea what love looked like.

Settling onto a small stool, she stared at Nathan's picture saved on her phone. It was them at Eloise's release party. His arms were around her thighs as he held her above him. A wide smile stretched his face as he looked up at her. She could still feel the warmth of his body as he held her, the strength in his arms, and the knowledge that he would keep her safe in the air above him. Swallowing down the lump in her throat, she clicked her phone off.

She couldn't do this. Squeezing her phone, she willed herself to stop crying. To get back out on the patio with its grimy sun and thirty-dollar brownies and finish this lunch with her mother. There wouldn't be some epiphany with Mitzie. She was not her mother. These were her choices. Just as she told Nathan, it was her life to live, and trying to be the opposite of her wayward mom was no better for her than being the same.

Returning to the table, she saw her lunch sitting there with a small to-go container next to it.

"Oh good, you're feeling better. I asked the waiter to box up half your lunch. That way, you can portion control better."

Ilsa rolled her eyes, opened the to-go box, and started eating out of that first. No, she didn't have to live her life in complete opposition to her mother, but dammit, she was going to eat every one of these forty-dollar ravioli.

Somehow, she managed to go to the store the next day. Her body felt like it was swimming in jelly. All her movements dragged against some unseen force. She talked to her employees, listened as Trinh updated her on business dealings, and even signed a few invoices.

But she wasn't really there.

By the end of the day, she sent all her employees home early and shut the store down. Trinh tried to stay late and talk, but Ilsa wouldn't let her. She knew her friend was worried, but Ilsa couldn't muddle what little mind she had left by blurring the professional and personal line with Trinh.

Greta Landis's assistant had emailed, letting her know the lawyers were currently looking over the contract and would get back to her soon with the terms. She should've been ecstatic. Instead, she felt numb. What good was this achievement when she was alone with her pinking shears and a five-day-old green juice to keep her company? Wrinkling her nose, she looked at the juice. How long had that been on her desk?

That's gross.

She picked up the plastic bottle and walked out of the office to throw it away in the large garbage bag by the front door. A knock sounded on the glass, and she shoved the mottled bottle into the bag before opening the door.

"Sorry, we're cl—" her words died out, seeing Eloise on the other side of the door, a large coffee cup in each hand.

"Hi, saw your car, brought you a coffee." She pushed into the room, thrusting the paper cup at Ilsa.

"It's seven at night."

Eloise shrugged. "So, don't drink it. You think I actually came here to bring you coffee?"

Glancing around the store, Eloise set her cup on the counter and went over to a mannequin wearing a purple wrap dress. "This is cute. I might have to get this."

Pinching the bridge of her nose, Ilsa counted to five in her head. "Eloise, now isn't really a good—"

Eloise interrupted her. "A good time to talk to your friend? It is, actually. Trinh called me. I don't even know how she got my number, but I'm glad she called. I knew you'd be bad since you haven't answered my texts. But I didn't think you'd be this bad."

"What are you talking about? I'm fine."

"Obviously not. I mean, look at you." She waved a hand in the air to indicate Ilsa's general self.

Ilsa looked down at her outfit. She wore an oversized T-shirt and baggy athletic shorts with a bleach stain.

"What, I can't try to be comfortable?"

Eloise sniffed before laughing, "Uh, no. *You* can't. I mean, you're not even wearing any accessories. For anyone else, it would be nothing but you? The perpetually overdressed one?"

Ilsa folded her arms across her chest. "What's your point?"

Eloise sat on a small couch, patting the spot next to her. "Tell me what's going on, and don't you dare say nothing."

Suddenly the urge to let it out overwhelmed her. So, she sat and told the story. Eloise, ever the good listener, nodded along and shook her head at the right moments, adding a gasp when she shared some ruder things said during the fight.

"Ugh, what a dumbass," Eloise said.

"Yeah."

"But so are you."

"Lou..."

"Do you love him?" Eloise asked.

Ilsa nodded. "It doesn't matter, though. We aren't going to work. I have too much shit getting in the way, and Nathan will always meddle and try to fix my shit. It's too hard."

"It's supposed to be hard. And easy. It's both. Nothing worth having is always going to come perfect. But it would be worth the work being with Nathan, what he does for you, and what you do for him. Worth your pride."

"I'm not too proud."

Eloise shook her head. "Of course you are. And he's got a hero complex. We all come into relationships with faults. No one is perfect, but your love can be."

"How did you become so wise?"

Eloise chuckled. "I'm not. Keller drives me crazy all the time. But I would rather spend the rest of my life bickering with him than quietly alone. He's worth the fight. You just have to figure out if Nathan is worth it for you."

"Of course, he's worth it," Ilsa snapped. "What kind of question is that?"

Eloise nodded slowly as if something had just occurred to her. "But you don't think you're worth it to him."

"He thinks I am, but..."

"Nope. Don't you dare finish that sentence. You are not letting your fear of not being good enough for him destroy what could be a real shot at happiness. You are kind, a good friend, gorgeous, driven, a mediocre cook, and a phenomenal designer."

"I'm an okay cook," Ilsa grumbled.

Eloise shook her head. "No, you're really not, but that's fine."

"You won't tell him about this, will you?" Ilsa asked.

Eloise scoffed. "Of course not. I'd never. I got you. Dolls before balls."

Chapter Thirty-One

RAYON
NATHAN

HIS MOTHER TOLD HIM once that no matter how angry she was with her father, she refused to sleep apart from him. He knew that his parent's relationship was overly rosy to someone like Ilsa. She may think that his whole upbringing had been, in fact, too perfect. Nathan wouldn't apologize for his past, and he sure as shit wouldn't act like there was anything wrong with wanting to take care of the woman he loved.

It'd been a week since Ilsa walked out on him, but it only took a few hours for the red haze to clear from his eyes and for him to see how royally he fucked up in confronting Thomas Gallegos.

Never once had Ilsa lied to him. She'd be by his side if he'd only listened to her instead of deciding what was best for both of them.

After her text that she was home safe, he didn't hear from her. He sent her a few updates, but it was nothing but silence on her end. Eloise let it slip that Greta Landis had reached out and offered the funding Ilsa needed.

Nathan knew Eloise liked him, but she certainly took the chicks before dicks adage to heart because she offered no more information, telling him she wouldn't say anything. Of course, that was after she chastised the band for being a total gossip in the first place. She railed at Theo for eavesdropping, at Keller for talking about confidential stuff in front of his bandmates, and at Nathan for being a general dumbass.

It was almost comforting to be lectured by her again. It took him back to the early days of the band when they spent their days on the road.

The promotion for their new album was ramping up, and his days were soon filled with appearances on talk shows, video interviews in the middle of the night across the world, and photo shoots for different publications. In his downtime, he worked out.

Tamara ordered them to go to the premiere of Aria Kingston's new season of her show. As he adjusted his bow tie, he glanced at himself in the mirror one last time. The circles under his eyes were dark from not sleeping well. His bed felt too large for him, and having unimpeded access to his blankets was too stifling. Running a hand over his clean-shaven face, he wondered if Ilsa was thinking about him.

Before he could second guess the experience, he walked out the door to the waiting limo where Keller and Eloise were waiting to go to the premier. Theo and Aria were separately arriving later to all the fanfare. He wondered how much longer Theo could pull off this PR relationship he had going on with her. Aria seemed nice, but Theo didn't need a nice girl. He needed one to put him in his place and knock him on his ass. Everyone had thought Safiya Khan was that, but from the rumors, she'd gone back to her husband. Hopefully, the man treated Safiya better than Theo did.

The red carpet was crowded with a mix of teen stars, a few musicians, and a smattering of reality show stars. Normally he'd have begged off but being the only member of Prevalent Notion not going would've stood out as him "snubbing" Aria, according to Tamara, so he went. They'd likely have a bar inside, at least.

Standing alone, he posed for a few pictures, signed a few autographs from fans who won tickets to the show and made his way to the theater. He stood inside the doorway with a double bourbon in hand, watching as Eloise and Keller made their way down the red carpet. They posed together. Even in her heels, Eloise was much shorter than Keller, but they fit together, always touching. He watched as Keller bent down to whisper something in Eloise's ear and saw her laughing.

He was happy for his friends. How could he not be? But the pain of seeing them happy in love when his chest felt like it'd been ripped apart was too much. Sipping his drink, he savored the familiar burn on his tongue.

A hand closed on his upper arm, and he turned to see Shelby standing beside him, a small silver purse in her hand.

"Hey, handsome, twice in a month. Aren't I the lucky gal?"

He bent down and gave Shelby a quick kiss on the cheek, pulling away quickly to show that it was only friendly. "What are you doing here?"

Shelby flapped her hand casually, "My manager set it up to be seen with the younger crowd. To remind them I'm also 24, not 34."

"Ah." He nodded awkwardly. Tipping his glass up, he drained the bourbon in his mouth.

Shelby looked around, "Where's Ilsa? You didn't bring her?"

He considered telling the truth, but it didn't feel right. Clearing his throat, he set his empty glass on a high table beside them.

"She couldn't make it tonight."

Shelby laid a hand on his arm and leaned in. "Well, her loss is my gain, right? Come sit with me. I'll introduce you to some people."

At that moment, a camera flash went off, a photographer circling the party for candids. Before Nathan could step away, the photographer was off taking pictures of two teen stars who just walked in the door.

Shelby shrugged. "All press is good, right? We're all here to be seen, anyway." She laced her arm through the crook of his elbow. "Come on."

After meeting a smattering of semi-famous people, it all blended in a smear of shiny hair, white teeth, and sharp jawlines. Nathan excused himself to the hall. The air outside was cooler, and he took a deep breath. He was already a few drinks into the night, and the bourbon was going to his head. Even though she hadn't responded to the messages he sent her, he needed her to know he was thinking of her. He pictured Ilsa seeing a picture of him and Shelby together. What would she think? Ilsa had trusted him before, but that was exactly that.

Before.

Now how would she react? Would she see the pain behind his eyes or only Shelby's hand on his arm and her eyes on his face?

Pulling his phone out of his pocket, he sent the text before he could regret it.

Nathan: *I know you said to give you time, and I'm doing that. But I wanted to let you know that Shelby and I were at the same premiere, and the paps got more pictures.*

Friends only. Despite what people might say, I am not dating her again.

The light dimmed to let everyone know they needed to take their seats for the premiere. Shoving his phone into his pocket, he made his way into the theater. Sitting down, Eloise leaned over Keller to mouth. *You okay?*

He nodded, reaching over to squeeze her hand once before the light went down and the show began.

Coming out of the show, he followed Eloise and Keller to the party, pulling his phone out of his pocket as he walked. He couldn't remember much about the show. Something about witches who worked at a special magical hospital or something. Aria was good. He remembered that. Otherwise, he couldn't tell you a thing about the show.

Seeing his notifications were empty, he shoved his phone back into his pocket before accepting a bourbon from Keller. Shifting on his feet, a buzz of nervous energy flooded through him. Was that...

No, not energy, his phone. He pushed his drink at Eloise as he pulled his phone out, his heart leaping into his chest to see that the notification was telling him the lives were refilled in his hidden picture game. Grumbling, he shoved his phone back into his pocket. Beside him, Eloise said something he didn't catch.

"Huh?" he asked, accepting the drink he'd rudely pushed at her.

"I asked, what's the matter with you?" Eloise asked, her brow furrowing. "You've been weird all night."

Taking a large gulp of his drink, he grimaced at Eloise. "I don't know, maybe my heart is broken, and I'm being forced to come to this charade of a show."

"Oh my God, why are you being so dramatic? You sound like Theo right now."

Nathan sulked at the insult, forgoing a response by taking another drink.

"You screwed up. You know you did. Stop being a baby about it and take a little responsibility."

"I tried. She didn't want to hear it."

"So, try again." Eloise turned to Keller. "Were you this bad when we had fought last year?"

Keller narrowed his eyes at Nathan and Eloise as if he were debating the right answer. "Worse. I was much worse—completely lovesick and useless."

"Except for the part where you went on national television looking like a male model. Son of a bitch," Nathan grumbled.

Keller let out a huff of a laugh. "Yeah, but that doesn't count. Inside I was way worse."

Rolling her eyes, Eloise turned back to Nathan. "She'll come around once she knows you're really sorry."

Nathan set his glass down on the table, grabbing Eloise's arms. "Did she say something? Do you know something?"

Flinging his hands off, she stepped back. "First, ow. Second, uterus before duderus. I'm not saying anything more."

Keller watched the exchange before him with a knowing smirk. Nathan raised a brow in a *come-on, man* gesture.

Keller put his hands up in surrender. "I'm not getting into this again. I'm team Eloise, even if that's taking an ovaries before brovaries track."

"Some friend you are." He grabbed the glass from the table, finding it empty.

He took his phone out of his pocket and sent a follow-up message to Ilsa before losing his nerve.

He would never lie to her. Now she'd know exactly how he felt, and he'd let her make the next move.

Eloise returned with two fresh glasses of champagne and a glass of clear liquid with a small lemon slice. Shoving the tall glass at Nathan, she raised a brow. "It's water. You're useless drunk and certainly not going to get Ilsa back, five bourbons deep."

"I have a high tolerance," he grimaced, sipping the bland drink. The water tasted like nothing but disappointment. She could have a least gotten him a Coke.

"What you need to have is a plan. Sober up."

He took another sip. "When did you get so bossy?"

Keller pulled Eloise close, kissing the top of her lavender-colored hair. "I like it when you're bossy," he whispered loud enough for Nathan to hear.

"You two are gross."

Eloise ignored him, giving Keller a quick kiss.

The limo pulled up to his house, and he got out, walking a few steps to the front door before stopping short. Ilsa sat on his front step, her head leaning against a pillar. When she heard the crunch of his shoes, she stood up. Every other time he'd seen her, she was well put together or fresh out of bed. The faded Prevalent Notion tee hung off her shoulder, and the shorts had a small hole in the leg. It didn't look intentional, but he was glad to see her like this. To know she was hurting like he was, that being apart from him was as hard for her.

"Hey," he said, not sure what else there was.

"Hey." She hugged her arms around her body as if trying to keep herself together.

"You want to come in?" he asked.

She nodded at him, stepping to the side to allow him to open the door.

He watched her walk inside and hoped against his better judgment that this might be the door to forgiveness.

Chapter Thirty-Two

Raw Edge

ILSA

WITH A GLASS OF Nathan's favorite brand of Moscato in one hand and her phone in the other, Ilsa burrowed deeper into her covers. It'd been two hours since Nathan sent his last text.

Nathan: *I love you. No matter what you want to do, no matter if you need me or love me back, I love you. Nothing will change that. I will respect you wanting space, but I'm here until you tell me you don't want me anymore.*

She had typed out a dozen responses before she ordered delivery of a second bottle of wine. The messages got more incoherent as she tried to type in her carbohydrate and sweet wine stupor.

She knew she shouldn't look up the pictures, but of course, she did anyway. Technology made it possible for the camera phone pictures Shelby and Nathan were on different Instagrams already. There was even a slide show of the best dressed from the premiere, featuring Shelby in a photo with Nathan. The caption said friend, but there was nothing friendly about how the actress looked at her Nathan.

Hers. He told her he belonged to her. Why did she never tell him that her heart was his for the taking? That she wished she could take back her stupid pride and let him in just a little. And while he screwed up, he hadn't ruined things for her completely.

Greta Landis was looking promising as an investor. After hearing that she met with the socialite, a few more investors also responded to her inquiries.

Eloise's words kept echoing in her mind. Did she want to work to be with Nathan? So many times, she told him she needed to make her own choices. But wasn't she taking this choice from him? How could she tell him she wasn't worth the effort when it was never her decision to make? He was holding true to his words. He never lied to her.

Her halfhearted excuses were wearing thin. She'd already fallen treacherously in love with him. It was too late for her. No time apart would make her feel better about being apart from him.

Half wine-drunk, she swiped from her messages to the ride-share app, ordering a car to take her to Nathan's. He wouldn't be home until later. She believed his words. If he said that he and Shelby were only going as friends, he meant it.

Stumbling to her closet, she surveyed her options. What does one wear when they're trying to reunite with their rock star lover? There was no style guide to help her here. She glanced down at her outfit. The faded Prevalent Notion T-shirt artfully ripped at the shoulder and black shorts that had seen better days.

Arriving at his front gate, she got out, waving to the driver that she was alright as she let herself through the side gate to his front yard. Coming to the front door, she stopped short. She couldn't let herself in. It didn't matter if she had a key. It wouldn't be right. Sitting on the front step, she leaned against the pillar and waited for him to come to her.

It was over an hour that she sat there alone on the porch. A million times over, she second-guessed the choice. She pulled up the ride-share app a dozen times, almost ordering a car. But every time she put it away.

She had always been determined. She was successful in business, in pageants, and in modeling. And now she was determined to see this through. If Nathan thought she was worth the effort, then she would try. She owed herself the chance to see this through. He had used his good upbringing as a hindrance to his understanding of her for so long, but why? She certainly had no idea what a loving relationship looked like, but Nathan did.

Maybe this time, she could learn from him. Maybe together they could be better.

The black limo pulled up outside his gate, and she watched through the ivy as he climbed out, wishing whoever was in the car goodbye. Was it Shelby?

Pain lanced her chest at the idea of petite Shelby in that limo in her green Elie Saab dress, her strawberry blonde curls pinned up to frame her sweet face. Taking a shuttering breath, Ilsa tried to compose herself enough to see Nathan. The garden gate clanged shut behind him, and he walked into the light of the porch, his black suit fitted across his muscular shoulders. His face was clean-shaven, and his full lips made a little "o" as he stopped in his tracks to look at Ilsa.

"Hey." His dark brows were drawn, and his hand clutched the keys as he looked from her to the front door.

"Hey." She hugged her arms around her body. Despite the night's warmth, a chill ran through her at his look of uncertainty. Maybe this was a mistake coming here.

"You want to come in?"

Stepping up on the porch, he put his key in the lock and swung open the door. Close to him, she could smell the musk of his aftershave and the bourbon and lemon on his breath. His face was clean-shaven and smooth. She knew if she reached forward and cupped his cheek, it would be warm against her palm.

But she wouldn't do that.

He stepped back, allowing her to go first into the house. Her steps were muted on his floor as she walked into his large living room. The taps of his dress shoes were loud behind her. Coming to the couch, she turned to face him, unsure where to sit. This house that only days before was like a home to her felt fraught. Was she still welcome here beside him?

He motioned to the couch, and she sat, sinking into the plush leather. Shouldering off his jacket, he hung it on the back of a dining room chair. Turning to face her, he loosened his black tie.

"Do you want anything to drink? Water, beer, wine? I think I still have some creamer if you want coffee."

"Do you have any sweet tea?" she asked.

His mouth quirked up in the corner. "I thought you said it was too sweet for you."

She shrugged. "I guess I've acquired a taste for sweetness now." She let the loaded statement hang in the air for him to hear what she was and wasn't saying.

His smile widened, and he left her alone on the couch to return a minute later with a tall glass of sweet tea. She took a small sip before placing it down on the coaster. Nathan sat to the left of her in an armchair. She wished he would've sat on the couch with her, but his expression was wary as he watched her.

Now that she was here, she had no idea what to say. How do you confess that you were wrong? How do you come out and tell someone you love them?

"I…" she gulped down the fear in her throat. Pursing her lips, she willed the words to come. "I got the funding from Greta."

Wait, why did she say that?

Disappointment flickered on his face, but he covered it well.

"I heard that. Eloise."

"Right." She agreed, picking up the glass to take another drink, the simple syrup and lemon clinging to her tongue. She missed this taste. It was all Nathan.

"Why did you come here, Ilsa?" He asked, his voice cracking on her name. He coughed to clear his throat as if it was painful to ask the question.

"Do you not want me to…"

"I always want you." He interrupted, his voice strong. "All the time, every moment I'm not with you. You have to know that."

Heat flushed her cheeks at his words. "I wasn't sure..."

Leaning forward, he pressed his hands together in a praying gesture, his words directed at his lap. "I don't know how much clearer I could've been. I told you I love you, that no matter what, I would love you. What else could I have said?"

"I don't know." She felt silly after he confessed how he felt.

"Did you think I was lying? That there isn't a moment, we were apart when I wasn't thinking about you?"

Tears threatened her eyes as she stared at him. "I don't know what I thought. I just saw your text, and I needed to see you."

"Because you missed me? Because you were jealous of Shelby? Why?"

"Because I..." her voice faltered, the last of her Moscato wine courage melting away. "Because I need you. I don't want to need anyone. I've worked so hard to build up this life, and then you come around with your kind smile, and ugly shorts, and sweet words, and I need you."

He was off the couch, kneeling before her, his hands on her cheeks. "Illy, listen to me. I am sorry for the way I handled the situation with Thomas Gallegos. I should've listened to you. But I won't apologize for wanting to care for you and protect you. That's the kind of man I am."

Ilsa nodded at his statement. "I know you are. It's one of the things I like most about you." She paused, taking a steadying breath, and looked him in the eyes. "That I love about you."

"You love me?"

"I didn't say that..." she trailed off, but his smile was stretching his cheeks at her lie.

"Yes, you did. You love me. I love you, and you love me."

Softening to his touch, she nodded. "Yeah, I love you. From the moment I saw you with Shelby, I wanted you. I think I loved you from that first terrible pick-up line."

He frowned. "My exes. Shelby—all of them—fade compared to you. Having you means more to me than any of them. What you and I have is real. This is it for me. You are all I need."

"You can't know that..." she hesitated. "What's going to happen when I'm not as pretty, or I get sick or bitchy?"

"I'll love you the same. That's how love works. We'll get through it together. I'm going to make mistakes too. We both are. But we'll work it out together. You just have to let me in. I know you didn't have a great example growing up, but I did. From what you've seen, being taken care of is transactional. How would you know how it feels when it's done with no expectations or demands—just love?"

Ilsa stilled. Was it that easy? Could she let him take care of her and trust that it would be okay?

"When you bring me food, that's taking care of me. When I get the AC fixed on your car, I'm taking care of you. But I want nothing in return. I do it because I care about you. Just like you care about me, no matter how much you fuss about it. You take care of your employees every day, putting their needs before yours. You took care of Eloise when she needed it. You take care of me every day. That's all it is, Ilsa. It's not a tally of good deeds for services. You're not a vending machine. Let me love you."

"Okay," she said slowly, the last of her walls coming down. She cupped his cheeks.

"Okay, we're good? Okay, you want to be with me?"

"Yes. Okay, all of it. I want all of it with you."

His lips descended over hers, kissing her with all his might. Her hands wove through his hair, pulling him closer. His arms wrapped around her waist as he pulled her down to the thick rug. As he kissed her, his large body covered hers. His weight pressed deliciously upon her. She could feel the hard lines of his thighs between her legs, the ridge of his growing cock as he kissed her. Running a hand down his arms, she marveled at how much more muscular he was.

"How are your biceps so much bigger?" she asked as his mouth traveled from hers down her throat.

"I had a lot of pent-up energy. I worked out a lot."

Squirming below him, she hitched her legs around his upper thighs, pulling him closer to her center. "I like it."

Bracing his hands on each side of her head, he looked down at her. "You want more?" his tone changed to something darker, sending waves of excitement down to her core.

She nodded at him.

"Take my shirt off."

She loved when he was like this. She unbuttoned his white shirt, letting the fabric fall away until his shirt was open. Discarding his button-down, he pulled his white tee over his head in a fluid motion. Did men know how hot that move was?

Sitting between her legs, she ground herself against him, feeling the ridge of his cock through his pants. His chest was hard, more muscular than it'd been only a week and a half before. Had it only been that long since she'd touched him like this? It felt like forever.

In their new declarations, every caress said the same thing. *I love you. I want you. Touch me more.*

Running a hand down his chest, she stopped at the front of his pants.

"Unbutton me," he demanded. "See how hard I am for you."

Her eyes were on his face, and her fingers flicked the front of his pants open. The only sound was their heavy breathing and the pull of his zipper. Cupping her hand around him, she palmed his length through his boxers.

"I missed the feel of your hand on me." He gasped. "Take it out. Feel me."

Pulling his boxers down, she took out his hard cock, a drop of moisture on the tip she slid down his silky length. Wrapping her hand around him, she pumped him inside her fist, never taking her eyes off him.

He fucked her hand twice before pulling away. "No, I need to feel you first."

He kicked off his pants and underwear until he was naked. She wanted a minute to appreciate his body, but he didn't allow that, covering her as his lips were on hers.

Grabbing her shirt, he pulled it over her head. She cursed herself for the days-old bra she was wearing, but she hadn't come over thinking they'd do this, and why hadn't she? She should have known.

"I haven't showered in a few..."

"You think I care? I want you clean, and I want you dirty. And right now, I want you on my tongue."

His words were all she needed. Arching her back, she unclasped her bra, the air cool on her skin. His mouth took one nipple in his mouth, his tongue swirling around the peak, her hips bucked against him. His mouth let go to move over to the other breast giving it the same attention.

"Nate, please." She gasped. Her clit was pulsing with need.

"I'm the one who tells you how this goes." He smiled wickedly. He kissed down her stomach, leaving a cool trail on her skin that the air chilled. Getting to her shorts, he played with the drawstring.

"I know you like dressing up, but these clothes are considerably easier to get off than normal."

She smiled. "Don't get used to it. I like watching you work for it."

"You're worth working for, Petal."

Between the lust thrumming through her and his words, she thought she might weep. "Please, Nathan."

Sliding her shorts and thong down in one motion, he kissed her bare skin, little feather-light caresses until he got between her legs. His tongue licked her seam as his fingers circled her clit.

"I'm going to lick this pussy until you come on my tongue, and then you're going to come all over my cock. Do you understand?"

"Yes," her voice was shaky with need.

"You don't come until I tell you to."

She nodded, losing all semblance of words until his mouth was on her clit, sucking it, while his fingers plunged inside her. As his tongue moved against her clit, she thrashed against his body. His muscular arm came down on her waist, holding her still as he worked her closer and closer to orgasm.

His fingers dived inside the tender part of her, coaxing her to completion. Pulling away, he looked up at her, the sheen of her wetness coating his mouth in the low light. "Come on my tongue. You don't get my dick until you come, understand?"

She nodded. She was pretty sure she was about to come with or without his tongue. He dove back down between her legs, licking and teasing until the string holding her together snapped, and the waves rolled over her. Explosions behind her eyes, and she cried out. Her voice echoed in the night as the climax worked through her. Her legs tightened around him, riding his face until she came back down. The burn of the rug beneath her added to the sensations of her orgasm. As she relaxed, he moved up her body.

His kiss was pungent with the taste of her on his lips. "God, you're gorgeous when you come. It's the most beautiful thing I've ever seen."

Lazily she wrapped her arms around him, pulling him close. His naked body was hard against her.

"You flattened me again," she quipped.

He smiled. "I'm just getting started."

Wrapping his arms around her waist, he picked her up off the floor, her legs wrapped around his hips, and walked them to his bedroom.

Dropping her on the bed, he stood above her, looking down. His dick was hard, jutting out in front of him. She propped herself on her elbows to give him a grin.

"You promised me something."

"So, I did." He went to the bedside table, pulled out a condom, and slid it over his length before crawling cat-like over her until he hovered over her body. "You'll get it, but I'm not fucking you. We're going to make love. I'm going to make love to you ten times over, and then I'll fuck you senseless."

His kiss was slow and tender as he pulled their bodies together. Their kiss never broke as he slid inside her, his cock filling her up. Slowly he began to move. It was beautiful torture. His hand cupping her cheek, he pulled away. "Look at me."

Opening her eyes, she found him staring at her. His green eyes warmed as they moved together, building closer to their mutual climax.

"I want you to look at me when you come. I want to see it."

Her breathing hitched as he drove into her, hitting the places she needed most. He pulled her up onto his lap, her legs tight around his waist. One hand in her hair, the other on her hip, he moved them together, never breaking their gaze. The position hit her clit just right, sending the last piece of her orgasm hurtling down.

"I'm gonna... I'm..." her eyes fluttering shut.

"Look at me." He demanded. Her eyes snapped open, and she stared as she hit the crest. She could feel him deep inside her, pulsing as he cried out with his own.

His grip on her hip tightened, and she wondered if she'd have a bruise. Spent, she rested her head on his shoulder, breathing in his scent, all sweat, cologne, and sugar. Laying her back, he rested beside her.

Once she caught her breath, she opened her eyes to find him looking at her, smiling.

"I guess Eloise was wrong. She said I needed to make some big gesture to win you back." Nathan said, brushing hair off Ilsa's face.

Wrinkling her nose, Ilsa looked at him. "Like what, singing on late-night TV? That's them, not us. Please never do that to me."

The corner of his mouth ticked up. "So, no dedicating songs to you on stage?"

Ilsa pictured it, his powerful hands gripping the mic as he leaned down to speak into it. The heat in his eyes as she looked through the crowd to find her. It wasn't half bad. "I didn't say that. Just don't do it if I'm mad at you. I would have been pissed if you tried to get me back that way. You are only allowed to dedicate songs to me when we are sublimely happy."

Gripping her arms, he pulled her up his body until she was lying on top of him. Brushing the hair from her eyes, he cupped her nape to pull her in for a searing kiss. His lips were firm on hers, and heat flowed through her body at his embrace. Pulling away, he held her face still to look at her. "You better expect a lot of dedications, because I plan on making you happy every single day for the rest of our lives."

A new warmth descended inside her. The statement was more than she ever thought she would want, but it was right. They were right.

Ilsa snuggled against his chest. Her nails on his nipple, she tweaked the pink tip. "You know, I was thinking we could have a spring wedding. You know, since flowers bloom when you walk by."

Nathan's face broke into a wide grin. "Is that your way of proposing?"

"Would you say yes?"

Pulling her up his body, he rolled her over onto her back. Taking her left hand, he pulled it to his mouth, kissing her palm. "I want a big proposal. With lots of food."

Ilsa rolled her eyes, "Of course you do."

"At a party."

Propping herself up on her elbows, she took his mouth with hers. Words broken between kisses. "I guess I'll have to start planning then."

Chapter Thirty-Three

French Seam
Ilsa-Two Years Later

TRUE TO HIS REQUEST, Ilsa proposed at a party for his 29th birthday. They were married in a small ceremony at a refurbished manor house a few miles from where he grew up. After a long discussion, she kept her name. He agreed she'd worked too hard at building her brand to change. His parents didn't quite understand, but that was okay. They still accepted her with wide arms, especially his mother, who tried unsuccessfully to teach Ilsa how to make a honey pecan pie.

Going back to his family home and watching them all together was an odd feeling. The warm-hearted teasing and how they would put their arms around each other as they talked. When Ilsa had gotten lost on her way to the grocery store, it was Nathan's father who talked to her on the phone, giving directions until she was back at the house. His soothing voice guided her home. When she arrived back at the house, he greeted her, telling her *I can't have my favorite daughter-in-law getting lost, now can I?*

When they left, his father hugged her, telling her to take care of Nathan and then telling Nathan to *keep the speedometer below a hundred* before letting them get in the car.

It was the dad jokes and the smell of sugar in the air. It was the freezer bag of bourbon balls his mother insisted they bring back to LA. It was the way his sister Ashleigh French braided her hair for her, and Nathan's nephew called her *Auntie.*

Hope bloomed in her chest at the idea that this was now her family.

She invited Mitzie and Doug to the wedding. Thankfully, Eloise was there to run interference when Mitzie started getting too showboaty. She invited her father, but she never heard from him. Eloise and Trinh stood up with her. The guys were his groomsmen. Nathan's nephew Kaiden was the ring bearer.

With funding from Greta, the extended line was launched to great press. Greta was already making back some of her investment. Ilsa gave the employees who stuck by her a raise and promoted Trinh to Chief Operating Officer so Ilsa could focus on designing and promotion.

Her clothes were being carried in Barney's and Neiman Marcus, with an affordable line being planned for Macy's in the next year.

Backstage after her runway show at New York's fashion week, Ilsa took a sip of the champagne that Deja had thrust in her hand a half hour before, and she kept setting it down to put out little fires. She wished her friends could make it, but Eloise was called away at the last minute, and Keller didn't want to be away from her. She knew she'd see them at their house near Seattle soon. The band had been invited to spend a few weeks at the new home the couple planned on filling up with babies. She suspected Eloise might already be expecting, but she'd have to wait until they joined them in a few days to find out for sure. Theo had gone ahead of them, skipping the fashion show. And it was just as well.

Ilsa had called in a favor and asked Safiya Khan, Theo's ex-girlfriend, to walk in the show. Safiya agreed, slashing her normally exorbitant fee for the runway to help Ilsa. Safiya was a professional, but Theo was an asshole who riled anyone up, his ex-girlfriend especially. Having a famous supermodel in the show helped with the publicity, and she had heard buzzing that her designs were getting good press so far.

Safiya had offered to stay behind and have a drink with Ilsa, but she begged off. She only wanted to see Nathan, who was waiting at the party. Deja came backstage, taking a dress from Ilsa's hand and replacing it with a glass of champagne.

"Get your ass out there and talk to people. We will take care of all this back here."

"But the tattersall dress needs to be..."

"Sent to Sakina Green, yes, I know. Get out of here." Deja placed a hand on Ilsa's back, pushing her out the door.

Grumbling about pesky employees, Ilsa changed from her all-black outfit to a light blue silk dress for the party. With its low back showing off her spine tattoo, she knew Nathan would love it. Every time she wore something with a low back, she was reminded of the moments in the bathroom before Eloise's release party, the tremble in Nathan's finger, and the heat of his touch as he helped her into her dress. The beginning of something new.

Walking into the party, she caught Nathan's eye from across the room and did a little twirl. The gleam in his eye told her he had the same moment in his mind. He had taken a later flight out because of a work meeting, so she hadn't seen him for three whole days. Making her way through the crowd, she was stopped every few feet by someone telling her they loved the show or asking questions. Her body was begging to be near Nathan, but duty called. It took over twenty minutes to make her way to him.

Nathan picked up her left hand, kissing the thin wedding band on her ring finger. "It was a great show, Illy." She smiled back at him, his wedding band of platinum and onyx on his finger.

Taking a sip of her drink, she surveyed the party. Another hour and she could call it quits, going back to the hotel room with her husband. Nodding at partygoers as they talked of themselves, Nathan stood by her side, supporting her. Until the party dwindled, and the bigger names moved on to the next big thing.

Nathan retrieved her jacket and held out his arm for her to take. Her heels were killing her. As they walked out, Nathan bent down low. "By the way, I got the go-ahead from Dr. Singh. I am officially swimmer free."

Ilsa's face stretched wide with a smile. "I still can't believe you did that for me."

Three months before, he went to the area's best urologist and got a vasectomy. The pain was worse than he expected, but when he complained about it, Ilsa threatened to talk to his mother, who loved telling the story of Nathan's ten-hour birth and how he had the largest head the doctors had ever seen on a newborn. He stopped complaining. Plus, Ilsa brought him all his favorite snacks and kept reapplying his ice packs while he watched reruns of Antiques Road Show.

"I did it for both of us. No point in you taking all the responsibility of not baby-making."

"Well, we should start on that, not baby-making asap then, shouldn't we?"

"Indeed." He held her coat on his arm, "Hey, before we go? Do I look like a trampoline?"

She frowned, "What? No?"

He nodded, "Okay, I was wondering if you'd want to bounce on me all night."

Throwing her head back, she laughed. This was her life. Dirty pick-up lines and sweet wine with the man she loved.

She was so glad she took the risk of falling treacherously in love with him.

Epilogue
Theo

Still rumpled from his flight, Theo got out of the car and looked up at the immense mansion. Never in all his years of searching for coins below the bleachers did he imagine he would be part of something that could lead to a house this amazing. Not that it was his house.

The waterfront mansion was a gift to Eloise from Keller, once again proving that his bandmate was a better man than him. He only wanted to give a woman a screaming orgasm and a ride home.

Well, almost any woman

No, he was not going to think about her. He worked hard to put that piece of his life behind him. If he didn't, the regret would eat him for a second dinner.

Walking through the open front door, he heard the chatter of people inside. Keller and Eloise had invited everyone up for a housewarming trip. With Keller and Eloise in marital bliss and Nathan and Ilsa just as bad, he felt like the odd man out. Sure, he had Aria, but he didn't actually want to be with her. That was all PR. His friends were getting lame.

Setting his suitcase down on the stamped concrete flooring, he made his way down the hallway, following the voices to the kitchen where Eloise and Keller were standing in a group of people he didn't know. This home wasn't far from where Eloise grew up, so she might've invited some friends over, though he couldn't remember Eloise talking about many friends aside from Ana and Xander, and he didn't see them. Just as well. They didn't like him. How was he supposed to know that he couldn't ask Ana if her pubes were red? Seems like a common question to ask a hot redhead.

He heard Eloise laugh, and then a low voice said something back. The sound was muffled enough that he couldn't make out the words, but he stopped in his tracks, his eyes on the group.

Stepping out behind Eloise, the small woman brushed her long dark hair off her shoulder. Watching her, Theo knew exactly what that hair felt like between his fingers.

He knew exactly how those green eyes looked as they gazed upon you. Fumbling on his feet, he knocked into a wrought iron coat rack, sending it toppling. He reached out his hand to catch it before it hit the floor, but it slipped out of his fingers. The clang sent everyone looking at him.

Some entrance.

Both the women looked at him, Eloise slightly annoyed and the other woman shocked.

"Teddy?" her voice was so soft he could barely hear it.

He opened his mouth, then closed it feeling like a wide-mouth carp. Clearing his throat, he realized that the group in the kitchen was watching him with concern. Swallowing hard, he attempted a small smile.

"Hey, Mattie."

The woman blinked a few times before turning to Eloise. "I should get going. Great talking with you, Eloise. Thanks for the beer."

Theo watched as she left, her long dark hair swinging behind her as she walked out the back door.

For the second time in his life, Theo let Matilda Lewis go, only this time it was her running away.

Acknowledgements

Thank you for joining me on this journey with Ilsa and Nathan.

To the following people, thank you for your help with research; Jamie, Heidi, Amber. Mistakes are mine. Cassidy, Kate, and Angie for reading it in its basic form. To my editor Heather E. Andrews. Liz and Jacob for responding to my ask of dirty pickup lines with a full novel worth.

Love to my writing friends, I couldn't get through those moments of darkness without your sweet messages and spicy videos.

My family. I love you all.

About the Author

Linnea March is a contemporary romance author who writes steamy stories about self-confident women and the rugged men who love them. She lives somewhere in the wilds of the Pacific Northwest with her husband, their two boys, and a plump dog. After fifteen years of teaching early childhood education, she put down the googly eyes and picked up a pen. When not writing, she can be found reading her way through an ever-growing pile of books while drinking copious amounts of coffee. She proudly refuses to use umbrellas.